I0780837

MAD GIRL'S LOVE SONG

by

ROMANY HEARTFORD

A Wild Ink Publishing Original

Wild Ink Publishing

wild-ink-publishing.com

Copyright © 2025 Romany Heartford

Edited by Andie Smith

Design and Layout by Abigail Wild

All rights reserved. No part of this publication may be reproduced, distributed, or transmitted in any form or by any means, including photocopying, recording, or other electronic or mechanical methods, without the prior written permission of the publisher, except in the case of brief quotations embodied in critical reviews and certain other noncommercial uses permitted by copyright law.

ISBN: 978-1-964885-02-5

Any references to historical events, real people, or real places are used fictitiously. Names, characters, and places are products of the author's imagination.

Mad Girl's Love Song is dedicated to every reader who has known the dark room.

And to Crispin—for the warmth of his hand in the darkness.

1

Everything After

Heli

THE ROOMS ARE ALWAYS the same. Repurposed and perched somewhere near the top of a facility building. The space we're in now was probably a store cupboard, once upon a time; it's small enough. There are two chairs facing each other, although the angle's off, like they're posing for a magazine. Tissues and a pot of fake flowers are crammed onto a tiny table between us. And the flowers are far from the fakest thing in the room. My latest therapist turns on her smile and asks the same question, while the back of my legs stick, uncomfortably warm, to the plastic leather of the chair. Pleather, I think it's called.

"Did you mean to kill him?"

"Excuse me?" I say, like I couldn't hear the first time.

"Did you mean to kill him?" She leans forward, trying to catch my eye. Her lips open, stretching the smile. Even her teeth are in on it, competing for my attention. They want my confession.

But I don't want to talk about it. Not again. So, I shift my gaze to the window; it's newly installed and opened an inch or so, although no breeze enters the room. Like, if you didn't have to, you wouldn't either.

I lift my body forward, just an inch or so, and peer at the window. It's as I suspected, hinged with metal bars, smiling weakly like a girl who's just been for braces but doesn't want anybody to notice.

"Heli?" The therapist's voice is a whisper, a rustle of noise in an otherwise still room. She slides the tissue box toward me, and I flinch back in my chair, a scream of sound. "Did you have a plan for that day?"

"Did I set out––to strike a fatal blow?" I say. "To stop the Doctor's big brain from functioning?"

It's always the same question. People are obsessed with what happened that day and whether I'd planned it. My eyes are stretched wide, dry, and I force myself to blink, imagining what I must look like from the outside. *Wild,* that's what the press calls me.

"Yes," the therapist says. "Did you intend to strike him?" Her hands twitch, unsure whether to clench or relax before she lifts them to dab the sweat from her face.

It's mid-summer and stuffy in this little room: no air-con, just an ineffectual window. The court assigned the therapist to help me. And until she, or they, deem me better, I am to be taken to this place, once a day where this woman will try to rebuild me, to put me back together. But I've heard it all before. And her hands betray her. They keep twitching, greedy for my story and all its gory details.

"I don't... don't..." I stop myself, looking from her trainers––white and unbranded––to her neat haircut. Her, my fourteenth therapist, doctor, psychiatrist, counsellor, shrink, the professional in my life, and wonder if she's serious. She can't think she's the first person to ask me this, so why bother? Truth is, there is no story. I've already said all I'm going to say.

"The court found––"

"Yes, I've read the court records, Heli. But," she pauses to work moisture around her mouth. "If this is going to work––you'll need to trust me. I'm asking you here and now––between these four walls––did you mean to do it?"

"But my condition." I'm stalling for time. Eventually, she might get me to talk. Not because I think she can mend me or fix my broken mind. But because there are things I need from her: acceptance mostly, time off for good behaviour, and I want time with Cai. It's boring keeping quiet and still. If the therapist asked something else, I might be inclined to speak. But the Doctor? I don't want to talk about him.

My eyes return to her trainers and her untucked laces, almost concealed into the sides. I'm not ready to talk about that day. Not even that year. I don't want to.

"I need to know your motivation," she says. "Your condition is not relevant. You were on medication at that time. Your symptoms were stable. Doctor Emma Vanardsdale vouched for all of that. Now," she says, "Let's start at the beginning. How did that day start––was it normal, or were you planning something?"

I look away, my breathing accelerating. There's a faint smell of freshly laundered clothes mixed with a musky, masculine deodorant. How can she say my condition isn't relevant? If I were able to talk to Cai about it, he'd call it like it is––this new therapist is an arsehole with a sweat problem.

"Ask me something else," I say, squeezing my eyes shut.

There's nothing to look at anyway. A too-small window, fake flowers, and white shoes. I am tired of it all. I've spent my whole life in stupid rooms like this one.

A tear slides across my cheek, and I hear her push the tissue box towards me. Maybe if I give her something she'll prescribe me a pill and I can go sleep it off in my bed.

"You know all of this already." My breathing is louder than my voice––a series of rapid ins and outs. "You must know about that day. From my notes." I hide the sound of my breath deep inside my chest. If only someone would ask a different question.

"I want you to tell me." Her lips form the question again, "Did you mean to kill him?"

"The Doctor's not dead." My teeth clamp together. He's here in this room. In every question she asks. She should be asking whether I'd kill him now if I had the chance. "I didn't kill him."

"But did you want to?" Her eyes gleam.

"Everyone wanted to kill him." I'd like to say she would too––*if she met him*. But I don't because I don't trust her with any of it.

"You acted on those feelings. Unless there was someone else involved?" She tries again to catch my eye, but I refuse to see. "Wasn't it you who removed the fire extinguisher from the wall and..." she begins to recite her version of events. About the miracle that means the Doctor still lives. I've heard it before, so many times. None of it is true.

"He was a monster," I interrupt. What was the word the press used for him? "A fanatic."

"Why don't you tell me about that?" She clicks her pen, a gesture so reminiscent of the Doctor and his therapy sessions, I want to gag.

"I don't need your help." I press my nails into my palms and look her in the eye. Her face is ordinary looking, a symmetrical haircut and faint powder lines on her cheeks. Boring.

"Let's start with something else, then. Childhood. What's your first memory in life?"

"Peony." My lips curve. Finally, someone I like talking about. "My sister, Peony."

"You know," she says after a while, putting down the pen––slim and unpretentious––her mirror image. There's a self-satisfied twist to her lips. "Perhaps Cai could accompany these sessions. Getting his perspective might help."

Just like that she has me, in a move she must have planned before the session even started. She knows, I think. This time I meet her gaze. She knows about Cai. And the thing that went down in the boatshed. And I wonder what it might be like to strike her too. There's nothing in the room with the weight of a fire extinguisher––just the fake flowerpot––but my hands will do. I pant, breathless with frustration for a minute. I'm seventeen now, still a girl, and not the monster in this story. "Cai wasn't there when it happened. They'd taken him away."

"Sira can come though, can't she? She spoke at your trial, right?"

"How should I know? I wasn't there." But I do know. Of course, Sira had been only too happy to stick her nose into my trial.

"I want to help you," the therapist's hand reaches to pat my knee. "But I need to know what happened. What we're dealing with. You need to trust me."

Would Cai tell her everything? All the stuff that was just between us. The truth. He always was a chatterbox; too trusting, when he of all people should have had his defences up.

I hold the end of my nose with my fingertips, it might have made a difference when they took him away. It might make a difference now.

My head shakes back and forth, and so, even though I'd rather be doing almost anything else, something changes after all. I drop my hand and let the words come. I start with that day in the school room, not long after I'd arrived, because Mal was there and really everything starts with Mal.

2

All the Stuff that was Just Between Us

Heli

We were not supposed to look.

"Keep your mind on your own work," Dr Fiennes said from his desk at the front of the school room.

But how could we do anything else?

Through the corners of our eyes, we snuck quick glimpses at Mal. He sat in the chair to my right. His shoulders slumped forward until his forehead hit the desk. The sound echoed. Despite the smell, I wanted to go and comfort him. I needed to. Mal looked so small, his body bent out of shape, crying and all.

"That's enough." Dr Fiennes's finger wagged before jabbing at his device. He was signalling for help, and they weren't coming fast enough. His frustration was all there in the crook of his finger. "Nosey parkers are not required."

The last time Mal had an accident, I went over to him, put my hands on his back--thin and damp and warm--getting right up and personal with his stink. What would he do if it were the other way round? I didn't think he'd follow their rules, sitting quietly, doing his work like nothing was happening. I put my hands on the desk and started to stand.

"That's your warning, Joe. Next time, no exercise." Dr Fiennes rapped the desk. "Eyes down––all of you. Focus on your books."

I dropped back to my chair. Mal would understand. Exercise time was sacred. It was a good hour in an otherwise crappy day. It hurt though; I was not good at sitting still. I held my nose hard, grounding myself.

Inhaling, I forced both hands to move towards the headphones, running my fingers over their surface––the scratched plastic circles and stiff foam padding. There was a voice lecturing on the finer points of the history of Stalingrad. Always a voice in my ear, telling me what to do.

"Heli," Dr Fiennes rapped my page––twice––with his ruler. "This is your warning."

"What? I haven't done anything."

"You aren't focussed on your work. If it happens again, you will lose your exercise privileges. Is that clear?"

"Yes."

Dr Fiennes was the strictest of the doctors. He policed the school room, and no amount of begging or crying could sway him. When he said something happened, it did. End of discussion.

I tried to concentrate, bending my back to the task and making notes in my exercise book: *the red army fighting for a ruined city*. I tried to breathe less before risking another glimpse to see if anyone had come yet. Last time it was immediate once Mal shit himself. But not today. I caught Cai's gaze, seated at the other side, his eyes flickered to Dr Fiennes at the front before he made a sick face.

I looked away. Cai's braver than most, but also kind of louder than he realised. And I was trying to stay out of trouble.

"Shitty bollocks." Across from me, Sira said the words over and over until she clamped her hand over her mouth, biting down on her finger. "Penis."

Sometimes I got the giggles when Sira blurted out but there was no room for laughter today, all the air was taken up.

"That's your warning, Sira. Now, take a breath. That's good control," Dr Fiennes said. "Mal, keep still. Someone will be here in a minute."

I turned back to my book. It was the only way to shut things out. Through the headset, the history teacher's voice was sour. It was pre-recorded so there was no way she could know I was distracted. Her tone said otherwise. She reminded me of the time limit. The source book was eight pages long, dense as tar. I released a sigh, emptying my lungs before they began to fill back up again.

Stalingrad, named after the Russian dictator Joseph Stalin.

My pencil scratched another note across my page.

Hard work has its own rewards.

That was one of the Doctor's sayings. I'd yet to come by any reward, but still I followed his instruction. A *good girl.* I didn't want to be here forever.

At the front desk, Dr Fiennes's head bent lower, exposing the neat circle of skin where he had begun to bald. He had this pained look like he couldn't believe his bad luck, as though it was him who was always in the room when Mal had an accident. On the table beside him was his device, a desk tidy and a line of Post-it Notes––the dull yellow kind. I had a desk tidy once, Peony's was pink and mine was baby blue, filled with pencils and a beloved rubber collection. They've all gone now.

Dr Fiennes looked up and I resumed my study.

Stalingrad, August 1942: the deadliest battle of the Second World War.

I made another note, adding the death toll.

Two million lost in a wrestling match between dictators.

I thought about the town where I used to live and its population––Mum, Dad, Peony, Gran, and God knows how many more. My eyelids fluttered. What must it feel like––to wait in a city with an army at your door?

My fingers stiffened when the sounds of the doctors' footsteps penetrated the lesson. White coats gleamed under the lights as they gripped Mal's arms. He wriggled and squirmed, fighting them off. And the rotten smell intensified.

"Get off."

Mal's hands slapped the table while the legs of his chair squealed backwards.

"We're here to help you."

"Bull-crap."

"It's for your own good," one of the doctors said. "It won't hurt."

"Stop making that noise," came a different voice. From behind it looked like Dr Devitt. The youngest of the doctors, and an unashamed science nerd. Sometimes I thought he was the best of a bad bunch. But today, he's just another part of the wall of white cloth.

Mal's resistance crumbled.

"Alright then."

They lifted him up and his limbs dangled, like a puppet's.

I watched, disappointed as Mal allowed himself to be taken, placid as a fish. I would have thrown things around––the headset at least––maybe a desk.

Dr Fiennes narrowed his eyes, indicating I should get back to it. He straightened his legs, and his head reared upwards from the front desk like a bird stretching for take-off. For a moment, I wanted to resist, making our eye contact last until it was uncomfortable.

"Line up," he said. "Now. All of you."

We arranged ourselves on the black, vinyl spots that had at some point appeared on the floor at the back of our school room. The spots kept order they said. We arranged ourselves like chess pieces.

"Silence," Dr Fiennes said.

"Silence," we repeated, "is healing."

What I really wanted to do was tell the doctors to be gentle with Mal. To remind them he was just a kid, fifteen, maybe sixteen years old. To tell them none of the things that had happened were his fault. But the only words that would come were the ones that were sanctioned.

"Silence," I said, my hands forming fists inside my pockets, "is healing."

Dr Fiennes patrolled the line, nodding his head until the business with Mal caught his attention. He helped their departure, using his device to open and then close the door.

"Back to your lesson," he said after a while and we trooped from our line-up on the black spots, back to our desks, headphones on, and notebooks out. I squeezed my pencil, forcing myself to listen to the droning history of Stalingrad.

"Heli," there was a voice behind my shoulder, and I jumped.

This time I hadn't heard any footsteps. I pulled the headset to the side. There it was again, the rush of dread that came so often in this place.

"Yes?" My mouth was stale with second-hand air.

"Come with me."

But I'd only had one warning. I had repeated the words and stood on the stupid spot. There was no need for any punishment. I glanced at Cai, my cheeks heating, but there was nothing he could do.

It was Dr Devitt, sent to escort me to the lab––probably. My heart pulsed. In this place, you never knew. A couple of days ago, they had taken Mal to the chair––mid-lesson. I wouldn't let that happen to me. I needed to do my time in the Facility––and get out.

"Come with me." His voice was sharp, like I'd been ignoring him.

"Science?" My voice clung to the back of my teeth.

When Dr Devitt gave a tiny nod, the headset gave way, and my hand dragged it from my ear. *Not today.*

"No talking. Tidy up––like you've been shown."

My breath squeaked as I released it. I pressed my hand over my mouth to silence it.

"That's better." Dr Devitt said, his eyes unblinking. "Order. Let's do things right."

"I shouldn't have to remind anyone that school time is for working and not daydreaming." Dr Fiennes glared across the room as though it was my fault people were distracted.

Placing the headset on top of the pile, I glanced at the other kids in the room, heads bowed over workbooks like in a real school.

"Let's go," Dr Devitt said.

Over my shoulder, Cai watched us leave. I smiled when he made the sign for luck, the corners of my face tight and heavy. In this place there was no such thing. But one day we'd find a way out.

3

THE CARVING

Sira

THE FIRST TIME I met Heli, she was screaming. Refusing to do the line-up, to chant the mindless *silence is healing* bullshit with the rest of us. Biting at the Doctor like an animal, and she was wailing——either she couldn't contain the sound, or her skin was on fire.

I remembered rolling my eyes at Wiley. Like the rest of us have learned, *silence might not be healing,* but you did the chant or suffered the consequences. Mya and the others told me to give her a chance because she was new. But I didn't think it mattered how many chances she got. Heli was one of those *look at me* kind of kids.

The other thing I noticed when she arrived was her hair. She'd cut it off, or burned it, on one side only; it looked weird. Different. Bright red too, and it wasn't even the brightest thing about her.

That day when Mal soiled himself, right there in the school room with us, Heli made it all about her. Hyperventilating when Dr Devitt took her out. Although, it wasn't the chair he was taking her to. She wasn't the one in danger. Safe while they put Mal in it. We all were. One at a time, that's the rule. I was not okay with that. But don't shoot me, I was just a kid, not the one making this shit up.

Heli's eyes met mine as she left, but it felt like she looked right through me.

When she was gone––the door closed and sealed behind her––Dr Fiennes's focus at the front returned to the Post-it Notes littering his desk. The same hard chemical smell that permeated this whole place, undercut with the waft of decay and rotten egg that Mal had left behind.

I picked up my pencil and tried to get back to algebra. It was hard. Maths was bad even in a normal school, numbers, shapes, and bits of lines never doing what they were supposed to.

At first, I didn't think the doctors cared about the work here. I didn't know whether anyone even opened our exercise books after lessons and checked on us. I knew better now. This place was all about checking. Square root of nine? I didn't give a fart. Maths wasn't my subject. So, I made it up. First rule of Cerletti, don't ask questions. Wrong was better than nothing. I'd learned that the hard way.

My desk was in the back row––below the brass plaque on the wall with the Cerletti logo engraved across it and the date the Facility opened last year. An outline of an old man with a big head. If I had the chance––and something sharp––I'd like to scratch a penis on the guy's forehead. You know the type of thing, carve it into the space stretching right up to where the Facility motto was emboldened: **Strides for Science.**

I had no idea what that meant, although science was a big deal. It was the only lesson we left this room for.

Me? I hated those sessions up close and personal like doctoring was a disease that was contagious. It was funny really--once upon a distant memory--I'd wanted to be a doctor. Not anymore.

Wiley nudged the back of my hand with his pencil. I checked on Dr Fiennes before turning to him. He's a skinny kid, must be because he never sat still. If they let him, Wiley would live outside, up a tree probably, or on some disused basketball court.

They cut his hair when he first got here, but it had rebelled already, growing fast and poking out in every direction like each curly strand has a mind of its own. Wiley mimed putting a gun to his head and pulling the trigger. I smiled, tipping my head to the clock. It wasn't long until lunch.

I looked down at the empty box, waiting for my answer, and scribbled the number five. Next to it, I added a decimal point and a two. It seemed more believable that way. Like I'd put some effort in, spent some time and worked things out.

While I was hard at it, Mal came back, his face blank, the line of his back slumped. Dr Fiennes got up from the front desk and tried to help him settle into his lesson. Mal was the only one who got the attention, special treatment you could call it.

Except it wasn't.

Not really.

It was like even they, the doctors, knew something wasn't working with Mal. Some part of their regime had gone wrong, and they were trying to fix it. *Look at us*, swarming around. They were buzzards alright, draining him dry. Mal was broken, good and proper, and you didn't need to be a doctor to see it.

Dr Fiennes's attention was on Mal, so I slid my hand underneath the desk and worked on the carving. I could only do a bit at a time. It's noisier than you'd think, sharp pencil tip scratching against cheap, rough wood. I'd gotten the top done, now I'm working on the long length of the shaft.

My momma found my collection once and said I had sex on the brain. Either that or the Devil had possessed me. But penises didn't feel like any kind of Devil work I understood. That, and they were the easiest thing in the world to draw.

4

THE COLLECTOR

Heli

ON THE OTHER SIDE of the door, we entered the long, white-walled corridor––a crooked spine for the Facility, travelling the length of the building. Dr Shalt was coming the other way, her heels clipping against the floor like they had a grudge against laminate boards.

"There you are." Dr Shalt stopped; her grey-flecked brown hair trapped behind a plastic headband. "He's waiting for you."

Her eyes flickered over me, but it wasn't me she was talking down to.

"Is everything in order?" Dr Devitt tried to reassert himself.

"Why wouldn't it be?"

"I just meant…" His cheeks flushed.

Dr Shalt had this way of making you feel like you were doing something wrong. You could be reciting the Lord's Prayer in your head, and she would look at you like she'd caught you taking a piss somewhere you shouldn't.

I let their voices fade into the background. Why should I care if Dr Shalt made Dr Devitt feel like dirt? My thoughts drifted to Mal. Where was he now? Getting cleaned up, maybe.

Mal was the quietest of the thirteen kids in the Facility. And every time they strapped him into the chair, he got worse. If he was incontinent before he came, I didn't think it was something you could ask.

"Don't you have somewhere to be?" Dr Shalt's voice cut in.

"Come on, Heli." Dr Devitt touched my arm, his other hand buried in his pocket.

Behind his round glasses––constantly slipping down his nose––he must have his own thoughts, buried and secret, like the things inside his pocket.

Further down the corridor we passed the forbidden door, the one kids weren't allowed through, and turned into the main hallway. If this were a normal place, not Cerletti, you'd call it a reception, the place where everything met. But here, there were no visitors, just doors and corridors: one to the science area, one to the dining hall and dormitory, one to the outside, and one back to the schoolroom and the Doctor's office.

The central space was high-ceilinged and sterile, a dome of purged air. Windows lined the walls, but they were narrow slits, too thin to let anything fresh or unvetted in. Don't even think about trying to climb out.

"Can I use the toilet?" I forced my thoughts into focus.

"Be quick."

I slipped into the empty stall and went through the motions, drying my hands on my clothes––plain as everyone else's. Splashing my face, I drank from cupped hands like a dog. It made me feel better, almost hu-man. I fumbled for the tablets tucked into my bra. They were small with raised markings: an R, a 1, a 5. Whatever they meant, I scratched them out with my thumbnail, then crumbled them into powder, flushing it all down the sink.

Drugs still lurked in my system from before I got here, a cocktail that made my skin itch and my hands shake. Some days they forced them down my throat. But sometimes I managed to hide them. Not at the front——but at the back, in the furthest recesses of my mouth. A flicker of rebellion that gave me hope.

Down the hall, a keypad guarded entry to the science zone——the doctors' domain. They took us in there twice a week for lessons and sometimes for their special experiments, observing us like mice in a cage.

I tried to catch a glimpse of Dr Devitt's code as he swiped his card, but he angled his body to block my view. The door resisted for a moment before opening with a hiss. He pushed it wider, and we slipped inside.

It was freezing, air-conditioned with a sharp smell like unperfumed cleaning chemicals. Sort of a relief after the stench of Mal. Sort of not. Everywhere there were cupboards and two wide benches that ran parallel to the walls——trays of chemicals and other equipment. On the display shelves at the far end, there were see-through jars filled with murky liquid and suspended body parts.

This one is a human tongue, the Doctor had once said. *And over there, a brain from a Victorian convict. Perfectly preserved except for the yellowed glass.*

I tried not to look at them, unease creeping in at the thought parts of me could end up in those jars one day.

Look at this one, a future Doctor might say. *It's the ear of the infamous mad girl, Heli…*

"There you are. In here, please."

It was the Doctor——collector of body parts and the one in charge. He made us call him the Doctor as if in a building full of doctors, he was the only one that mattered. Cerletti was his creation, his brainchild. He could've picked any title, but he chose that. He had his clipboard with him--he always did--ready to scribble notes as he watched his experiments unfold.

My fingers hovered near my nose. While Dr Shalt stole small kindnesses, the Doctor belonged in a gothic novel, and not just because of his bizarre collection. He was a machine, driven by cold, clinical routines.

"If you could, get things ready, Dr Devitt."

The Doctor ushered me through one of the many doors. A long table stood in the centre of the room covered with piles of coloured plates--plastic, like the kind clowns juggle at a circus. I had the urge to hide behind them, to shield my face. Questions floated, untethered like balloons, but I knew better than to ask.

The Doctor pulled up a chair.

"Heli?" he said, my name was sharp and uncomfortable in his voice. I kept my eyes on the plates. "Can you look at me?"

"What?"

"Remember, you're here so we can help you." He folded his hands over his clipboard. "The Cerletti Facility strives for reformation."

"I don't need reforming."

"The law says otherwise. Do you remember the fire?"

My chest tightened. The fire wasn't something I could face. Not with him. I dropped my gaze.

"A groundbreaking treatment plan. We are taking strides for science."

The engraving on the plaque behind my chair in the schoolroom said something similar. **Strides for science.**

"If you want to get better, you'll need to work with us."

The Doctor said he wanted to make us better, to fix the unfixable things in our brains. That's what he wanted. I just wanted to get out.

"What are the plates for?"

"It's a puzzle," he said. "I'll record your speed and accuracy. I just need you to follow the instructions without getting distracted."

"Right."

Puzzles beat some of his other lessons.

"It's mathematical. Use your brain first, hands second."

I almost took it literally––imagined using my feet or even my tongue. Pleasure was rare, it made me reckless. I stepped forward, picking up the instruction sheet.

The plates were smooth and cold against my hands. I tried to follow the steps from the instructions. But it was hard.

"Stop." The Doctor's pen hovered, ready to scratch on his clipboard. "Now, Heli."

The plates spun out across the table, a tumble of colours.

"That's quite a mess," he said. "Think first. Act later. Start again."

I sifted the red plates into one pile and the green into another, organising them first by colour and then by weight––trying to get the maths right. But the instructions made no sense.

Frustration boiled over, and I slammed a plate down. It split into sections––not the bad kind of broken; it was meant to. I checked the others––they all had the same mechanism. The Doctor took notes while I pieced them together, following his instructions. But it wasn't my brain that cracked the puzzle, it was my uncontrollable emotion.

Dr Devitt entered. "Everything's ready."

"It's the only way left," the Doctor replied. "Come along, Heli. Let's try something else."

Fear tightened in my chest as I followed him. Back by the shelves of body parts, the door to the room with the chair was open. Inside, under dim light, two figures moved. I recognized Dr Shalt by the gleam of her plastic headband. She tapped a needle against a tray. The chair loomed, half-reclined like a dentist's but with straps for wrists and ankles. My heart clenched.

Please, not me.

"I'm not going in there," I said.

"This way." The Doctor gestured, impatience in his voice. "Hurry up."

He opened another door into a storage room––tiny, windowless. My breath came fast. Anything was better than the chair.

The overhead light buzzed and then I saw it: a monkey perched on the bench, scratching itself.

"You've left us no option," he said, "but to try something different."

"Oh."

"Be careful. No sudden movements."

But I didn't listen. I stepped forward, reaching to stroke the monkey, longing for the wet nose and warmth of Elvis, my dog back home, when the monkey's arm snuck out, surprising me. A long, furry arm with giant fingers pinched hold of my nose. Pinched and didn't let go.

I tried to breathe. A whining sound like a burst balloon.

"Get the needle," the Doctor said. "Quickly."

"No," I wrenched the monkey's fingers back. "Don't hurt it."

"It's a hallucination," he said. "Keep still."

I touched my nose, already enlarged by the experience; pain dripped from my eyes. My arm hurt too. Something had stung me.

"Some ice, I think," the Doctor said.

"Ice? Why?" Shock overwhelmed my brain. There hadn't been a sting––they'd lured me in with a monkey, then jabbed me with a needle.

"Ice will help your nose."

"My nose." My fingers reached across to where my arm hung heavy at my side. How could he talk about my nose after what he'd done. "What happened to my bloody arm?"

"Heli," he said. "We do what we do to be kind. If you don't like injections, you need to take your tablets."

"What about the monkey? Did you hurt it?"

"There was no monkey. Now you will be escorted back to the school room. Dr Devitt, one moment please."

I put my jumper back on, wincing as I pulled it over my sore arm. Looking around the room, there was no trace of the monkey. And how did the Doctor know I wasn't taking my medication? They checked my mouth; I thought I'd fooled them. Unless they had cameras in the bathroom, the thought crawled beneath my skin.

"Everything's ready," the Doctor continued, speaking outside the door to Dr Devitt. "After lunch, we'll proceed with the boy's next treatment in the chair."

5

The Dark Room

Heli

CERLETTI RULES DICTATED THAT our days were full of order. Every minute was accounted for––sleep, meals, blood tests, lessons, exercise, and back to food again––down to the time we were given to take a shit.

We all followed the same routine, except when the Doctor called us for therapy. Those sessions were solitary. While the science zone occupied one end of the building's long, white corridor, the Doctor's office was at the opposite end––isolated, soundproof. You never heard a thing from inside, the thought made bile bubble at the back of my throat.

The walk to the Doctor's office was the longest inside the Facility. The room itself was the same shade of white as everywhere else––when they set up this place, there must have been a mandate about the dangerous effect of colour.

Cerletti white dominated—from the doctors' coats to the spotless walls. In the space behind his desk, the Doctor displayed his trinkets and achievements. The room reeked of chemicals, the same stench clinging to the Doctor's breath. It was the perfume of the Facility, and I hated it.

"That's quite a record, young lady," the Doctor used his pen to hover over his notes. "Two fires, one--of course--very serious. And several others violent--"

"I told you all of that."

The Doctor liked to talk about what he called my *past misdemeanours*. It didn't make me proud hearing him read it all back.

"You don't..." I waved my hand. What good did it do to relive the past? "You don't need to shame me."

"Tell me." He clicked his pen. "On a scale of one to ten, how strong is your urge for destruction."

"Zero."

"Zero?" He pulled a face, indicating his disbelief. "Not even a small fire?"

"That's what I said, isn't it?" I stared at the window.

Although it was hard to see much, even in the Doctor's office the windows were regulation--narrow, high and out of sight. I tried to see outside. Murky, grey sky and the shadow of a tree, a whispering promise. To be anywhere other than here in the room with him. My eyes squeezed tight.

"I'm not planning on starting any more fires."

"And why do you think that is?"

"It's not because I'm happy if that's what you mean."

"When I mean something, I'll tell you. Relax. These sessions are designed to help you work through issues arising from your misdemeanours. I'm not here to judge."

What a liar.

I gave up on worrying about what little I could see through the window and scuffed my feet together.

"You have been sent here for your reformation."

My head jerked up. The Doctor talked about reforming us often but how we got here very little.

"By who?"

"After the fire, it was recommended you would make a good candidate for our trial. With your parent's" consent, of course."

"Trial? What trial?"

"It is the work we are doing here to resolve adolescent abnormalities."

"You think we're all abnormal."

The Doctor's lips moved, and big words tumbled out.

Were we abnormal? Sure. Sira was nosier than your average person and Mal had his problems. Joe was a bully. But were we any different from other kids? The Doctor thought so.

Looking at the window again, I wanted to go outside where there might be a chance to talk. I longed for fresh air and the scent of the sea.

The Doctor tapped his pen. "What reason would you give for the zero?"

"I feel different, I suppose." My hands tightened and I shoved them underneath myself. If I said I still thought about fire, he'd prescribe more drugs. "I guess I'm not in that place anymore. I'm not as angry."

"And how does that make you feel?"

"Excuse me?" I'd just told him how I felt. Why did he need these things to be said over and over again?

"What reason would you give for this 'different' feeling?"

"Maybe my meds." My hands twitched beneath me. It was like sitting on a creature that couldn't be calmed––that wouldn't be still. That was my meds too.

"It's good you recognise the need for medication––without it, you won't get better. And what about the urge for violence? On a scale of one to ten, how would you describe that?"

He'd asked the same thing last week. The thing with violence was––I'd never hurt a fly. It was other people who called me violent. What would I call it?

Self-defence.

"Heli?"

"Zero."

"Zero?"

"That's what I said."

The Doctor wrote something before looking up. "Have you heard of the dark room analogy?"

"No."

Perhaps I had in a therapy session once before. It didn't matter.

"It's a metaphor," the Doctor's pen fell still, "where you exist in one room, but the curtains are drawn––so everything is dark. You can read and talk, lay on the bed, but it's all done in darkness."

"You can't read in the dark."

"Don't be smart;" his fingers twisted. "That's the point––everything is made harder, more difficult, by the dark room."

"Why don't I just draw the curtains?"

"You can't," he said. "Sometimes you want to, but you can't."

"Am I still in the room?"

"The treatment here," he put his pen in his pocket––a sign the session was over. "The medication, therapy, and routines will help you. Complete reformation," he nodded, "Strides for science––that's the key."

"What about the chair?" Even my hands stopped shifting to wait for his answer.

"Electric shock treatment is part of our plan to fix the things in your mind, where talking therapies can't help," he said. "But you're not ready, not yet. Now––have a sweet."

He pulled the packet from his drawer and placed it on the table. Every session ended with a sweet. Today's had stripes. I felt awkward. The sweet was a trap. Except I couldn't work out why when I was already captive.

"Is that it?"

"Take your medicine. Follow the rules." The Doctor eyeballed me. "And we will see your progress continue."

I took the sweet––might as well––and waited to be accompanied back to the school room with candied mint and a hint of toffee sticky against my tongue.

It was quiet when I returned, all the other kids were concentrating on their work. Even Cai didn't look up. The mood was so still––a rigidity that came from fear––I was worried that they'd put Mal in the chair again while I'd been with the Doctor.

We'll proceed with the boy's next treatment.

But I couldn't remember when it was that he'd said it.

After the lesson, I pushed towards Cai, waiting when they put us in pairs, and luck must have been on my side or something because Dr Fiennes didn't even look in our direction, as he assigned us together.

"And last of all," he said, pointing. "You two. Your exercise hour starts now. Make sure you're back on time."

"Come on," I grinned at Cai, and he followed me outside.

I inhaled the sweet scent of mud and heather, letting it push back the sterile stench of the Facility. But the sight of the wire fence ahead reminded me that even outside, we were still under Cerletti control.

For one hour a day, we were assigned a partner and sent outside. It was the closest thing to freedom we knew. Except this was the Cerletti Facility and nothing was what it seemed. Sure, sometimes we messed with our route, walked left from the main gate, first towards the lighthouse, then over the rocks near the harbour, choosing one way instead of the other. It was not against the rules. But we were only as free as a zoo-bound orangutan––to roam one side of its cage before the other. There was no power in movement. Power was the enclosure.

"Where's Mal?" I asked.

"They took him," Cai said. "He hasn't come back."

"He's gone to the chair again?"

"I guess so."

Poor Mal. It didn't seem right to be outside while he was trapped with the doctors. I sprinted across the grounds towards the gate.

"What's the hurry?" Cai's breath was heavy as he caught up with me.

"I need to get away from this place."

When I'd asked about the chair––the Doctor had said *not yet*. How could I stay here, knowing it was coming? I mean––what if I shit myself too?

"What's going on?" Cai said. "You look––"

"It's nothing."

The Cerletti building was surrounded by iron fencing except for a tiny section at the back where the land fell away to rocks and ocean; I guess they thought they didn't need to bother with that bit.

We reached the gates that stood open for an hour each day, two hours on Sundays; the path beyond a smiling strip of stones and mud. There was not so much as a hint of dampness––even though I could have sworn it had rained last night.

"You can talk to me," Cai said.

His eyes crinkled, maybe from concern, maybe from sunlight breaking through clouds, I couldn't tell.

"Why did my mum agree to send me here? I'm not so bad." My throat was tight. My words scratched and I tried to lower my voice. "I asked the Doctor about the chair, and he said, not yet."

"No. Did he say when?"

"We've got to find a way out. You and me. Mal too." I looked at the horizon line, the place where the sky met the sea. Escape, we talked about it from time to time. But we were marooned on a tiny island. Truth be told, I didn't even know which ocean we were in.

Cai's hand on my back rubbed a circle: "My mum doesn't want me either."

"Mums are supposed to love you, no matter what." I leaned against his hand, letting its warmth soothe me. "You know, sometimes I really miss my dog. Something to cuddle, you know?"

"Yeah."

"Elvis," I said. "We named him that because he looks like he has a quiff--his hair stands up no matter what we do. It's real cute."

"I've always loved animals," Cai said, although his hand dropped, and my back felt cold without it. "More than people usually. That is until--"

"Did you know there's a monkey in the Facility?" I stopped on the path, scanning the stretch of trees for a glimpse of bright blue ocean; the strange encounter in the science zone with the monkey's sharp, pinching hand replayed in my mind. What if there really was a monkey? And we weren't the only ones trapped.

"No there isn't," Cai laughed. "Why would they need monkeys when they've got us?"

"Well, something pinched my nose--the other day," I paused. "When I was with the Doctor." What day was it? Yesterday--the day before--earlier? A tremor passed through me. Sometimes I couldn't remember things, and now even the days were blurring together. "Look."

I pointed at my nose.

"It does look red."

"I told you."

"But you probably did it to yourself."

"Me?" I stopped on the path. Days mixing up was not as bad as imagining things.

"You're always doing it."

"I guess sometimes, I do." The Doctor said *violence towards yourself counts.* I punched Cai on the shoulder––just a light one, a tap if you will. "Come on," my voice was a whisper. "I think I'd know the difference between a monkey and my own hand."

Except I didn't––did I? Earlier, when the Doctor asked about the darkened room, I'd lied about that too. I'd heard about it plenty––with other therapists from the time before. Of course, I had. The thing was the conversation had revealed something else important. I wasn't the only liar.

The Doctor said the only route out from the darkened room was to take medicine, stand on spots when he said so, and obey all his other rules. It wasn't true though; the only fix wasn't his. There were other ways.

I thought again of his collection of body parts and shuddered. If I lived in a darkened room, it was no wonder I'd gone mad. Except darkness wasn't the real problem at Cerletti, was it?

6

FRIENDS

Heli

SCIENCE LESSONS WERE USUALLY with Dr Devitt. He was the one with the strongest teacher vibe. Enthusiastic, like if he didn't have to wear the Cerletti white uniform, he'd be head to toe in teacher's tweed and leather patches. The other kids moaned, but spending time alone with him in the lab didn't bother me. It was preferable to the school room.

Heat emanated from the lamp, illuminating the small segments of frog where we'd pinned them to the slides. Frog's skin was made from kaleidoscopic swirls that marshalled into patterns under the microscope. I wondered how long ago the creature's life had been taken and by whose hand.

"Did you kill it?" I said.

"Excuse me." Dr Devitt pulled back from the lens, squinting in the glare from the lamp.

"The frog––did you kill it?"

"Ah, I see." Dr Devitt laughed as though I had said something funny. "Did I go out and catch it for our biology lesson––you mean?"

"Sure."

"No. I am a scientist––not a hunter-gatherer." He paused. "Besides, its species is not indigenous to the island."

"What does that mean? Indigenous?"

"Frogs don't live here."

I nodded while he removed his glasses. Dr Devitt wiped them with his lab coat––without glasses––his face looked strange, younger, somehow vulnerable.

"Let's look at the abdomen next." He changed the slide. "What can you see?"

"Not much. It's blurry." After a moment, I asked, "Do you like it here?"

"Most of the time," he said, turning the dial on the microscope. "Sometimes, I miss the regular things. Cinema, take away, library."

Dr Shalt's small heels clicked across the lab floor. I glanced from the shadow of her approaching figure to Dr Devitt whose cheeks had pinkened. He bent over the microscope, burrowing his face against the eyepiece.

"I've adjusted the focus," he said. "You should see the shapes within the stomach clearer now. It's very beautiful, actually, a bit like the inside of a kiwifruit."

"Are you aware the bell has rung?" Dr Shalt said.

"I see," Dr Devitt replaced his glasses before glancing at his watch. "No, I was not in fact aware. Right then, Heli, it must be your exercise time, straight away."

Dr Devitt's cheeks glowed, and I got the impression he was hurrying me to the door, out from the science zone, and along the corridor, back to the rest of the kids waiting by the front entrance. He acted as though it was my fault we were late, and he was the one who needed to be somewhere else. Examining the frog wasn't too bad, but I wouldn't risk missing a moment of my time outside.

I was partnered with Cai. I didn't mind too much who it was——as long as it wasn't Joe. Even under the Doctor's routines——Joe was a psycho and good at not getting caught. The bigger kids: Mal, Joe, Sira, Mya, Cai and me, were probably a similar age. Although Cai was the biggest. Tall, where I was short, rounded where I was bony; *sharp and angular from nose to knees*, my Gran would say. I tried not to think about the things she used to say, although the venom of the past had no respect for boundaries.

"Where shall we go?" Cai asked as we headed towards the Facility door.

I shrugged. "Harbour, I suppose. Maybe have a swim."

"Heli?" Dr Shalt stepped into the space between us. "Need I remind you of the rules again? Perhaps you should stay behind to write them down——"

"It was a joke." I raised my hands. "We can't swim without bathing suits."

"Ha, ha." Her smile stiffened. "Take care, young lady. I shall be keeping an eye on you."

As though to prove her point, she looked me up and down, her presence a blockade in the doorway and the fleeting freedom of exercise time. I glanced behind her to the other kids, streaming outside into the sunlight——what was she waiting for?

"Yes, Dr Shalt," I said. "I'm very sorry." She smiled, and after a moment, stood aside, indicating the door and her permission to use it.

"Wait for me," I called to Cai, hurrying to leave before the door was closed.

At the gates, the Cerletti building sat behind us in the centre of the island surrounded by a craggy series of paths and heather-spotted land that dropped away to rocks and sea. From the rocks near the lighthouse, there was a good climb down to a shingle beach and a harbour. Although we called it a harbour––it was just a jetty that stuck out to sea, trailing bits of old rope. Boats must have landed there at some point, but we never saw any. Down on the beach was the best bit of the island but you had to walk fast to make it out and back in time.

I watched the kids on the path ahead––the group of them––together, laughing and gesticulating. Wiley bounced like a dog eager for his walk. Mal walked with his hands in his pockets, his thin shoulders slumped. Joe and Sira laughed, their arms almost touching. Well, she was welcome to that idiot's company.

I couldn't catch them and was left behind, my breath scratching at my throat. There's a show I'd watched a few times with Peony and Mum. *Girl Time*. At first, it had been just them, but when I was old enough and learned to be quiet––they had let me join. The show we'd watched was about a teenage girl chosen to slay vampires and her gang of mates. They called themselves the Scoobies. Mum said that was a reference to a cartoon gang of kids that outsmarted villains and had talking dogs.

I watched the others separating as they exited the Facility gates, drifting left or right, past the wall, in their twos. I wanted to be a Scooby. Part of something. The chosen one.

"Hey," Cai said. He was waiting behind the fence.

"Hey," I said. Most of all, I wanted to have a dog again, something to bury my nose in; it didn't even need to be the talking kind.

"Penny for them," Cai said.

Penny for them. It was the sort of thing my Gran used to say. A ridiculous expression, suggesting you would trade your secret thoughts for a penny.

I looked at Cai and the sea on the distant horizon, shoving thoughts of my Gran away. If she could see what really went on inside my mind, she'd have a heart attack. And that might be worth it, for a penny. I wondered what Cai had been like before he came here. I wondered whether we would have been friends.

"Come on." He poked my side. "You're too quiet today. It's freaking me out."

"I was thinking about my family if you must know." The words surprised me because we weren't supposed to talk about the past. To mention the things, we'd done which had led our families to give up and send us away. *You have to put Peony first.* My Gran had told my mum: *It's too late for this one.*

"Oh hell," I said as tears started to make their way from my eyes to my chin.

The Doctor said discussing family was triggering. It was the one rule I kind of understood. My mum didn't fight to keep me; she let them take me like an unwanted pair of shoes.

"What's wrong?"

"Sorry, I wasn't..." I felt teary. I stared at Cai as he shimmered and flickered. "I didn't mean to." But it was too hard to blame my parents; it must have been my Gran's fault I was here. She convinced them I wasn't worth holding on to.

"It's alright;" Cai blinked.

I stared at him, surprised he had stuck around. Boys usually got uncomfortable around crying. His eyes were the darkest shade of brown, huge pupils in the centre made them look almost black. He pointed towards the lighthouse, where it loomed on the far side of the island.

"Everyone is down there already––or on the rocks," he said. "We should get a move on, or we'll run out of time."

"Alright," I scrubbed my face against my sleeve.

We scrambled across the seaweed-strewn rocks, passing Sira and Joe where they had stopped to scoop at something in a pool with their hands. In the bright light, Sira's face was calm and smiling; her tics were better when she was outside.

"Why don't boats ever come here? Like, how do they know they're not welcome?"

"The lighthouse," Cai said, pointing. "Some kind of boat code."

The lighthouse was a focal point for the island. It wasn't much of a house, just a post with a big light that flashed day and night, warning boats off.

"What about pirates?"

He smiled. "Who'd want to come here? Cerletti isn't a place for day-trippers. Or smugglers."

"I suppose. Let's go for a paddle."

"Heli, you know we're not supposed to."

"What's the harm in getting our feet wet?"

Cai and I took our shoes off, rolled up our trousers, and waded out into the sea. Water spray whipped cold against the skin of my legs, and I zipped my coat up.

"Heli. Hey, Heli."

I turned. It was Mal waving to us from the beach.

"Come on," he said. "The bell's going to go soon, and we won't make it in time."

"We've been summoned," Cai turned.

"Who's your partner today?" I called across to Mal while wading back. He was alone on the shore. Pebbles crashed against my ankles and slipped underfoot; it was hard to go any faster.

"Just hurry up, will you?" He waved his hand.

"What's up your butt?"

"I don't want to get in trouble," he said. "Dr Shalt reminded you about the water before you left."

"Yes, but that was with my bathing suit." I grinned, but Mal didn't look amused.

I pulled my socks and shoes back on--leaving my toes numb and sandy within. We'd have to jog to make it back before the bell. Worth it though.

"It's getting warmer," I said. "It's maybe spring now. And the water's--"

"I've told you before," Mal said, shaking his head. "We are not going swimming. Not even if it gets really hot."

"I thought you loved swimming." I followed him across the pebbles towards the path. This was the weird thing with Mal, you thought you were having a cosy chat and then he got angry. "You told me once you were part of that swim team."

Mal's face went still, his brown eyes closing. "I don't do that anymore."

"Why not?" I asked as the three of us cleared the last of the rocks, slipping around the lighthouse platform, and heading for the path back to the Facility gates amid the outside scent of mud and heather. "Shall we run?"

"We'd better," Mal said.

"Don't you miss swimming, though? I mean--I know there's no swimming pool here--but one day you could swim again."

"How many times do I have to tell you? I don't want to." Mal sighed. "When I was on the swim team, they wanted me to be someone I'm not."

"But do you ever think that if we weren't at the Facility...?" My question trailed away. I didn't know how to put it.

"Think what?"

I wanted us to be friends, to know who Mal was before he came here, and for him to stop getting cross. I glanced at Cai, but he was too busy running to be of any help.

"Well, do you?" I said, uncertain now because Mal already looked pissed. "Do you ever have a thought?"

Mal rolled his eyes. "No, my arms and legs just move of their own accord. Of course, I have thoughts."

From the other side, Cai pantomimed a Princess's nose, and I sniggered.

"Do you think about this place?" I tried again. "About what they want with us."

"It's best not to think too much."

"Is it?" I gripped Mal's sleeve and together we stared at my hand on the fabric of his jacket: another rule broken.

We weren't supposed to touch each other. The Doctor said there would be the most severe punishment for anyone found transgressing this rule. We didn't know what it would be, and so far, were too scared to find out. I glanced backwards, a flicker of shimmering blue-grey water floating towards the horizon. "Are we ever going to get out of here?"

"Mollie did."

My breath caught and I turned to face Mal. "What do you mean Mollie did?"

"Here one minute, gone the next. It was before you came." He took his jacket off and tied it around his waist. I did the same, it was warmer off the beach, away from the wind. We were close enough to the Facility to slow our pace a little; the warning bell hadn't even rung yet.

"What'd you mean?" I said.

"They said Mollie must have drowned but I reckon she was too smart for that."

"But if she got out, then we could too." I took a step backwards, the sides of my toes rubbing against my socks as my mind spun. Escape, was it really possible? I tried to rebalance myself.

"You alright?" Cai put his hand on my back, steadying me. I straightened and inhaled the cold, fresh island air. "Excited at the thought we could escape?"

"No," Mal ran his hands through his hair: "No," he said again: "It doesn't help to think like that. Mollie was, I don't know. Different. Smart, super smart. I'm not Mollie, you aren't Mollie."

"But--"

"We're never going to leave this island. Better to face it. Kids like us don't get to have normal lives."

"Why not? It's not like it's the bloody law."

"Isn't it? Who sent you here?" Mal's face was more animated than I'd seen it before; the tops of his cheeks dark with colour, his eyes spread wide, brown centres afloat in the white. "We aren't normal kids."

"Speak for yourself. You're the one who–"

"Says Little Miss Fire-Starter. What was it you said the papers called you?"

"Don't," I wrapped my arms around myself. I'd told Mal about the fire and the newspapers in confidence. He'd only brought it up to be mean. "Why would you..." But his face was drained of colour, his eyes wet. "I'm sorry," I said because I hated it when he cried. "I'm sorry for saying those things about you—"

"It's ok," he shrugged. "I'm sorry too."

He showed me then, stopping on the path just before the Facility gates. With his hands––brown and delicate with pale-tipped fingers––he folded the sleeves back on his top, revealing the dark skin of his arms: the ruined flesh and silvering lines, some more vivid than others.

"I know I'm not normal," he said again. "You can make up your own mind about yourself."

I looked from his arms to his eyes, blood rushing inside my ears––bubbling and hissing. I felt dizzy. It made me uncomfortable thinking about Mal doing that stuff to himself. My hand hovered around my nose.

"I don't think I can." Jagged shapes shifted on the edge of my vision. "Isn't it normal to feel pain?"

"Pain is normal. But we aren't normal kids. You know that."

"We could be." I released my nose and reached for his arm. "You said it was up to me. We don't have to be what they say we are." The Doctor said we needed fixing, that our minds were broken.

Mal shrugged my hand away, rolling down his sleeve. "There's the bell. Let's get back before they close the gates."

"We're not all the same, you know? Look at Sira––she's practically better. Even the Doctor says so." My lips were dry and salty. We passed through the Facility gates, groups of kids dotted further along the path. "She'll be going home soon."

"No," he said. "No, she won't."

"Why not?"

"Haven't you figured it out?" Mal's face went blank. "If Sira's proof this place works, she's not going anywhere."

"What do you mean?" I called, but he sprinted towards the others and the Cerletti building. "Wait a minute."

"Come on," he shouted over his shoulder. "We'll be late."

I followed, uneasy. Not normal. I swallowed, tasting salt. Isn't going anywhere. The words lodged in my mind. Someone named Mollie got out, didn't she? That's what mattered.

Inside the Facility, the bell rang again, and we filed toward the dining hall, passing the Doctor in the corridor.

"Heli," Mal whispered from behind me. "Don't tell the Doctor you've been paddling. He said last time––no more trips into the sea."

"How would he know?" I glanced down at my legs. My wet feet rubbed inside my too-small shoes hidden beneath my trousers. The Doctor couldn't see the salt on my skin. He'd have to lick it to know––a disturbing thought.

The Doctor stepped forward. "No talking. Line up."

I needed to warn Cai, next to me, so I nudged him, not hard, just enough.

"Silence," the Doctor said.

"Silence is healing," we repeated.

I forgot about it until after dinner when the others went to reading time, and I was sent to see the Doctor. Had Cai given us away and told the Doctor about the paddling?

"Sit down," the Doctor gestured to a chair. "Have you taken your medicine today?"

The truth was no, but I wouldn't say it.

"Yes, Doctor." There was no choice but to lie.

"Once the meds build up in your system, we'll see a decline in your violent tendencies."

"Violent?" I jerked back, startled.

"Yes, like shoving people in line before dinner."

"I'm not violent." My hands twitched, and I fought to stay calm. "That was just..." But I couldn't admit what I'd been hiding. I looked away. The display cabinets behind him blurred. "I did the chant."

"Only when your symptoms are stable," he tapped his fingers. "You need to take your tablets. We can't keep injecting you."

"What do you mean––keep?" I only then remembered the incident with the monkey. It scared me, how much I forgot.

"When your blood test indicates no medication, we've had to inject you. It's happened three times," he said, pausing. "Second, and most important––you must want to get better. You do want that, right?"

I stared at him. Of course, I wanted to get better. Just not turned into someone else.

"Is something wrong?"

"You said––*not yet*."

"Excuse me?"

"Earlier, you said *not yet*. Are you going to use the chair?"

"The chair requires significant time from a doctor. For now, we use it for one patient at a time. Understood?"

"Yes." Relief hit me. As long as Mal was in the chair, there was no room for me. I was glad––even grateful––someone else suffered so I didn't have to. I hated myself for that.

"Though we hope to bring on another doctor soon," he continued, slipping his pen into his pocket. "Then, we can extend the chair's use. Now, time for bed."

"Yes, Doctor." My gaze flicked to his desk, hoping for a distraction. But he didn't offer a sweet. Instead, he escorted me down the corridor.

By the time I reached the bathroom, I was shaking. Tremors radiated through me. Avoiding the stares of kids brushing their teeth, I locked myself in a stall. I thought about punching the wall, but last time that didn't end well.

Violent.

I forced my fingers to unclench, closing my eyes. When would it be my turn in the chair? The Doctor never answered.

A new doctor was coming, and then they'd be able to extend their use of the chair. I thought about the Doctor again––evading questions. Mal said someone called Mollie got out. I forced myself to sit on the closed toilet and pulled my legs tight, under my chin. I needed to find out what had happened to Mollie and follow her example.

7

WOOF WOOF

Heli

A DAY OR TWO slipped away before I could ask Mal about Mollie again. Yesterday, I'd been paired with Cai for exercise time, and he wanted to walk to the far side of the island––the part where the iron fence ends in a sheer drop to the ocean. Not as good as the beach, but in the wind, the waves slammed against the rocks, and the view was intense.

"Let's go the other way," Mal said, nodding toward the Facility gates, away from the kids heading to the beach. Ahead, Sira and Joe were having the same debate.

"No," I said. "I went that way yesterday. I want to get my feet wet."

"Not this again." Mal shoved his hands in his pockets but began to follow the others down towards the beach.

He wanted to needle me about the rules, but I didn't care about them––or the doctors making them. Being good wasn't working anyway.

"Tell me about Mollie," I said, catching up.

"There's nothing more to say," he gave me that look like he knew what I was thinking and didn't like it.

"How can you say that?" I forced my hands to stay at my sides. "How did she get out?"

"I don't know," Mal pointed at Wiley, Mya, and Cai down on the beach already throwing sand. "Let's join them."

"Alright." We clambered over the rocks onto the pebble beach. I knew he was dodging me, but maybe one of the others would talk. Mya had been at Cerletti almost as long as Sira.

"Look, can you see it?" Wiley bounced, shielding his eyes. "Over there."

Clouds, dull like smoke, scudded across the sky, revealing glints of orange light. The tide was at its lowest, exposing brown, scummy sand, littered with seaweed. A swirling wash of water that left bubbling craters in its wake. Except for the land behind us, grey waves stretched in every direction, fringed with white foam.

"Oh," I said, spotting it. "There."

A small boat bobbed on the waves, too far to see us––probably––but close enough to make us hold our breath. I lifted my hand, excited by the hint of something beyond Cerletti's reach.

"I can't see it anymore," I dropped my hand. "For a second, I thought... If a boat came here, maybe we could leave."

"It's the lighthouse," Cai said. "Anyway, there's nothing to see."

He turned away but I kept looking just in case.

"Hey," I said, remembering Mollie and how she got away. "Did Mollie find a boat? If she did maybe we could too."

Mya gasped, her eyes darting to the Facility, as if the walls could hear. "Why is she even..."

"Heli," Mal tugged my arm. "It upsets people, bringing it up. I shouldn't have told you."

"But Mollie escaped! Don't you get it?" I couldn't keep the frustration out of my voice. "We need to talk about it. Don't you want to leave this place?"

Wiley came over and dumped a handful of sand over my head. "You're it," he said darting away.

Everyone's tight-lipped stance on Mollie only made me more determined. But I chased after Wiley for now, managing to get some revenge with a fistful of sand down his back.

Running around with the others was a distraction but a part of me ached for greater freedom. I wanted to go for a swim. I wanted my feet to leave the island, even if just for a moment. And I wanted to break a rule; maybe I even wanted to find out what would happen if I did.

"Let's go for a swim." I hesitated near the water's edge, longing for the chance to get wet. "Please."

The encroaching waves covered my feet where they broke and receded, sucked back out to sea, shifting sand and seaweed together. Despite the grey day, there was a suggestion of warmth in the flashes of sunlight.

"It looks lovely and cold," Cai said grinning.

"I have to do something." I took a few steps backwards and began to strip off my top. Up and over my head. My arms twitching, I threw the top behind me. I didn't care what anyone else wanted. My feet needed to leave this island––even if just for a few minutes. "It's dead calm out there."

"I've told you before––don't," Mal said, running over. "It's not calm. Look at the waves––the way they're breaking is dangerous."

"It's beautiful." I took off my trousers.

I could feel his eyes on me then, all their eyes, even while they pretended not to look. Cai, I thought, might have liked what he saw.

I stood still and glanced at my pale skin--almost translucent in the cold, veins and bones exposed beneath. I squeezed my eyes shut. Other bits and body parts, hidden for now. Inside my head, I pictured the Doctor's collection--housed in the jars, back in the lab--and my eyes popped open.

"I have to."

I needed to get as far away as possible from weird science and doctors. My feet tensed, bare skin against the pebbles. Without the Doctor's interventions--what kind of girl would I be?

Faint hairs stood erect on my arms, and I wore Facility underwear that did me no favours. God only knew what Mal thought. I always had the impression he wasn't into girls. Didn't stop him from staring though. I raised my arms and turned a slow, deliberate circle. And again, the wind teased at my hair. Let them look. I didn't care.

"What's she doing?" Wiley skidded to a stop at the water's edge. "Don't go into the sea, it's not safe. You'll drown."

It was a long speech for Wiley, but I was past caring.

"I just want a swim. I won't go out of my depth."

"No way, Heli," Mal said. "It's too dangerous, even on a calm day. Island tides and currents are totally unpredictable."

"I won't be long," I said. "Just a quick dip."

"Get Sira," Mal said.

When Wiley ran off, I laughed. As though the presence of Miss Goodie Two Shoes would change anything.

"I'll come with you," Cai said.

Behind us the Cerletti building dominated the landscape. Without it, the island would be wild, remote, breathtaking--a paradise. But the

Facility was inescapable, its single-storey structure stretched all the way to the far side of the island.

I turned away from the dark imprint of the building in the distance and closed my eyes. The Doctor said I must follow his path, trust his judgement. But I didn't trust him.

"I need to go somewhere other than here. To be free in the water. My skin's too tight." And that was the total truth. My fingers rubbed over the skin of my forearm, near enough to draw blood, before opting to hold my nose.

"Just have a paddle?" Mal said. He began to take his shoes off. "I'll come with you for that. Put your clothes back on––eh?"

"A paddle is not freedom." I released my nose. "Why not have a swim with me?"

"I don't like the sea. It's rough and wild and freezing cold. Heli, please," Mal held out his hand. "Let's just paddle. I don't want to swim anymore, not anywhere, and especially not out there."

"You don't like the sea?" My body started to shiver, and I rolled my eyes at Cai. Mal could be infuriating. "What are you so scared of?"

"It's cold and unpredictable," Mal sat on the pebbles at the water's edge. "Too risky."

"Come on." Cai finished stripping off his top and started to sprint. "I'll race you."

"Alright." I smiled, looking out, really looking.

There it was on the horizon, the shimmer of a faraway land. An impression. No bigger than the smudge of an artist's thumbprint. I wanted to get to that place: somehow. Get closer anyway. I raised my arms and threw myself at it. Never mind what Mal said. I wanted to get in the water with Cai. Get all of me in it and get away from the Facility, the doctors, and even the other kids. Just for a minute––to be free.

"Wakes you up," Cai laughed as the water swirled around my ankles and I went deeper, stepping towards another place.

Anywhere but here.

Although it was cold. Really cold. It was a shock, and gasps poured from my mouth. F-words, too. There was a strong current wrapping itself around me. For a moment, I felt a spike of fear. But I liked being held. The water was strong and powerful. And I pushed against it, letting it hold me. I wanted to let something--anything really--take hold of me.

"Hey, Cai." I waved my arms at him. "You're right--it wakes you up."

Salty water spat from my mouth as a wave crashed over me, dropping me from its embrace. My feet sank into the seabed, and I pushed back, splashing my arms.

"Their loss," Cai pointed at the other kids on the beach.

One of them called me wild--maybe all of them--their voices were lost in the roar of the sea. I supposed I was wild, although not like they meant it.

Wild.

I hated the word. They meant my behaviour, the splashing and my refusal to give in. To me that wasn't wild; that was hope and it was all that I had left.

"Hey, Heli. Stick to the shoreline," Mal shouted, but after a while, he joined us.

"You took your time."

I sprayed Cai and Mal with water, and they splashed back. Just for a minute, a hint of a smile played between us.

"Mal," I threw a handful of water and dark green seaweed. "Are we friends then?"

"Sure," he shook the seaweed from his head.

"But you think I'm wild." It was a single, sad thought that echoed around my head. Maybe Mal didn't see me the way I saw myself. The idea took shape, growing bigger, like when you light a candle.

Then, there was a surge of water coming at me from above and below. A series of waves slamming down. One after the other, the ground slipping away from underneath. I tried to regain my footing, but the waves kept coming. A terrible weight. I went under for a minute, maybe more. Hands pulled me backwards, another one under my chin. I struggled to reach the ground, my feet kicking at nothing but water.

"Get off," I tried to pull free and turn on my stomach. But I couldn't do that either. "Help."

The clouds darkened in the sky, turning angry and vengeful.

"I'm sorry." Seawater burned from the back of my nose to my throat. I closed my eyes and saw the Doctor's collection––the body parts trapped inside jars, forever preserved in nasty chemicals. I'd only wanted a moment of freedom. "I'm sorry."

"We have to go sideways," Mal said. "Kick your legs if you can because you're heavier than you bloody look."

Then it was hard work, physical work like I'd never known before; I kicked my legs while Mal dragged me. After a while, I had no clue whether we were even going in the right direction.

Everything was tinged the same dull grey colour as the sea. My limbs were heavy and bloated from an excess of salt water. All the while, there was the constant pressure of a hand under my chin.

"Think you can make it from here?"

I grunted and heaved myself back onto my front with Mal's hands helping me. I kicked my arms and legs. A slow, painful swim back in. Even though I could see the shore, every stroke was an effort. The wash of brown rocks, pebbles, and seaweed grew closer. I reached for it, the sea keeping a tight grip, dragging me backwards, undoing the distance I'd managed to gain. I might have given up if it hadn't been for Mal.

He'd said he hated the sea, but he must have been one hell of a swimmer--a champion--before he gave it up.

"Hey," I tried to speak but my lungs were full of water and a wet cough exploded from my throat.

"Come on," he held my wrist and tugged onwards. "You're nearly there."

When spongy sand sunk beneath my kicking knees, relief flooded me. I looked around for Cai. He was just behind.

We lay on the pebbles; the mud-like sand was long gone and buried beneath a weight of water and changing tide. My head was on Mal's chest. Cai lay flat beside us, quiet for once; the cold swim must have knocked him out, sending him to sleep. My eyelids fluttered, my legs an aching numbness from the kicking and the cold.

"Jesus Christ," Wiley said.

"You are going to be in big trouble," Sira said.

I don't know when she arrived, but it didn't surprise me she had nothing nice to say. I buried my head against Mal. His skin warming beneath my cheek, and there was the comforting beat of his heart. I never wanted the moment to stop.

"Come on," Mal said, when the faint ringing of the warning bell came from the Facility.

"When the Doctor sees us," I said. "What will happen?"

"Trouble." Mal picked up his shoes. "The usual."

"Why don't you swim anymore?" I whispered. "Like, you're so good at it."

"It's complicated."

"Fine," I rolled away, looking for my clothes.

I couldn't understand Mal. One minute we're the best of friends and the next… silence.

"We've got to go," I nudged Cai with my toe and his eyelids fluttered open. "You, ok?"

"Yes," he got up, tiny threads of seaweed stuck to dry skin, the beginnings of muscles in his shoulders as he pulled on his top and I made myself turn away.

"You're relentless," Mal said after a moment, throwing me my trousers.

"Is that a good thing?"

"I don't like my body," Mal said, gesturing to himself.

I looked, like I really looked, but I could see no good reason not to like anything. It was all perfectly ordinary and boy-like to me.

"He wants to be a girl," Cai said under his breath.

"Oh," I said. "Really? You'd rather be a girl?"

"No, it's not like that." Mal shook his head. "I don't like girls' bodies either."

"Charming." I shook my head and the three of us finished dressing while the other kids sprinted from the beach. The warning bell was going; we would have to be quick if we were going to make the gates.

"Do you know how on display you are in swim trunks?" Mal said.

"I've never thought about it," I tried not to laugh. Inappropriate laughter was one of my many failings, but you've got to admit it was pretty funny. "But I guess you would be."

"That's why I don't swim."

"Can't you just choose a bigger pair?" I glanced at Cai, walking on the other side with his hands in his pockets.

"When I was a kid. Maybe eight or so," Mal said, "I saw my dad in shorts. He had these long, dark hairs on his legs. I was teasing him about looking like a gorilla and I think someone said something like--one day I'd look like that too."

"Like?"

"The gorilla," he said.

"Oh," I said. "There are worse ways to look."

"I wouldn't be so sure," Cai said, hurrying ahead.

"Hey," I put my hand on Mal's arm, a little stung by Cai's tone. Maybe he felt bad for convincing me to go in the water. "He doesn't mean that." And I leant forward to kiss Mal--full on the lips. Not a sex kiss, just one between friends, and what could have been, if things had been different.

"Thanks for saving me," I said.

"I can't stand this place," Mal said as we scrambled back over the rocks, trying to catch the others on the path. "I hate everything about it. But this," he breathed in and threw his arms back: "this has been a good day." He flicked the back of my head. "Unexpectedly."

"Charming," I flicked him back. "But if you can have one good day, you can have others."

"No," he said, "haven't you been listening to the good Doctor? We are here for reformation. Not good days. They want to rehabilitate me. Help me to function in our marvellous world," he kicked at a loose stone. "But I don't want to be anybody's dog."

"Woof, woof," I said, and we laughed. I got the part about gorillas, and I supposed he wasn't keen on the Doctor turning him into a dog either.

We ran, our feet scrambling over the last of the rocks and then the pathway, the wind cold in our hair. The Facility loomed closer, its shadow stretching toward us. And even though we made it on time, the Doctor was waiting.

8

Yellow Brick Roads

Sira

Heli always claimed she didn't know where we were. It's not that I didn't believe her, not exactly. Some of the other kids said it, too. But come on, there were clues.

We were surrounded by water; it could have been an island near America or some tiny spit of land. But I'd travelled a long way from home, and I didn't need a yellow brick road to work out we weren't in Kansas anymore. Given the accents of just about everyone else here, I'd say we were somewhere off the coast of Britain.

I was one of the first residents at Cerletti; I guess that tells you everything you need to know about my folks. They gave me up, no questions asked, as soon as someone mentioned an experimental Facility and a chance of getting their potty-mouthed kid reformed. I guess my habit of drawing penises didn't fit with my momma's hope of winning beauty pageants. I actually arrived on the same boat as Mollie. Two girls, same wide eyes, and no place else to be. Of course, Mollie didn't stay long.

You've probably heard about what happened to her, already. Although afterwards, the Doctor told us not to talk about it. When she'd gone, or died, or whatever; it was all I could think about. Getting out.

I wasn't the only one who talked about escape. Everyone did. But no one dared push it like Mal and Heli. Did she really think she could wade through the cold water to reach dry land? The sea doesn't forgive mistakes.

Joe and I were partnered that day, it was about the time things were getting started between us. We were with the other kids at exercise time, but not really.

Joe hadn't said a word as we walked from the Facility towards the pebbled beach and sat on the edge of the path, the bit that overlooks the rocks, our feet dangling over the side. That wasn't unusual, and to be honest, I liked the quiet. The faint sounds of the others' running feet on the beach, the spit and hiss of throwing sand.

Joe's hand brushed against my knee. It was an accident, probably, until he did it again. This time, he left his hand there, warm and deliberate.

I stared at him, trying to work out what I felt. Things had been a little uncertain down there since the drugs from this place had kicked in. At first, it had been a relief, sharing a room with eleven others and all that. Nobody wanted masturbation on the table for discussion with the Doctor. I was happy enough to shake hands with the Devil and accept his trade.

Everything felt numb at the Facility. Now, I wasn't so sure.

Joe was tall with a mop of dirty, blond hair. Piercing eyes like he had stuff to say but couldn't work out any other way to tell you. He didn't usually smile all that much either, unless he was kicking someone, out of sight of the doctors.

"Is this, ok?" he asked, his hand soft against my thigh.

It was the nicest thing anyone had said since I'd arrived at Cerletti. Like he was soliciting my permission, as though he cared what I thought.

"It's ok," I said and lay my hand over his, although I God damn nearly fell at his feet.

There's a saying where my dad came from--a Chinese proverb to respect always the silent woman. But proverbs were no match for Tourette's. My momma didn't agree with it either, coming from the swamps.

She had her own stuff to deal with, only second place in the beauty pageants of her youth and a daughter who wasn't hell-bent on fixing things up nice for her. Momma believed if she could get my hair shiny enough, all the other problems would just melt away. She didn't take it too well when I pulled long, dark strands out in fistfuls and cussed without control. Long streams of bad words and expletives. But it's not like I could help it. I never set out to disappoint them. Too loud for my dad's tastes, not shiny enough for my momma. My parents dragged me from one psychologist to the next. It was only a matter of time before they accepted the Doctor's invite.

The warning bell rang, and Joe and I tagged along with the other kids. No longer holding hands, but from time to time we caught each other looking and smiled. The funny thing was, I hadn't cussed once.

Heli and Mal were behind us, straggling. By a miracle, we all cleared the gates before they shut, but inside the walls of the Facility, the Doctor freaked out.

"Stop right there," he said, pointing his pen at Mal and Heli who were trying to avoid his attention at the back of the line. "What is this dishevelled state and wet hair? On the spots."

I hurried to the first one, assigned to me on account of my ability to pass myself off as docile and obliging. Watching the other kids assemble alongside, I noticed Heli and Mal trying to rearrange their wet hair on spot numbers three and four.

"You've been swimming." The Doctor slid his pen into his top pocket and began his slow march along the line, waiting just outside the building.

Trouble was coming––I could feel it gathering like a storm, and I didn't want to get caught in its tailwind. I hung my head, willing myself to disappear, and the other kids followed suit. Except Heli, I assumed.

"What were you thinking?" The Doctor came to a stop beside her spot and said. "Have I not been clear about the dangers the sea imposes? It is not a playground. It's as likely a graveyard."

"It was my idea," Heli said. "Please don't blame––"

"Indoor exercise only from now on," the Doctor lowered his voice, frowning. "Until such a time when you can be trusted again. The sea is particularly unpredictable and dangerous on small islands." He stepped backwards and rocked on his feet before raising his hand, beckoning with a finger. "Dr Devitt, there you are," he said. "Tonight, please arrange a talk for everyone about the hazards of drowning. The shortness of time before our bodies shut down in the cold. The overwhelming power of the ocean. We certainly don't want a repeat of..." He looked away, his jaw tensing. "Enough. Take them out of my sight. Straight to the dining hall."

"Please," Heli reached for the Doctor's arm. "Please, please don't punish anyone else. It was me. My idea. I wanted to..." Her hands interrupted her, holding her nose, gripping it tight until she could no longer speak.

I walked past, keeping my back straight. Their punishment horrified me, the prospect of being kept inside. I wasn't sure I could have handled it. No time outdoors at all. No fresh air. It was true what they said, there was no place like home, and our road out from Kansas was lined with neither yellow bricks nor dancing munchkins. I didn't think even the Wicked Witch was capable of the things the Doctor did to us. But Heli had known what she was doing; she must have when she'd run into the waves, and yet it was hard to see her convulse on her spot. Why didn't she realise the only way to avoid trouble was to do what she was told?

"Enough," the Doctor said. "I've made my decision. And it's final. You will atone for your irresponsibility. Now, all of you, follow along after Dr Devitt, straight to the dining hall before I cancel dinner for everyone."

Heli released her nose with a long whine like a punctured tyre and rejoined the line with the rest of us. She prodded Mal's back as we walked, and I heard her whisper,

"Do you ever imagine they've got it wrong?" she paused, "and it's them and not us that are mad?"

"You're funny," Mal said. "But no. I never imagine they've got it wrong."

There was a faint smell of overcooked cabbage coming from the dining hall and I rolled my eyes at Joe, hoping he'd see it too. Heli was trouble and best avoided. But he scowled like nothing had happened between us and flicked his fingers into Wiley's back.

Wiley blanched but kept moving, keeping Joe's attack to himself. I was hurt for a moment but covered it as quickly as I could. Everyone else was distracted by Heli's antics on the beach and the fuss she made at getting caught. It reminded me of the need to tread carefully; I got why Joe had snubbed me, we would have to keep it a secret or they'd take that away too.

9

Noses

Heli

I HOPED THE DOCTOR would relent on the punishment, at least after a day or two. We all hoped. But he didn't and the days spent without going outside stretched towards six, seven, eight. It was hard to realise the value of something––to grasp and appreciate it––until it was taken away, lost and stolen.

"In a moment––it will be exercise time." Dr Fiennes rolled his sleeves at the front desk of the school room. But his words didn't hold the usual promise of fresh air, sunlight, and the beach. "Joe, collect the books and pencils. The rest of you pack your things."

"Mal," my voice cracked. "Mal? I'm sorry."

Joe appeared. "Don't beg." He leaned in, his breath sour. "You're so pathetic."

"Keep your nose out."

While I didn't understand why some of us were at Cerletti, it occurred to me that the two people with the most obvious of problems were also the least likeable.

Joe and Sira.

I wanted to tell him exactly what he could do with his opinion and bad breath when Dr Fiennes appeared, his hands resting on my desk. The top of his bald head bared down.

"That's a warning," Dr Fiennes said. "Heli, you will conduct yourself by the rules or you won't have any exercise time at all."

"But——"

"That is final." He stared at me until my eyes closed. Anything to shut him out. "Are we clear?"

"Yes, Dr Fiennes."

My hands crept beneath my thighs, and I sat on them, disgusted with myself. My tongue flickered across dry lips as I tried to steady my breathing. Mal stood with his arms crossed, his gaze distant, shoulders stiff. He'd barely spoken to me since that day we went swimming. I wanted to apologise, despite everything, it was hard to regret lying with my head on his chest, down on the beach after he'd rescued me. That moment had felt like true friendship. But the tight set of his jaw told me not to bother.

My gaze skittered to the window. It was bright outside; sunlight flooded the school room, making the dust dance. It was too nice of a day to be stuck inside.

Even though it was the last thing I felt like doing, I got up to help Joe with the books and the pencil sharpening, hopeful that maybe——if I was good enough——today the Doctor would allow us to go back outside.

"It's my job," Joe shoved my hand away. "Stop it."

"What's your problem?" I wiped my hand where he'd touched it on my jumper. Joe was a typical bully; he only wanted people to do his chores when he had his hand at their throats. I lay my fingertips on top of the pile of exercise books. "I'm just trying to help."

"Help yourself, you mean." Joe glanced at Dr Fiennes, who was tidying his own things at the front desk, before stabbing a pencil into the back of my hand.

Pain exploded, sharp and blinding. The pencil jutted at a 45-degree angle, wedged between skin and bone. I gasped, my vision blurring, rage twisting with humiliation but I swallowed the scream.

"What's wrong with you?" Tears burned and I blinked, furious.

"What are you doing over there?" Dr Fiennes's voice cut through the haze. "Line up on the spots."

Blood bubbled around the pencil, and I wrenched it free. Joe smirked, as if daring me to say something. But I wouldn't give him the satisfaction.

"Silence," Dr Fiennes said.

"Silence is healing;" we repeated, and I dropped my head, fingers pressing against blood from the swollen flesh of my hand. My eyes closed and warm water trickled. There wasn't even the promise of fresh air and the beach to cheer things up.

The Doctor and Dr Shalt stood at the far end of the corridor in the fake reception area, dragon guards at the door, protecting the treasure of the outside world. Together, they refused to let us even see it––to take a peek, a glimpse, not even a fleeting glance.

"Doctor," I stuffed my damaged hand inside my pocket, pain pulsing as it brushed the lining of my trousers: "Do you think maybe today we could go back outside?"

"No. Wait on the spots over there, Heli."

"But please, it's been a week, I think. And I'm sorry. Really sorry."

"I said no," he repeated, pointing at the spots.

The other kids were ushered through the Facility door, even Joe, who of all people didn't deserve it right now, while the three of us were marshalled back along the corridor, isolated from the others and kept inside--again. I wouldn't even mind the business with Joe and the pencil if the Doctor had changed his mind and let us go outside.

In previous days, we had been taken to the reading room and made to sit, today Dr Fiennes led us further along the corridor and stopped at the forbidden door that was usually the domain of the doctors. He swiped his card and opened it. I hurried in after him, curious about what we might find.

But it was only another white corridor. He took us into the first room.

"You can have a good run around in here." Dr Fiennes put his door card back in the pocket of his coat. He looked at me. "Burn off some excess energy."

It was a small space, empty of furniture--just a narrow skylight up high and down low, long, white, stuck-on lines that marked out a court. And there was a basketball hoop on the wall opposite the door. I almost laughed, imagining the doctors running, sweating in their white coats, glasses slipping down their noses while they tossed a ball about. Or worse, they might come equipped for exercising in ill-fitting, white shorts and sweat bands. A grotesque image.

"Who do you think uses that?" I nudged Mal and pointed at the net. "I mean--gross. Do you think they wear sweatbands?"

He shrugged, stuffing his own hands deep inside his pockets.

"Oh, come on, that was funny." I resisted stamping my foot. But really, it was hard enough being stuck inside without Mal refusing to talk. After what had happened with Joe in the school room, I needed someone to be on my side, someone who'd listen.

"Come on." I gestured at Cai for the ball. "Heads-up, Mal." I hefted the ball in the air, ignoring the pain in my hand as I balanced it. "Say something."

"Something," Mal muttered, sitting against the wall and drawing his knees to his chest.

"That's not what I meant," I said. "I want to talk."

"I'm not in the mood."

I threw the ball, but Mal ignored it, and it bounced into a corner while he rested his chin on his legs, rocking back and forth. There was nothing else for it other than to fetch the ball and throw it back and forth with Cai.

"He's having a bad day," Cai said.

"We're all having a bad day." I rubbed the swollen flesh on the top of my hand; a scab had formed. "There's no need to take it out on other people. It's not my fault we're stuck inside."

"Isn't it?"

"Don't you start." I kicked the ball at Cai's head, but he dodged out of its way. No one was listening.

Cai didn't ask about the commotion with Joe in the school room, and if he noticed how I winced whenever the ball caught against my hand, he gave no sign. I couldn't bring it up myself. It would be like admitting to a weakness. Joe's voice echoed, telling me I was *pathetic*.

Although I felt like crying, I put my energy into pounding up and down the court and throwing the ball. Whenever I passed near Mal, I looked over, hoping he'd change his mind, but he was locked into his own head, and I had no clue how to help. I'd wanted to ask Mal about Mollie again, but what was the point when he refused to talk.

When the other kids returned, loud and annoying, their pockets full of forbidden sea glass and shells, the anger that had been growing since a pencil pierced my skin began to burn. A seething resentment at Joe larking around with the others, his face flushing with pleasure from the outside. It wasn't fair. I'd resisted the Doctor's accusations of violence since I'd first arrived at Cerletti, but now––I couldn't deny it––I wanted to punch Joe. I wanted to take my swollen hand and wedge it in his face––hard. Maybe I wanted to punch all of them. All the other kids––one after the other. To take something and break it, to wipe away smiles, to remove treasures from pockets and smash them. Most of all, I wanted someone to notice what Joe had done. To punish him.

When the Doctor on duty at the door emptied their pockets and put their loot in the bin, I rejoiced, my heart lifting. I was glad to see the pleasures of outside limited, to see the other kids' faces crushed.

"Don't bring things back inside," the Doctor tutted. "How many times do I have to tell you? These belong to the natural world. They are not to be taken."

"Good riddance," I nudged Cai. He too was transfixed by the sight of things that belonged outside, on the beach, or on the path. "You know, it's kind of ironic…" I remembered the Doctor's collection of things on a shelf in his lab––things that didn't belong in a jar.

"What is?"

"Nothing."

I pushed the thought away. It wasn't welcome inside my head.

"Silence," the Doctor said.

"Silence is healing." We chanted together, for once glad for the distraction.

Life at the Facility was even worse without time outside, and while Mal sulked, I was no closer to working out a way to escape.

The hours shifted from one thing to the next. All other aspects of the Facility continued, undisturbed by our punishment: schoolwork, science, sessions with the Doctor, and a new assignment.

Chores, the Doctor declared, would help us learn some *responsibility.* Even Sira's disorder had submitted to the Doctor's renewed drive for order and fallen into line--her twitching limbs, grunts, and facial tics, sometimes rude or funny words, had almost stopped--or maybe I'd stopped noticing.

When my session with the Doctor finally came, I clung to a fragile hope: maybe if I gave the right answers, he'd let me out.

"Heli?" the Doctor cleared his throat until I looked up. We sat together on either side of the table in his office. "Save daydreams for your free time."

"Yes, Doctor."

The display cases and framed certificates behind him on the wall cast shadows in the mid-morning light. The Doctor was up to his usual tricks and lying again; there was no *free time*--no thinking time--at Cerletti. Even reading had been shortened to allow for the new chore rota as though he believed busyness would be our remedy.

"Let us return to the violent outbursts." The Doctor's pen stilled over his clipboard. "Tell me--how do you feel about those?"

"What outbursts?"

"Several times--for example--you have been caught shoving other children in the line-up."

"I wouldn't call it violent." My hand hovered around my nose, but I wouldn't let him derail me. It was ironic how he accused me of violence while Joe stomped around the place, attacking people with pencils. "If you'd let me go back outside, I'd--"

"Being inside is no excuse. You exhibited violent behaviour before the punishment. A punishment--I might add--that is entirely your own fault."

"But..." I hesitated. The image the Doctor painted was not the same as the one I had of myself. *Violent behaviour.* "I sometimes get angry," I said. "That's true." The rest of it wasn't though. "Although, I don't like the spots or chanting."

"We use chanting to embed automatic good habits," he said, "so we learn to listen and to concentrate and," he looked at me, "to be polite."

My hands shifted, and I screwed them into fists, studying the scab that formed where Joe had stabbed me. It still hurt when I moved it.

"But it's hard to be stuck inside while everyone else gets to breathe fresh air and collect shells." I looked at him the way I'd once looked at Dad, begging him to get Peony and me a dog. "And I'm not violent."

"Is there anything else you'd like to say?" The Doctor made a hard, sniffing sound--like he was short of breath. "Any more truths?"

"There are people in here who have actually been violent. Where-as--the worst thing I've ever done is think about something. Like some-times when the others come back from being outside... But you have to understand, I haven't acted on it. I've wanted to," I said, "but I haven't been violent."

"And how do you feel about having these angry thoughts about the other children?"

"How do I feel?" The Doctor--whatever I did or said to direct him elsewhere--would stick his nose deeper.

I looked at him, scrutinising the shape of his features, his every crease.

"Something amusing?"

"No," I shook my head. "There's nothing funny about being stuck inside."

"I see." His hand continued making vigorous notes. "And do you hold yourself to account for this anger?"

"I..." My throat spasmed. It was his fault I was angry, and what was more, I squashed my anger--carrying it inside--small and silent. I changed myself to suit him. And yet, nothing was enough. "I don't think so."

"In that case--perhaps we'd better consider this session at a close." He finished writing on the sheet of paper hidden behind his clipboard, making the strange nasal sound again.

But there was something else I wanted to know. Something I couldn't contain.

"There is one other thing." My hand shifted, stretching outwards. I froze, repelled.

"Yes?" he said.

"The monkey," I said, my voice barely a whisper. "Will I see it again?"

"Monkey?" The Doctor's voice was soft and curious. "There are no monkeys in the Facility."

"But I saw it." The memory was vivid. "It pinched my nose."

"I see," he held his pen aloft, balancing it between the tips of his two forefingers. "You must listen carefully. There are no monkeys in the Facility," he paused, letting the silence stretch. "At least none that anyone else can see."

My lips trembled. What was he talking about? I remembered the monkey--its small fingers pinching my nose, the sensation so real it made me flinch. I didn't trust the Doctor, but things didn't add up. Memories slipped through my mind like eels, elusive and hard to hold on to. The Doctor told lies, but I couldn't forget how Cai had laughed, too, when the monkey was mentioned. My eyelids fluttered shut. Who could I trust--him or myself? Of all the places I could have ended up, why here? It was the court's fault, the fire's fault, my Gran's fault.

"Would you like a tissue?" the Doctor asked.

"No."

"Knowing the monkey only existed inside your head--how does that make you feel?"

"Not good," I said, because how could I escape here when the Doctor said what I saw was not what he saw? My eyes squeezed tighter. In the darkness, I heard his pen click back into life.

"And do you remember experiencing these symptoms before?"

"You mean, before--"

"Before you came here, yes."

"No." My head shook, invisible hands shuddering through me, forcing my eyes open. The first thing I saw was the Doctor's shadow as he leaned forward, taking notes. "No. Never."

"Not even on the day of the fire?" He looked up. "Think carefully. You don't remember anything unusual that day?"

"Doctor," my voice wavered, timid. I hated this topic; he knew it. "I haven't seen my family since that day. Except at court..." I hesitated; Peony hadn't been there. "At least, I don't think I have." I looked at him for confirmation. He nodded, so I went on, "If there had been an animal--how would I know if it was real?"

"Did you see any animals?"

A swallow made a lonely sound in my throat. "No."

"Then I think we can conclude there were no unusual visitors that day. Not animals, anyway." He scribbled a note. "And what about people? Do you remember seeing anyone else that day--someone who might've encouraged you to do something?"

A memory lurked, just out of reach. At Gran's house, Peony had asked me to burn things––mementoes from an ex-boyfriend. A t-shirt, perfume, a cuddly toy, photos. Fire. Maybe she thought I'd keep it under control. But fire does what it wants.

"Heli," the Doctor pressed. "Was there someone else?"

"No," I paused. "But even you could be a figment of my imagination––like the monkey." I closed my eyes, wishing him away.

"I'm still here. As real as you." Silence stretched, then he might've offered his hand: "Touch me if you like."

"No, thank you." As he pulled back, I sought out the small window's faint light. "Will you let me outside again? Or at least let Mal and Cai out––it wasn't their fault. It was my idea to go swimming."

"When the punishment has been completed," he replied, his breath a hiss in the dark. "You broke the rules. Tears won't lessen the atonement required."

"And the monkey... will I see it again?"

"I don't know. But delusions are often echoes of real things. You didn't invent the monkey entirely; there was one––a toy monkey––for distraction during injections."

I groaned. His words made me feel worse. Delusion; distraction; fabrication.

"How much of what I see is real?"

"Not all of it."

No kidding. My hatred for him grew––this man who collected kids for experiments only he understood. Who lined us up, kept us inside, and put us in electric chairs.

"But it's the parts that inspire violence and destruction we must be most alert to."

My breath rattled in my throat. It was the things he said about me I hated most. "Tell me something I don't know."

"It depends on how regularly you take your medicine." He snorted. "Your carelessness with your drugs makes things worse. You have to want to get better. Follow the rules. No more unauthorised swims, for example."

"I do want to get better. You know I do. It's just--"

I screamed then--raw and guttural--anything to end the conversation. Within moments, he pressed the alarm--a blare of sound --and they descended. A swarm of doctors, hair pulled tight, needles gleaming. The medicinal scent thickened. I thrashed, my chest tightening, unable to breathe. If I was broken, I would never leave this place. Cursed to stay inside, walk the corridors, stand on spots.

Dr Shalt's needle pierced my vein, a scratch of cold. I tried to bite her but failed. I was a mad girl, the Doctor had said, my mind played tricks. There was no choice but to accept it. In this place, escape was impossible.

10

FIRE

Heli

THE BELL'S HARSH RING shattered the darkness. Smoke choked my senses, heat bearing down like a weight. I buried my head beneath the pillow, gasping for breath, desperate to escape.

"What's that noise?" Sira's voice was distant. "Bollocks, bollocks, wank," she muttered.

The weight of the pillow lifted from my head.

"Heli, let go of it."

"Why don't you get lost?" I gripped the pillow, as though it could block her out entirely.

Sira leaned closer, her features shadowed in the half-dark.

Her face twitched. "It's time to get up."

The lights blinked on, and the bell stopped. My hands stretched forward, pushing away from the bed. I drew deep, smoke-free breaths and started dressing. My clothes were already folded––a plain white T-shirt, brown trousers, and a hooded jumper. Yesterday was hazy, just flashes: the Doctor's nose, a needle, my missing sister.

The dream always worsened after an injection. Fire. Without it--no court, no social workers, no Facility. Fire was the gateway.

We dressed in silence, the routine a comfort.

"Hey, Sira," I tried. "Sorry about earlier. Didn't sleep well."

She turned to Mya instead, her expression sharp and irritating.

"Yes," I said, louder. "I do want to talk." I pulled on the last of my clothes and marched towards her bed.

"What do you want to know about Mollie?" she asked, catching me off guard.

I shrugged. "What was she like--I suppose?"

"Funny, smart, annoying. She slept in your bed." Sira smirked. "Time's up. Bell's ringing."

My hands tightened, knuckles turning white, as I lined up for breakfast. The greasy stench of sausages turned my stomach. The echoing clatter of cutlery and murmur of voices pressed in. I gripped the cold fork, unease coiling sharper than hunger.

After eating, we shuffled back to the black vinyl spots on the floor. I focused on the shapes I could make--one circle, two shoes, and the way my shadow stretched long in the dim light, pulling away from me. Around us, the room felt like it was folding in, the silence heavy with the faint buzz of the fluorescent lights above.

Dr Fiennes stood at the door, his smile exposing a pale flash of teeth. He guided us forward with brisk motions, our line creeping toward him.

"Good morning, Heli," he said, his voice too bright against the dark morning.

"Morning," I muttered, my eyes fixed on the ground, avoiding his smile.

Maths.

I flipped open my workbook and slipped on the headset. Maths used to be my least favourite, but now I liked its black-and-white certainty. Cai's empty desk sent a jolt through me. Was he in the chair? My stomach churned at the thought, but no––it was his turn with the Doctor today. Still the chair loomed large in my mind, its presence a constant threat.

"Line up. On your spots," Dr Fiennes called after a while, his voice firm. "Silence."

"Silence is healing," we chanted.

Joe called out; his voice louder than it should have been. "If silence is healing, why'd you make us chant?"

Dr Fiennes stopped in front of him, his expression cold.

"It's just a question," Joe muttered, cheeks red. "Chanting's not silent, is it?"

"We follow rules to create positive habits, Joe. Do you understand?"

"Yeah, sure," Joe gazed at the edge of his spot peeking out from his shoes.

"In that case," Dr Fiennes said. "Silence."

"Silence is healing," we repeated.

I glanced at Cai; surprised Joe's outburst had evaded punishment. He widened his eyes, while his lips sounded the silence chant.

But Joe's reprieve didn't last––after lunch, they came for him, while the rest of us went back to class.

After geography, Dr Devitt took me to the lab, a space of chemical smells, wooden benches, and glass jars holding things I tried not to look at. Sweat gathered under my arms as we mixed compounds, and I kept glancing at the door. It was shut and I wondered whether it was where they'd taken Joe.

"Hold this," Dr Devitt handed me tweezers.

"Do you know where Joe is?" I asked, trying to sound small.

"He's having treatment," he replied, not meeting my eyes. "Focus on your work."

Encouraged by his answer, I continued, "What happened to Mollie?"

Dr Devitt froze, removing his glasses. "Focus on your own recovery, Heli. Follow the Doctor's rules."

"Please," I said, my thoughts like the rush of pebbles when a wave hits. Each one pulled me in a different direction. "I'm sorry about going swimming. Can I return to outside exercise?"

"You'll need to speak to the Doctor," he said. "I think he might be inclined toward leniency if you apologised again."

"But--"

"Enough," he snapped, turning back to the experiment.

Sweat trickled down my spine. The bell rang, cutting through the tension.

The door opened, revealing the small room with the chair. Doctors disconnected cables from some monitor. Someone had been in there. Had it been Mal again, or were they using it on Joe? I felt a pang for Mal. For Joe, it was more curiosity.

I wanted to talk to Cai--more and more, I found myself wanting to talk to him. My cheeks flushed at the thought. I should be planning how to get out, finding out how Mollie had done it. Instead, I kept picturing Cai, his lips close to mine. But Cai wasn't there when I reached the line-up, and neither was Joe.

In the gym, Mal and I kicked a ball around, a sad excuse for exercise. It was too hot to be trapped inside.

"You've not been in the chair then?" I forced a smile, glancing over my shoulder towards the door. Where was Cai?

"No."

Sweat dripped down my neck, the heat oppressive in the enclosed space.

"It's him in the chair then." I sat on the floor, tears welling.

"Come on, he'll be alright," Mal said, tossing the ball. "At least play."

"I don't want to." The image of Cai strapped into the chair wouldn't leave me. "Why can't we go outside?" I called to Dr Fiennes, my voice cracking. "At least open the window."

"It's not that hot," Dr Fiennes replied. "And only one of you is doing any running."

I watched Mal balancing the ball, his ribs showing through his damp shirt. "Are you eating?" I asked.

"It all comes out the other end," he said with a bitter laugh.

"I'm sorry," I twisted my hands together.

"Sorry enough to play?" He threw the ball at me, forcing me to catch it.

"You could use a haircut," I said.

"Says you."

"Mal, it feels like the walls are closing in." I got up and threw the ball to him. It landed at his feet, a hollow sound. "I've got to get out before I go mad."

"Too late," he said as we threw the ball back and forth, the bounce echoing. "You're already mad."

"I'm glad you're not in the chair," I said. "This time."

"Me too," he admitted, "though I feel like an arsehole for admitting it."

"The Doctor said––one at a time."

"Guess he changed his mind."

"I need out," I whispered, leaning close and flipping the ball from my fingertips in a chest pass.

He caught the ball, his voice low. "I've got a plan. An ultimate solution."

"What is it?" My heart raced. "Can we escape––like Mollie?"

Mal's gaze darkened: "Oh, I'm going to be like Mollie alright."

The weight of his words pressed heavy.

"Can I come too?"

He hesitated, his hand twitching on the ball. "Maybe try your meds first? See if you can leave through the front door."

"I have been taking them," I lied. "I didn't want to, not until they told me what happened... There was a fire at my Gran's house. They think I started it. But I didn't. You believe me, right?"

"Sure. I believe you," he said, his voice soft.

"My sister, Peony––I don't even know if she..." My voice cracked. "They think I'm lying. That I'm mad."

"It's okay," he said. "I believe you."

"Will you help me find out?"

"Maybe," he replied. "But for now––"

"Time's up," Dr Fiennes interrupted. "Get your things."

I turned back to Mal, desperation heavy in my chest. "If I could just speak to my––"

But Mal's face had gone pale, his eyes wide with fear.

11

MIDNIGHT WALKS

Sira

IT STARTED HAPPENING MORE and more. Midnight walks between our beds while the other kids slept. Although sensors were set up for unexpected movement, we'd learned to skirt them. Every step pulsed with adrenaline. The risk was worth it for the reward. Not just the thrill of sneaking around but the intimacy of it, skin pressed against skin--touching in new places--the comforting warmth of being held.

I had just made it back to my bed, slithering across the floor, hugging the walls. My hand was clamped over my mouth--stress made me more likely to cry out--when I heard her voice.

"Why won't you talk about Mollie?" she whispered.

"Heli?" I said, yanking my blanket up and sliding beneath it. "For God's sake. Bollocks. Bollocks."

She must have heard me sneaking back. I bit down on my finger, pulling the blanket tight over my head, and hoped the rapid beat of my heart wasn't loud enough for everyone else to hear. I wondered if Joe could hear anything on his side of the thick grey curtain separating the girls from the boys. Probably not, he slept like the dead.

"Please, it's creeping me out," Heli said, her voice a thread in the dark. "Since you told me she slept in this bed."

"Go to sleep," I said, trying to steady my breath. I hadn't risked sneaking back from Joe's bed only to get caught talking to Heli.

"But why tell me that and then refuse to talk about her?"

"I'm tired," I hesitated. "Maybe in the morning." Although I'd already told her what I remembered about Mollie.

I wondered if she'd try to threaten me. She had me at her mercy now. If she came right out and accused me, I could tell her she'd imagined it. Everyone knew she hallucinated––talking to people who weren't there. But could I be that cruel? The Doctor had promised severe repercussions for touching each other. He'd already punished us once, even using the chair on Joe––I wasn't about to let Heli get me in the same trouble.

"Do you know how she did it?" Heli pressed, her voice as insistent as a building storm. "Did she talk to you about her plan?"

I rolled over, our faces just inches apart in the dark. I could make out the vague shape of her. "No, Mollie didn't talk to me. We were friendly but not like that. I guess she thought the more people who knew, the greater the risk."

"Pretty smart," a new voice whispered, and I stifled a gasp. For God's sake. Did everyone know what I'd been up to?

"What are you doing awake?" I asked. It was a miracle one of the doctors hadn't come in with all this talking.

"I heard you," Mya replied.

Her bed was on the other side of Heli's. I squinted into the darkness, trying to make her out, but she was either too small or the room was too dim. Mya was here for anorexia––her parents sent her to Cerletti after the other clinics failed. Tired of the cycle, she'd return plumped up only to waste away again. Now she was still skeletal, but the Doctor claimed he was pleased.

"Everyone says that," Heli continued, relentless. "Mollie was smart––"

"Exactly. She didn't tell anyone her plans," Mya cut in. "She just disappeared one night."

"She left at night?" Heli said.

"Yeah––ask Mal. He knew her best."

"Happy now?" I yanked the covers over my head. I didn't care what Heli threatened, I wasn't saying another word tonight.

12

BOOKMARKS

Heli

WE STOOD TOGETHER AT the door, waiting for Dr Fiennes to finish packing away his stuff. And once he'd stopped moving, Mal seemed to shrink--even smaller--his shoulders slipping down the wall like the weight of the room was flattening him.

"Mal," I nudged his foot. "What's going on?"

"What?" Mal took his time to reply, his face shifting to watch Dr Fiennes. "What do you want?"

"I'm sorry," I whispered. "It's my fault we're stuck inside."

"Forget about it."

"Why do you look so scared?" My heart pulsed, a frantic plea. "I don't understand." Dr Fiennes slid his device into its case and the air thickened. "If it's about the swimming. I'm sorry. I didn't mean to cause trouble. You know," I indicated the inside space, reaching my hand backwards and pressing at the wall. Rolling my eyes, I pulled a face, thinking it would get a laugh or at least raise a smile, but it did neither.

"It's ok," Mal said. "Now, for God's sake––shut up." Dr Fiennes was heading over to us, his bald head gleaming even in the falling light. "He's coming."

"Why are you being mean?"

His eyes narrowed: "Because I've got my own shit to deal with." A tremble went through him.

"But someone else is in the chair," I said, feeling panicked again that it might be Cai and not Joe they were subjecting to it. "I'm your friend," I said.

My hands reached outwards, hoping to resurrect the previous closeness. It was Mal who had saved my life that day on the beach, and just now, he'd promised to help me. He was my friend.

Mal squeezed his eyes closed, leaning his head against the wall.

"Line up now, in silence," Dr Fiennes took his exit card out.

"It's supposed to be one at a time," I didn't mean to yell. It just came out. Follow the rules they said. But the doctors kept breaking them.

"That's a warning, Heli." Dr Fiennes swiped his card through the door. "Back to the hallway to line up with the others, on the spots. Mal, it's time for your session—I'll take you down."

I looked at Mal. No wonder he was scared if Dr Fiennes was taking him to the chair. No one knew exactly what happened in that thing, except for Mal, who didn't talk about it. The chair was a relic from the olden days, resurrected by the Doctor to reform our minds, to shock us into submission. If you looked at its impact on Mal, it was a shock alright.

Later, in the reading room when Mal returned, he was pale and silent, and there was still no sign of Cai. The gnawing in my gut wouldn't stop. I needed to see him.

I grabbed my book and rested my head on the table. My limbs ached to move. I glanced at my legs--shrinking, withering. Soon, there'd be nothing left of me.

"What are you thinking about?" Mal nudged my shoulder. We were supposed to be reading, relaxing our brains before bed. But there was too much going on and I couldn't keep still. "You're clenching your fists," he said. "Careful, Dr Devitt is watching."

"Nothing much." I tried to release the tension in my bones. "I've just been sitting in one position for too long."

"Are you sure?"

"Oh, thank God. Cai," I nodded, distracted because he had finally returned. "At last."

"No talking," Dr Devitt took his glasses off, wiping them on his sleeve. "Settle down, Heli. There's only ten minutes until bedtime. Do you think you can manage that?"

Cai dragged a beanbag over and I leant close, "Where have you been?"

"What are you talking about?" Cai's dark eyes were serious. "You know where I've been."

"No," I glanced at the book in my lap. "I don't know where you've been. With the Doctor somewhere?"

"Of course," he nodded. "With the Doctor."

"Oh." I looked at my book. Had he told me that and I'd forgotten? Things slipped from my memory like sand through a fishing net.

Doctor Devitt did a lap of the room and came closer.

"Heli--eyes on your book," he said, passing back to the front. "All of you remember to use your bookmarks so I can see you're following."

I lifted mine. I was reading *Great Expectations*. Cai's book was *Of Mice and Men*. I'd read that one a while back; it was alright, considering our limited choices.

"Cai," I whispered. "If the Doctor's using the chair on more people, I think it's time to really go. Mal says he has a plan. But I think we should try and find a boat or something."

"Alright," he said. "Although first we need to be allowed back outside. That's step one."

"Of course," I nodded, reassured we had the beginnings of something. "Step one," I nudged Mal, wanting to share the idea with him. "Get back outside."

"That's not going to work," Mal said, under his breath, his eyes shifting back and forth while he rubbed his stomach like his guts hurt.

"No harm in trying."

"There's plenty of harm," he said. "And where would we go? No one wants me back home and it seems no one wants you either."

"You're being mean again."

"Are you even talking to me?" his dark eyes narrowed. "Are you even listening?"

"Hey," I said. "Stop it."

"I told you before––there's only one way out of here."

"One step at a time."

"You think I can't say no––like down on the beach. But I'm telling you now, we are stuck in here until the Doctor deems us better, or we die."

I raised my eyebrows at Cai, unsure if he could hear Mal's comments. The repeated use of the chair was making Mal worse, and it was even more reason to find a way to leave.

13

THE OTHERS

Heli

Strip lights, always flickering at the start of the day, hung over the table where we ate. Three times a day, we sat in our assigned places like clockwork. Breakfast was always ready––thirteen plates, thirteen pieces of toast, the same count every day. I knew them in my sleep. Hard-boiled eggs with grey centres, rows of cups, and plates. I wondered how many spare plates they kept––how many more of us kids they'd catch.

Today, a staff member, in a crisp black and white uniform, was putting up a sign in the corner. Occasionally, we'd see one––cleaning or setting the table, always avoiding eye contact.

"What's that?" I nudged Cai.

"Who cares?" Joe hunched over his toast like he was hoarding a secret.

"No one's taking that from you," I pointed to the blackened crust of his slice.

Wiley sniggered and Joe's leg shot out beneath the table. Wiley doubled over, holding his knee.

"Seriously? Was that necessary?" I glanced at Dr Shalt––she was on duty but didn't notice.

"What are you going to do about it?" Joe's grin widened; black crumbs stuck between his teeth.

"Heli, pass the salt," Mal's voice cut through. He gestured, oblivious to Joe's scuffle.

"For God's sake." I shoved the salt his way. The other kids were back to eating, acting like nothing happened. Even Wiley, his laughter choked down with his breakfast.

I focussed on Sira. The first time I'd met her, she'd twitched so hard, she couldn't stay still on her chair. Now she was quieter; a shadow had wrapped around her, holding everything tight. It was a shame. I missed her outbursts—swear words flying like bullets. No one invented obscenities like Sira.

"Great," Mal shook the empty saltshaker. "Just perfect."

"Mal," I whispered, trying to catch his attention, but he ignored me, lost in his own head; he had been since that swim. "Fuck's such a boring word, don't you think?" I looked at Cai and Sira.

"There are more playful ones," Cai smiled. "Why don't you give us a few inventions, Sira?"

"Excuse me––Dr Shalt?" Mal stood; his voice louder than he probably realised.

Although, she didn't even pause her typing. She was seated near the small, high-up window. A beautiful smear of colour on the glass.

"Yes?" She finally glanced up, her smile thin and practised.

"No salt."

"You've had your allocation. Sit, or you're out of time."

"But we've only just––"

"I said––sit."

"Yes, ma'am."

We froze at his tone, knowing it wouldn't end well.

"That's a warning, Mal. Don't call me ma'am. We're not in the army." Dr Shalt's smile sharpened. "Everyone, time to clear away. Now." She clapped her hands, and we hurried to cram in our last bites. Her voice stayed cool and firm. "Straight away. Or you'll miss lunch, too."

Mal's face darkened. His untouched breakfast scraped into the bin, and my stomach knotted. If he would just talk to me, we could plan our way out of here together.

"Mal," Dr Shalt said. "Take that plate to Heli."

Although we had nearly finished cleaning up, we jumped at the bell signalling the end of breakfast. I dropped the last of the greasy plates into the bowl to soak, hating the feel of the slippery residue on my fingers. I slipped an extra egg into my pocket when Dr Shalt wasn't looking.

"Hey," I whispered when Mal came over. "Want this?"

"No thanks," he said, his face shadowed, clothes hanging loose on his frame.

We lined up to leave, catching sight of another cleaner. Two staff in one day––rare. I nudged Sira, but she stiffened.

"Hands to yourself, Heli," she said, although her voice was low enough to dodge Dr Shalt's radar.

"Says you?" I tried to tease.

But her face twisted into a grimace, spasming.

"Sorry. I didn't mean––" I mouthed, regret washing over me. I just needed a sign that not everyone had given in to the Facility's rules. I hadn't meant to trigger her.

The cleaner carried out the tub of dirty dishes, avoiding eye contact. It was a treat to see someone different––fresh, novel––dressed in a neat black and white uniform, like a dentist or a flight attendant. She was pleasant in her ordinariness. But who'd take such a job here?

"Lesson time," Dr Shalt said, opening the door. "But not for you, Heli."

My heart pounded. Had she seen what had happened with Sira?

"The Doctor wants to see you," she said, indicating him, where he lurked in the corridor.

The Doctor stopped in front of me. "Tomorrow, you'll go outside for exercise."

I blinked, glancing at Mal trailing behind the others across the line of black vinyl spots.

"But what about the others?"

"This is a reward for your behaviour since the incident. You and Sira together can supervise Wiley––he hurt himself yesterday. The responsibility will do you good." His smile lingered. "Keep him away from the rocks. No danger, Heli. None at all."

I tried not to think about Mal and Cai. It wasn't fair.

"But––"

"Would you rather stay inside?"

The thought of sun and wind made me hesitate. "No, Doctor."

"After the incident earlier, Mal will stay in. You'll follow Sira's example. Now go into the school room. Education first."

14

A TALE OF DERRING-DO

Sira

WE NEARLY GOT CAUGHT a few times. The more I fell for Joe, the less I focused on everything else. I still wanted out––the Doctor's plan for us was hooey––but Joe made me distracted. Sometimes, I was even happy.

The reading room had stiff-backed chairs, half a dozen bean bags and a shelf of books that promised more than they delivered. I made it through the first chapter of Hard Times, but Pride and Prejudice lost me after a page, and Moby-Dick turned out to be the biggest letdown. It was just about a sailor––not at all what I'd imagined. The only thrill was when a guy's leg got bitten off.

Dr Devitt sat at the corner table with headphones on, listening to something on his device. He tapped his fingers, making notes, the blue light from the screen casting shadows on his rigid face and reflecting off his glasses. By then, I'd given up missing my phone, so I wasn't jealous, whatever Dr Devitt was doing, it wasn't making him happy.

Heli glanced once, then twice, in his direction before she dragged her bean bag across the floor all the way towards mine.

"Where've you been?" she whispered, her hands twisting together. "It seems like ages."

"I've been with the Doctor," I squinted, the beginning of a tic forming. Heli often talked about how she hadn't seen you for ages when you'd only been gone an hour. "Completing my assessment." I leant closer. "Actually, he told me someone new was coming to the island––another doctor––apparently, she wants to see how much progress we're making. All the wonderful things going on at Cerletti. You'll have an assessment, too. We all will."

"Another one?" Heli screwed up her face. "How many doctors does it take to fix a sick kid?"

Heli's hand tugged on her nose like it often did before she turned to look around the room. Mal slumped on a black bean bag on the other side of the shelf, all the way to Mya, who sat bolt upright in a plastic chair as she flicked through the pages of *Moby Dick* like she was looking for a picture. If she was closer, I'd warn her not to bother.

"Do you really talk to the Doctor?" Heli said, her fingers fidgeting.

She didn't need the extra emphasis on the word *talk*. I knew what she meant. Although talking was not really optional with the Doctor. He asked questions, and I replied. That's how therapy sessions worked. And no one asked things like the Doctor did. It was his master talent. An art form. Sometimes, I tried to look at his clipboard and work out whether he'd pre-conceived the questions. They felt rehearsed, but there was never any confirmation of this. I even asked him about it once. He flipped my enquiry around. *Would you prefer it if my questions were planned, Sira?*

"I don't say anything to him." Heli's hands were moving fast again in time with her words. "I keep my mouth shut. I try to, anyway. Sometimes I say more than I mean. Well, he writes things down--I don't know what--on his clipboard. I bet you talk though." Her finger points at me. "You're his pet."

"Yes, we talk. I answer his questions; he makes notes." Perhaps this place was making me better. I spasmed less, not beauty pageant perfect, but less than I used to. We didn't talk about the darkest things though. The things that kept me up at night. Things I've never told anybody.

"I'm not letting him and his pen into my mind any more than I have to." Spit danced on Heli's lips on the word pen, her skin luminous even in the semi-dark of the reading room. The shorter half of her hair brushed against her bean bag as she moved. "Well," she said, "what do you talk to him about?"

"Heli," I said. "I don't really want to--"

"No need to look like that," she hesitated. "Besides, it's me who needs advice," she paused. "Tomorrow--the Doctor said I could go back outside with you and Wiley."

"What? Just you?"

"Yes. So how do I tell them? I feel bad because it was my fault--you know--the day of the swim."

"I guess the person you really need to tell is Mal." I tipped my head towards him. He looked lost in an overwhelming black beanbag like he'd laid down in the dark and it had swallowed him. "He's even thinner than before."

"That's what I'm talking about," Heli said. "It's not fair. But after the stupid thing with the salt, I don't know how to..."

Joe's single tap on the wall made my heart quicken. "I have to visit the toilet." I said, unable to meet her gaze.

"Oh, ok." She shrugged.

When I returned, sliding back into the reading room as quiet as a mouse, Joe hung back. He'd said he'd follow me after a minute. My book was where I'd left it and so was Heli.

"What meds have they got you on?" she asked, her voice a whisper.

"What?" I said, eyeing the door. Joe should have arrived by now. If he took any longer, Dr Devitt would get suspicious. "Why are you talking about––"

"You're sweating," she said. "I thought it might be the meds."

"Yes," I said, my shoulder spasming. My tics were worse when I was anxious, and I couldn't work out what was taking Joe so long. Sweat gathered under my arms, too. If Joe took much longer, I'd need a shower.

"Back home," Heli said, "they started me on something for ADHD––these tablets." She looked off into the distance like she could see someone there. "They said I was hyper. Couldn't sit still––my teachers hated me. But the meds––well, they made me feel like I'd just got off a roundabout. Sweaty and dizzy. All the time. It was horrible."

"What about now?" I eyed the door.

"I'll take what they give me," she said, her eyes flickering to the left. I thought she was probably lying. I could understand that, not everyone liked the feelings that came with being doped. "As long as it's not Ritalin, that's the ADHD drug. Feeling nothing is better than spinning. Constant––non-stop––dizziness."

"Hey." Mal pulled his bean bag over, lay across it on his front, balanced his book on his head, and pulled a silly face. "What are you doing?"

"Just talking," Heli said. "You know."

"I thought you were doing better," he said. "Taking your meds like a good girl."

"I am," she smiled––a slow, lazy smile. "Tell me a story––will you? A tale of adventure and derring-do. I'm bored of this book."

"Derring-do?" Mal glanced at Dr Devitt, but his headphones were still on. "You talk crazy, girl."

"You know what a story is."

"A story, you say? Well, how about this one?"

I could hear Mal whispering words, but I didn't catch any of his meaning because Joe reappeared at the same time, rubbing his stomach. He stopped by Dr Devitt and gave him some cock and bull story about an upset tummy. Relief flooded through me; a tidal wave so strong I had to close my eyes to avoid getting washed away.

The next day, the Doctor ushered me into the group heading outside with Heli and Wiley. Usually, we went out in pairs, and Heli figured the Doctor trusted her to keep an eye on Wiley. But I had a feeling it was more about us keeping an eye on her.

At the gates, they took off down the path while I jammed my hands into my pockets, happy to hang back. The heather lining the trail was in full bloom, a haze of purple mingling with softer, paler shades that shimmered like jewels in the sunlight. When my momma used to drag me around cities––sprinting down streets, chasing cabs or getting stuck in traffic jams––I always wished for quiet. A place without the bustle, the overflowing bins, and the noise. You know what I mean, where every sense gets hammered: the greasy smells, phones buzzing and too many people. But right now, I'd have taken all that, even one of momma's pageants.

"Watch the rocks. They're slippery."

But I might as well have been talking to myself. Wiley and Heli bounded over the rocks like a couple of puppies, oblivious.

"Wiley's usually great on these rocks, right?" Heli said, turning. "Like a little crab. So, how did he fall?"

"I don't know," I muttered, my eyes darting around until they landed on Joe, who was down on the beach with Mya. A knot tightened in my stomach. What were they doing down here while I was stuck playing babysitter?

"Ball sacks. Ball sacks." The words slipped out before I could stop them, my face twitching uncontrollably. "Sorry. Scrotums. Sorry."

"Don't worry about it," Heli said, moving closer. Her tone was casual like it was no big deal, but I felt every word like a weight. "Did someone push Wiley?"

"Why would you say that?"

"Was it Joe?"

"No. He didn't push... I never said anything." I turned away quickly, hiding my face behind my hands. Joe had been there that day, sure, but I wasn't about to share that with Heli. Besides, why would he push Wiley? He'd come over to see me.

"What's he got over you?" Heli pressed, stepping closer.

"Stop it," I said, the words sharp and loud.

I turned and walked away––more like a hop, really, as if something sharp had jabbed my toe. The spasms were running wild, completely off the charts. I forced myself to breathe, trying to reel it back in, but the obscenities kept slipping out. It stung deep; things were usually better outside. The open space was supposed to help.

Heli spread her arms wide as she moved in the opposite direction, stepping onto the pebbles.

"The tide's out, look," she called, her voice carried by the wind.

"Come on, Wiley," I said, following her down onto the beach. Once we'd all cleared the rocks, my breathing relaxed a little. Down on the pebbles, I gathered the white ones, slipping them inside my pocket. If I could get them past the Doctor, they'd make a great blank canvas for my artwork.

"Look," Heli said. "Back there."

"Where?"

"There." Heli pointed to the rocks where we accessed the beach. They stretched all the way along this side of the island. A small pathway cleared by our feet, where we climbed from the path to the beach. Heli steadied herself against the swirling, sucking motion of the sand. "Can you see it?" she asked.

"Yes," I said. Near the harbour, hidden within the rocks, was a door.

"What do you think is in there?" Heli's voice dropped to a whisper, her eyes darting back and forth. "Why would they hide it?"

"I'm not sure," I said. "Storage?"

"Is it there?" She turned around, her cheeks pink. "Like really there––or," she dropped her voice to a whisper. "Am I seeing things?"

My eyebrows raised, the last of my twitches now under control. I wasn't sure what to say, I hadn't thought she knew.

"It's there," I said. "Shall we go and look?"

"Should we leave Wiley though? What if he falls?"

"He's alright throwing stones in the sea. He's not a baby. Come on––there's a new place to explore––after all this time." I grinned, a break from the monotony of our routine was welcome.

On the far side of the rocks, a battered wooden door lay hidden, easier to access from the beach, but still climbable from the rocks. It was tucked, out of reach of the water. I scanned the surroundings, setting the pathway to it in my mind.

"Heli," she jumped when I nudged her. "Has the Doctor ever said anything to you about the chair?"

"Only that it was one at a time until a new doctor came. But the other day, I thought they might have put Joe in it?" Her face scrunched up. "Maybe I got it wrong."

"No," I said as we walked across the beach to the door. As we got closer, it looked pretty wind-battered. "You got it right. They did put him in."

"I saw it once, you know," her voice trailed away like she wasn't quite sure. "It's in a windowless room with no light. I saw it through a doorway in the science lab. There were two doctors there. Dr Shalt was one of them, and she was preparing a needle. Have you ever seen it?"

"No," I said. The Doctor told me once electric shock therapy wasn't compatible with my condition. That's pretty much the only thing Tourette's has got going for it, but I worried what the other kids would think if they found out I was protected from its reach. It made me feel bad, guilty, like I'd done something wrong.

"Do you want to open it?" Heli pointed at the door.

"Sure."

I reached for the handle, twisting it hard where it was rusted with salt. The door was part of a small wooden hut.

"Sira." She rested her hand on my shoulder. "I think the chair had restraints. I want to ask Mal about it, but I'm not sure whether I should. It makes me think of an--electric chair--you know the one?" She mimed being fried by electric shock, and a cold shiver passed through me. "That kills you."

I thought about Mal, left behind at the Facility. He was on his own. Again. Whatever that chair did, it looked to me like it was killing him one way or another.

I opened the door. It was a small boatshed. My heart shifted. There was plenty of rope, tarpaulins, nets and buoys--for all the use they were to us.

"There's no boat," Heli said, disappointment heavy in her voice. "I thought--"

"Let's get out of here," I said, glancing over my shoulder. "We've stayed too long already. We don't want to get into trouble."

"No, we don't." She ran her hand along the wall. "Still, it's good to know this place is here."

"Why?" I said, surveying the greenish walls and piles of old fishing equipment, abandoned like the stuff people leave outside a charity shop. "It's horrible--damp and smelly."

"But it's somewhere you can close the door and just be," she said, waving her arms. "You can be alone."

"You can do that in the bogs."

"It's not the same."

"Do you want to talk some more about the chair?" I asked as we shut the door.

"No," she shook her head. "Come on, let's find Wiley."

Wiley was skimming stones and ran towards us when we emerged from the old boatshed.

"Shall we start climbing?" I turned to Heli, surprised to find she had tears on her cheeks. "What's the matter?"

"As if you care."

"What'd you mean?" Her tone stung because this afternoon had felt pretty nice, stumbling on secrets together. "We're friends."

"No, we're not," she said. "At least not since you started sneaking off all the time."

"What are you talking about?" My grip on the rocks faltered. If Heli had noticed, the chances were someone else had too. "You're mad with me because I'm trying to get better."

"That's what you think of me?" Heli sniffed. "I don't care whether you twitch or not. Say all the swear words you like. I think it's funny. But you are always sneaking off."

"That's not true," I paused: "And that's not why you're crying."

"I'm not," Heli sniffed. "It's just the wind. Can we talk about something else?"

"What do you think will be for dinner?" I asked. "Maybe they'll show us a movie like they did that one time."

"So long as it's not black and bloody white."

Outside the Facility building, we lined up on the spots.

"Well done, Heli," the Doctor said, walking along the path. I cringed for her; what would I do if he lay his hand on me? Patting me like a dog.

"There's no need to look like that," the Doctor said, coming to a stop beside her. "This is not a thing to endure. A prison. You have behaved responsibly. Well done."

Heli's fists clenched like she wanted to punch him.

"You understand that your place here is a great privilege."

"No," she said, her voice full of fury, "it's not."

"In you go," the Doctor said, as though he hadn't heard. "Straight to the dining hall."

Joe gave me our signal and I excused myself to visit the bathroom. It was a relief after the day so far. Heli could keep the grungy boatshed; I much preferred the privacy of the bathroom.

"D'you mind if I go back first?" I asked.

"Again," he brushed his finger along my cheek. "You'd better make it worth my while."

I kissed him for a long minute. "It's just Heli was asking questions earlier on the beach," I said: "I don't want her getting any more suspicious."

"No one will believe what she says, she's a lunatic."

"Better to be safe than sorry." I pressed my finger to his lips and hurried to the dining hall.

Inside, I found my seat at the table, glancing around for our chaperone. It was Dr Devitt, sat in the corner, tapping at his device. My hands reached for my cutlery to eat the chicken stew. Dr Devitt was the least observant of the doctors.

"Good, isn't it?" Heli said, her plate nearly empty. "No movie though."

After a moment, the screech of Dr Devitt pushing his chair back echoed over the room and we all turned.

"What's going on?" I whispered.

Dr Devitt's face had paled in the blue light of his device. He stood and began patrolling the room, his gaze flicking back and forth from us to the door.

"What's the matter?" Heli said. "You look like——"

But she stopped when the door interrupted her. And the Doctor's shadow fell over the room.

"Sira," his voice cut through the room. He beckoned with a slow, deliberate hand.

I glanced at Heli, panic rising. Tears pricked my eyes. I'd worked so hard on being good and now——one mistake and it was over.

"Now, please," the Doctor's icy tone promised punishment. My legs felt heavy as I stood. Whatever waited for me beyond that door, it wasn't good.

15

BLOOD

Heli

A SCREECH OF SOUND, too loud in the quiet, as I pulled the grey curtain down the middle of the room. It was my job. I couldn't remember if someone had told me to do it, or whether I'd just known it was my role--an assignment, the daily chore. But the curtains couldn't keep the nightmares out that followed--screams, crackling flames and faces fading behind smoke.

Maybe it had been Mollie's job before I arrived. I didn't hate doing it. The curtain was a thickish material--grey, the colour of naval ships and cheap metal. With a sharp tug, I could bring it down from the ceiling. But the disruption wouldn't be worth what came next. I forced my hand to unclench, my knuckles aching from the grip.

We slept in a huge dormitory in the middle belt of the Cerletti Facility; girls were on one side of the curtain and boys on the other. My bed was between Sira's and Mya's.

Mya, on one side, was quiet enough, although Sira groaned on and off all night. The Doctor may have gotten a handle on her Tourette's, but sleep was no defence. It was always humid in the room, too, no matter the weather. Too much breath from too many people. Other gases, as well; the thick curtain was no match for them.

Some nights, I slept ok; other times I turned from one side to the other, shifting my arms and the flattish pillow beneath my head--trying to mould it into some kind of shape. But it was a lost cause. The beds themselves were simple, camping ones that folded in half on days when we cleaned, offering little solace in between. Once a week, when we stripped the sheets, you could see the dark green fabric stretched tight over the thin metal bars, throwing a canopy over the floor. The sheets had softened over the time I'd been here. If you washed something enough, it gave way.

Once a week, we were assigned a longer exercise session-- two hours outside instead of one, in what we thought of as Saturday, the week's highlight. I had no idea if it was an actual Saturday; we had lost track of days--dragged behind them like the load of a donkey.

"Two hours today," Dr Devitt said. "I'll assign you into three groups. Listen carefully."

I waited to be assigned to a group.

"Heli, Mal--and Sira--you're the inside group. Come along. I will bring a ball."

My stomach sank. No outside time again. No wind on my skin, an illusion of freedom. I didn't care about the ball. It was a rubber excuse for fresh air.

Sira's face crumbled, as the others ran for the door. I couldn't watch.

"Dr Devitt," I said, "can't we go outside? The Doctor trusted me the other day and Sira hasn't done anything--"

"No," he said, "you cannot go outside."

"But——"

"I'm not going to argue about it." Dr Devitt had been terse since the mysterious business with Sira last night. "In one way or another, you have all proven that you cannot be trusted."

His voice carried the weight of authority, labelling us untrustworthy——a verdict that was inescapable. Sira hadn't returned after the Doctor took her away last night, not until this morning when he'd brought her into the school room. I wondered what had happened because Sira never broke any rules.

In the corridor, further along, Dr Shalt was in conversation with the Doctor. I kept my gaze averted as we made our way towards the only room with any kind of space for running. Dr Shalt's posture was stiff; her face animated as she spoke to the Doctor. She glanced over at us as we passed, and for once the smile slipped. Her face was furious——reddening and blotchy.

"I'm not their mother," Dr Shalt said, her voice sharp. "You have always been clear that our role is not parental. And if this continues..." She glanced our way, her voice lowering to a hiss: "It will compromise the experiment."

It pleased me to know that things were not going Dr Shalt's way, but the rest of their conversation was lost as we moved past.

Sira and I collected the ball from Dr Devitt who set up a computer table in the far corner.

"What happened last night?" I whispered, leaning in. "Was it because of the boatshed?"

Sira's eyes flicked to the table. "Don't," she said, her cheek twitching.

"Fine, don't tell me. Let's not be mates." After the other day outside with Sira, I'd thought maybe we had become, not friends exactly, but friendlier.

She grunted, her eyes twitching before she pulled her jumper off.

"Give me your jumper, too," she said, "we can use them for a goal."

"Weather's shit outside anyway." I grinned, relieved she wasn't making a big deal about being punished. That was the thing with Sira. One minute she was busy sucking up to the Doctor and the next she was alright again.

But after a few minutes, Mal sat on the floor in the corner and refused to join in, which just left Sira and I.

"For God's sake, Mal," I threw the ball towards him, but he ignored it, and it rolled into the corner. Sira jogged over to retrieve it.

We threw the ball for a bit, between the two of us. There was some satisfaction at throwing it hard, making Sira sweat and pant as she ran. But then I went over to Mal.

"Hey," I said. "I wanted to tell you something. When I was allowed outside, I found something." I paused hoping to garner a glimmer of interest. "There's a boatshed."

"With a boat?"

"No," I shook my head. "That would be too easy. But it's a start."

"No," he said. "We're just as trapped in this hole as before. Only now we know they once had a boat to store."

"Step one," I said. "Exit the Facility––that should be easy enough, we just need to steal one of the doctors' pass cards. Step two––we can make a boat. There are bits we could use in the boatshed."

"Are you joking?" Mal shook his head. "Do you know how to make a boat?"

"It doesn't need to be an actual boat. Just something that floats. Then we can monitor the sea for a gentle tide. You know all about those."

"That's the worst plan I've ever heard."

"What was Mollie's plan then?"

But Mal wouldn't say any more. I looked over my shoulder to find Sira had sat down––unwelcome as a long-tailed rat. She sniffed, pulling at her ponytail.

"What do you want?" I asked.

"What else am I supposed to do?" She wiped her face on her sleeve, her cheek twitching. "You don't have to talk to me. We could just play ball again?"

Mal's response was to pull his jumper over his face and turn towards the wall.

"Now look at what you've done." I tried to push her away from us, but she wouldn't budge. "Fine," I sighed. "If you want to talk, tell us where you were last night."

"I was caught," a solitary tear slid down her cheek.

"Caught? Where? Outside?" I dropped my voice to a whisper, glancing at Dr Devitt. Maybe there was something to be learned from Sira.

"No. Going into the boys' toilet."

"What? Why would you want to go there?"

But she wouldn't say anymore, and I was trapped between them, both lost in their misery. It was actually better when exercise time ended, and Dr Devitt sent us to perform our chores.

In the laundry, a tangled heap of plain tops and trousers waited to be folded. Everything was drab––white, brown, grey, sometimes black––as if whoever chose our clothes had never seen a sunset or a rainbow. I wanted to tie-dye them, streak them with pinks, purples, and oranges like splashes of fire on water. But here, there was no room for colour.

When I first came, someone else did the laundry. We'd toss our dirty clothes in a bin, and they'd come back once a week, neatly folded. Then, one day, without warning, the doctor assigned the chores to us. Now, every day was a ritual of folding dull fabrics, the smell of soap competing with the cold, sterile scent of the Facility.

At least I never had to deal with Mal's mess. Someone else––some invisible helper––took care of his soiled clothes. Or maybe they just threw them away. But where would they get new ones? There were no shops on the island.

My hands paused over a pile of t-shirts. Laundry was thankless. My mother used to say: People only notice laundry when it's not done.

Mum.

Once she slipped into my mind, I couldn't stop the memories. They came, rapid-fire, each one hitting the bull's-eye. Her laugh, wild hair like mine but brown, not red, and her scent, sweet and sharp like orange peel. I was folding strangers' clothes in a white-walled Facility on a secret island, and she was... where?

My hands started to shake. I doubted I'd ever see her again. The thought choked me, and the walls pressed in. She must have agreed to send me here.

It had been a weird day from the start. Peony and I were getting along, like we hadn't in years. Normally, she'd pick at me, mocking my clothes, my music, and my taste in everything. But that day, we were allies. We were at Gran's, a united front against a common enemy.

My jeans protected my legs, they had said later. My arms hadn't been so lucky. Everything else––gone in a flash, a heartbeat, maybe two. And I never saw my sister again.

I finished folding the last of the t-shirts, wondering why laundry made me think of that day. Had I been washing clothes then, too? I turned a top over in my hands, staring at the dull fabric. I couldn't remember everything, just that it wasn't me who started the fire.

The flames weren't the reds and oranges they write about in poetry. They were a colourless, searing force, turning everything to smoke and shadow. My sister was caught behind the inferno, hidden in the blackness. We'd been burning things––her idea. Peony's letters, photos of her with her ex-boyfriend. I tried to reach her through the flames. Gran tried, too. When I closed my eyes, I could still smell burning paper and scorched fabric; I could see the melted white soles of her shoes.

A murmur of voices broke through the memory. I blinked, looking down at the shirt in my hands. Each one had an initial, a small white "H" that meant it was mine. I stacked them into neat piles, sliding them into cubby holes where our names were written in marker pen.

"Heli?"

I froze, my heart stuttering. Was this what the Doctor had warned about––phantom voices, things that weren't really there?

Footsteps shuffled through the doorway.

"There you are."

"Dr Shalt?" I turned.

She held something in her hands––a package, pale pink against the sterile white of the room. My chest tightened. Could it be? A letter, a message from Mum, or…?

"These are for you."

She handed me the package of crinkling plastic. A bright, unnatural pink. My mouth went dry. It was a pack of sanitary towels, the same brand Peony used to hide in her drawer. My stomach churned. Another part of me, my body, wasn't mine anymore. They watched everything.

"Can you tell, then?" A blush spread up my neck, and I gripped the package, fighting the urge to drop it, to shove it away.

"Of course not," Dr Shalt replied with her smile stretched to a tight, thin line. "But you're of an age now. These are just in case."

"Oh." The heat burned in my cheeks. I didn't know where to put it, how to hide it. My mouth opened, then closed. I searched her face, hoping she'd offer a solution.

"It's time for dinner," she said.

I'd have to stash the package under my pillow or in my bedside drawer. There were no shelves in the bathroom, no place safe from prying eyes. What if someone found it? The plastic package rustled, whispering like an unwanted secret.

"Will it hurt?" I tried to keep my voice steady, but the thought made my stomach twist. I could handle most things, even the toilet parts, but blood made me queasy.

Dr Shalt arched an eyebrow, amused. "It happens to all girls," she said. "If you have more questions, ask the Doctor."

Sixteen, I guessed. I must be sixteen. It was strange how time slipped away––dates lost without a calendar to mark them. Peony had been fourteen when she got hers. I remembered Dad once bringing home supermarket-brand pads and Mum laughing, saying, We're not poor. They'd both cracked up, teasing him. Now I was, alone, clinging to this pink package that marked me out, even in this place of outcasts. My mum would have made a joke of it, made me laugh. But here, it was another part of my freedom wrapped in plastic.

With the package hidden under my sweater, I scurried toward the dormitory, but the door was locked. The bell rang, echoing down the hall, and I had no choice but to head to the dining hall. The others lined up. I pressed the package against my body, praying no one would notice. In my worst moments, I never imagined Dr Shalt handing me sanitary towels. Not like this.

At dinner, I tucked the package under my chair. Mya's head turned, her gaze catching the edge of pink. My grip tightened around my fork. Did Mya have her period, too? Or Sira? I thought about asking, but Sira and I weren't exactly on speaking terms. I needed to know where they hid theirs if they had them. Why were they wrapped like that anyway––cheerfully pink for something that should be blood-red?

After dinner, we had reading time. Cai and I settled into bean bags, side by side, but the pink package sat like a guilty secret between us. It caught my eye every time I shifted. I hated it. I wanted to fling it across the room. It should have been Mum giving it to me, making a joke, laughing like she used to.

"Hey," I whispered, touching Cai's arm. He leaned closer. "Do you have parents?"

"What?" He pinched his nose, snorting a breath. "What kind of dumb question is that?" His eyes flicked to the pink package. I dared him to ask. "Have I got parents?" He shook his head. "I haven't got time for the birds and bees talk."

"I know about the birds and bees." I shuffled away.

We talked every day, Cai and I, but the hard stuff stayed buried. There was no way I could talk to him about the pink package, about how just the sight of it made me feel alone, discomfort clawing at my chest.

"I know about sex, thank you very much." I moved my beanbag further from his, closer to where Sira and Mya were. "That's not what this is about."

"Good," he grinned, "because I don't have time for that either."

"As if." My cheeks burned hotter. I'd only wanted to know if he thought about his parents, too. I didn't know whether he'd deliberately misunderstood me. Pink packages in white rooms were enough to make boys uncomfortable. "Let's just read our books, okay?"

"I'm not the one trying to have a sex talk."

In silence, I turned the page, almost dropping the book in surprise. Someone had drawn a penis through all the words. I traced my finger over the indentation before closing my eyes. No one here talked about their parents. No matter what the Doctor told me about the fire, I was sure it hadn't been me that started it.

"Sira," I whispered, moving even closer. "Are your parents still alive?"

"As far as I know," she said.

"Why are you here then?"

"Because they were ashamed of me."

"Stuff like this?" I held up the book with the line drawing of a penis. She giggled.

"I forgot about that one."

"My parents said they'd have me back once this place had fixed me," Mya said, pulling her black bean bag over.

"How would they know if you were better?" I closed the book, trapping my fingers inside the pages.

"I'd be fat."

"What about your parents, Heli?" Sira's cheek spasmed. Just once. "Will they want you back when things at this place are done?"

"There was a fire," I said, shaking my head. My parents hadn't put up any kind of fight to keep hold of me. But maybe, if my Gran was out of the picture, and I found some way to contact them–to convince them. "Fire's why I was sent here."

"Is that where you got those scars?" Mya said.

I nodded.

"Sorry."

"Not your fault."

Mya glanced from the pink package to Dr Devitt, typing on his device in the far corner and said, "I don't like it here."

"Me either," I rubbed my forehead. "Do you think we're stuck here forever?"

"No." She shrugged. "Have you got your period?"

"Not yet," I said. "Have you?"

"No," she shook her head, before continuing: "The Doctor says I don't weigh enough. She has though." She nodded at Sira.

"Where do you keep your stuff?"

"In my drawer," Sira said.

"I'll do that too," I smiled, it felt like we were getting somewhere. "You know, we don't have to wait for our parents to want us back." I leaned closer to them both. "If Mollie escaped, we can too. Not by ourselves, but maybe together."

"Haven't you worked it out yet?" Sira reached to tug her ponytail. "Mollie's dead."

"They can't all be dead."

"Who?"

"Everyone they don't want us to talk about," I said. "It's too convenient--"

"Oh, shit," Sira said.

"What?"

I turned to look at her, but she was watching Mal on the other side of us. I followed her gaze.

"Get off," Mal said, his voice cracked, raw and broken as they pulled him to his feet. "Not again," he sobbed, his legs thrashing. "Please. I won't go. I won't."

He was crying. Big, fat, noisy gulps of air. Now I wished I'd spent reading time with him and taken the chance to ask him why his skin looked so grey.

"Hey," I stood up from the beanbag, my legs trembling. "Leave him alone."

From behind, a pair of hands pressed my shoulders, and my knees buckled. The drop to the beanbag took the wind out of me.

"Stop that," Dr Shalt said to Mal. "I said, now."

Other doctors appeared, surrounding Mal. Dr Fiennes and the Doctor too. Three white-coated forms held him as he cried.

"Don't make me go," he said. "Not again. Please."

Before he fell silent.

"Sira," Dr Shalt said, "please open the door? Quick now."

"Don't you dare..." I tried to grab her arm to stop her.

But she did it anyway and they took Mal from the room, his eyes closed, and body trembling.

16

A SPECIAL VISITOR

Heli

I woke up with a strange, clawing sensation in my throat like I'd swallowed something alive, a spider maybe, and now it was trying to crawl its way back out. I swallowed hard, trying to force it down, but the feeling clung. A reminder of what they'd done to Mal last night.

"Get up. The bell finished ringing ages ago." Mya and Sira stood beside my bed, fully dressed, hands braced on their narrow hips. Their eyes were sharp. "If you don't come, they'll punish us."

"I don't want to." The words slipped out, flat and bitter. It wasn't fair, not really. It wasn't me they'd put in the chair.

Sira leaned closer, her smile stretching too wide, forced like she was trying to hold back some panic underneath.

"I think I can smell bacon," she said, her voice faltering. "Come on." She glanced at the door. "You must like bacon."

Breakfast was a rotation—egg and toast one day, maybe a sausage or banana with yoghurt the next. But never once had they given us bacon.

The others whined about the food, craving pizza and chips, but for me, food was fuel. It didn't matter what it was as long as it filled the hollow ache in my belly. Not that it could make up for being cooped up inside while the others ran free. It had been over a week since Sira and I stumbled upon the boatshed. The Doctor had let me outside on a whim and now I was being punished again. I turned my back on her, on her jittery smile. There was no reason to get up.

"You've got to get dressed," Sira's tone slipped into the familiar whine of a dog wanting its walk. "They're coming."

Her finger jabbed into my back, hard, a sharp reminder there was no more hiding under the covers. The grey curtain had already been pulled back, someone else had done it.

"I don't want to." My limbs felt like the bed was trying to swallow me whole. I wanted to stay put, to disappear into the mattress and let the day pass without me. But Sira's face had gone pale, her lips trembling. Fear crept into my chest like ice spreading through water.

"You've got to," she repeated, her voice wavering. "Otherwise, they'll punish all of us. Get up, Heli."

"Who pulled the curtain?"

"What does it matter? Just come on. I'll help you."

"That's my job."

So, I got up. Not for me. For her, maybe. I didn't care what they did to me anymore. I'd had enough. But somehow, I got dressed, feeling the stiffness of the fabric against my skin. I slipped into the back of the line just before Dr Shalt unlocked the door and herded us into another grey day at the Facility.

Standing behind Mal, I realised I should have got up sooner. He looked smaller than before; his shoulders hunched like a bird with a broken wing.

"Hey," I whispered, but he didn't turn, didn't even flinch when I pressed my hand against the small of his back, feeling the sharp ridges of his spine beneath my fingers. He didn't acknowledge me at all. "Hey," I tried again, my voice a rasp. "Mal--please, talk to me. What happened last night? Was it...?" I swallowed, forcing the words out. "Was it the chair?"

"Leave me alone," he said, his voice a thread, unravelling into the silence. He cradled his stomach, retreating to a place I couldn't reach.

I couldn't argue with that. I didn't have the strength. His misery hit harder than any of the Doctor's punishments. I wished we could go back to the beach on that single afternoon when escape from these walls had seemed possible. We'd shared something that day--him and I--laying on the pebbles, my cheek against his chest. If the Doctor let us out again, I could show him the boatshed.

After breakfast, they lined us up on the spots outside the school room, and the Doctor stepped forward.

"A special visitor is coming." His voice was heavy with self-importance, his pen a weapon inside his pocket. "To observe us--our routines and practices--and the progress we are making. Our strides for science."

My heart sank. Sometimes, he talked to us like we were still five. *A special visitor.* I guessed it wasn't going to be Santa Claus.

"Dr Emma Vanardsdale will look closely at our Facility, at the provisions and routines we give you. At the success of our programme in helping you play a role in society and live a fulfilling life, with your differences. She'll want to see results, so I expect you all to cooperate."

Silence stretched across the corridor, bowing our heads under its pressure.

"You must speak with pride about what we have achieved, the progress we have made, our efforts to rehabilitate what had previously been a hopeless cause." His smile sharpened like he really believed he'd accomplished something great.

I scanned the line, but all the others had their heads down, expressions on their faces tucked away.

"After your schoolwork," the Doctor continued, stepping closer––his pen contained in his pocket, a gleaming grey presence against the white. "Everyone can have the opportunity to go outside. All of you, together, in two groups. Even you," he nodded at me. "But I would like your word that you will give Dr Emma Vanardsdale your full cooperation when she arrives."

I scanned the line again as the Doctor's words settled over us like snow, the promise of time outside.

"So, what do you say?" the Doctor's feet shifted near my spot.

"Yes, Doctor," Sira started the agreement, and one by one, the rest of us vocalised or, in Mal's case, grunted our acceptance. I didn't really know why the Doctor had bothered asking, getting consent from us was usually the last of his concerns.

"Well done," he smiled. "Now, silence––"

"Silence is healing."

My heart pulsed between the chanting. *Outside.* The true value of it wasn't apparent until it had been taken away. I hadn't liked it, but at least I had understood why the Doctor did it the first time, after we'd been found out going swimming, but not the second. He'd let me out that time with Sira and Wiley like he wanted to remind me of what I was missing.

I looked around at Mal to acknowledge the good news together. His lips moved, but his gaze was far away. He had grunted, after all. Maybe later I could get him to talk when we were outside.

"Silence," I said, my voice a whisper, "is healing."

When the bell rang, we were sent outside in the promised two groups. It was a change to the Doctor's usual policy of placing us in pairs. I was so grateful to be outside I didn't give it any thought. My group made it to the rocks first--all of us running without speaking--while the other group lagged behind.

At some point, Wiley had found a stick and was throwing it back and forth with Mya. Mal was at the back, his head low.

On the path that led along to the rocks, I waited for him, the tumble of the waves below. I wanted to check that he was ok.

"I hate her," I said, remembering how Dr Shalt had taken Mal last night.

"You'll have to be more specific." Cai stopped, his breath coming hard and fast.

"Oh," I said, my breathing speeding up again. "It's you."

"Charming," he smiled.

"I was waiting for Mal."

"Fair enough," he said, balancing on the edge of the path like it was easy. "Who do you hate?"

"Dr Shalt." My voice was sharper than I'd intended but he didn't react. I watched Mal's approach in the distance, slow and heavy. "She takes pleasure in it."

"Yeah," Cai said, his voice was quiet. "It's the smile."

"And that awful lipstick." I shook my head, sitting on the cliff's edge and leaning back into the wind. The waves lashed the rocks below our feet. We wouldn't be able to go onto the beach today; the tide was wrong. The rest of my group was climbing down the other side towards the small jetty where it jutted out to sea. "A smile used to mean something. You know?"

"Still does."

"No, it doesn't. Dr Shalt has spoiled it." How could someone smile when they were doing that to Mal?

"She's not the first." Cai stretched his foot out, balancing his weight before springing to the first rock towards the harbour. "There's daggers in men's smiles."

"What?" I squinted at him.

"Shakespeare. It's funny what pops into your head, isn't it? Things you thought you'd forgotten." He turned to look at me. "Anyway, just so you know, people have been smiling funny for years. Are you coming?" He indicated the harbour.

"No," I shook my head. "I'm waiting for Mal. I'm worried about him."

"See you in a bit then," he said.

Then something strange happened; his hand leaned in from the rocks and touched my leg. Squeezed it so gently I wondered whether I'd imagined it. My pulse fluttered in my throat. I thought he was giving me some kind of signal, but then he was gone, heading down to the jetty with the others.

"Mal," I said.

He stopped beside me while I pushed myself up. It was obvious he didn't want to talk, so I decided to try another tact.

"Shall I show you the boatshed?"

But the tide was wrong, so we had to make do with lying on our stomachs, hanging over the edge of the rocks. The faint outline of the rusty door and rotten wood below.

"See?" I said, pointing at the outline of the door. "I told you it was there."

Mal didn't respond, his gaze lingering on the rocks, distant and hollow. A gust of wind carried the faintest trace of something metallic, blood maybe, or rust.

17

DRIED BLOOD

Heli

THE SCHOOL ROOM WAS hot when we entered, hotter still by the time Mal arrived late and took his seat. Dried blood, dark and flaking like crushed rose petals was crusted around his mouth. A silent cry for help. My chest tightened as I watched him, but his eyes were fixed on nothing. He looked like he'd been bitten by something savage––some kind of tussle, an altercation or a fight. Perhaps he had bitten his own lip. I didn't know many people who'd had a fight, nor which was more likely. I wondered if he'd lost his cool with the Doctor and something bad had happened.

My heart thumped inside my chest––grinding, anxious, overstimulated. Thinking about the various ways Mal might have sustained the injury didn't help.

My guts clenched violently, and I doubled over. I'd have to ask him myself later.

Cai dropped his pencil, and for a fleeting second, he mouthed a single word, "Chair."

I nodded, my limbs sticky and twitching. The pain in my stomach was fading to a dull ache.

How was it possible that the chair got worse?

"Lessons are to be conducted in silence. That's a warning, Heli," Dr Fiennes said from the front desk, and my eyes turned down. "All of you should have your headsets in position now. Mal? That's your warning, too."

Dr Fiennes took the unusual step of rising from his desk. His forearms exposed in short sleeves; he patrolled the schoolroom. I shifted, my skin slick with sweat. There was no reason for him to pick on either of us; we hadn't done anything to deserve a warning.

Dr Fiennes came to a stop behind Mal, breathing down his neck. Eventually, Mal got the hint and lifted his headphones. As the hours passed, it grew stuffier in the schoolroom. So much so, it was a relief to be taken out after lunch to have my therapy session with the Doctor. The corridor was cooler, and the Doctor's office better still, thanks to the metal box in the corner belching out cold air, its engine whining with effort.

"Bit primitive," the Doctor said, "but it does the job."

I looked at him for a moment; the box should be in the school room where the majority of people were. But I said nothing before turning my attention to the wall behind him. The objects of his affection were still where they had been the last time.

I squirmed in the chair, squinting at his display. There was a damp, sticky feeling between my legs and a pain in my guts. Although, one of his framed documents caught my attention——a black and white picture of a stern, old man with a huge forehead and some text beneath. I could read only the first three words before the font grew too small: **the Kalinowski Method**. I tried to work out the next word, sweat pooling along my spine, sticking the backs of my legs to the chair. The Kalinowski Method didn't sound good.

"You don't like it here?"

I looked at him. What could I possibly say? "I'm hot."

"We can discuss it, if you would like?"

"You don't see us as people; all you care about are routines." The words came one after the other. "You sit in here, hogging the air con while we're boiled alive in the schoolroom. To you, we're not even human. We are here for strides for science. Your strides."

"That's not what I think," the lines around the Doctor's eyes crinkled before he reached for his pen like they wanted to appear trustworthy, friendly even. "And you are not being boiled alive. We want to help you. The better we understand the science behind things––how our brains work, what makes some people behave differently––the better a place our society can be."

"Like the brain in the jar?" I wondered how he'd explain what had happened here in his report for the new Doctor coming to visit, to inspect and scrutinise the Facility's work. The words and phrases he could use to explain the inexplicable.

"Yes. Exactly like the old convict's brain." He rocked his pen back and forth. "We examine things so we might understand them. It is easier when children work with us. When we work together. Do you think you can do that?"

It was hard to counter such an argument.

Do you want to make society a better place, Heli?

Of course I wanted a better place, but you know what I really wanted, Doc? I wanted my family back. I wanted to cuddle my dog. I wanted annoying questions about my day I could roll my eyes at. I wanted time with Peony and hot chocolate with little pink and white marshmallows. I wanted music and beach BBQs. I wanted Christmas.

"It works a little like John Stewart Mill's *The Harm Principle*." The Doctor relaxed his pen. "Have you heard of John Stewart Mill, Heli?"

"No." Of course I hadn't. He made me feel bad, inadequate in my lack of knowledge. I didn't really want to listen to him anymore, and so I retreated to my quiet place, coiled up somewhere deep inside myself. *Peony*--most of all, I wanted to know what had happened to my sister after the fire. I wanted to see her. But the Doctor's voice penetrated.

"Individual liberties must be curtailed for the collective good," his tone was almost gentle. "It's the only way to protect society from harm. And here, we are protecting you from yourselves."

"What? Like Stalin?" My mind snagged on an old history lesson. Bad men liked to argue that what they did was done for your own good.

"No," he laughed. "Not at all like Stalin, young lady. Stalin acted for his own interests--alone. This is more than a political theory. It's a philosophy. That all decisions should be made in the interests of the majority and not the individual. Like during a deadly pandemic." He threw his pen hand wide. "Suppose that in order to make a vaccine, it might require the sacrifice of a few to save the lives of many. You'd agree that the sacrifice was worth making, wouldn't you?" He made a note on his clipboard, and my stomach clenched; I wanted to punch him. "How could you not?"

"How could I not." I looked down at my legs, squirming and damp in the hot chair. The fan continued to whine, but its efforts could not cool me.

"Someday, I hope we'll work together to make scientific advancements. Consider the others: Mya, Joe, Sira, Mal--they have all come to see that the best way is cooperation."

"I don't think that Mal--"

"If we can understand what happens inside the human brain to make you different," he said. "If we prove that our methods here are effective--"

"You know something? Mal doesn't look so good today. I'm worried--"

"Nosey Parker." He shook his finger. "You must trust that we have Mal's best interests front and centre."

"He doesn't look so good."

"There's no need to shout." The Doctor leant forward, frowning. "These sessions must focus on your recovery, Heli. No one else."

"I'm sorry, it's just you never tell me anything." About what was happening to Mal or about what had happened to my sister after the fire.

He pursed his lips. "Once we get the side effects of Mal's treatment under control, all will be well." His fingers flicked his pen. "Time is up."

"Wait." My heart thumped now that the Doctor was talking. "Please, I really need to know about my sister. Where is she?" My heart pulsed.

After the fire, they'd taken her to the hospital. And after some legal intervention, not to mention my Gran sticking her nose in, I was sent here.

"We have been over this," the Doctor said. "There was a fire. Your sister survived, but her injuries were life changing." He slipped his pen into his pocket. "You must put what happened into the past. You belong here now, Heli. This is the best place for you."

I looked at him.

"Do you understand?"

"Yes, Doctor." I nodded, my chest relaxing. Peony was alive; of course, she was. But I'd been so afraid.

When I reached the toilet, I found the cause of the stomach pain and the sticky feeling between my legs. Looking at the blood, I was surprised to feel as calm as I did. I stuffed some toilet roll down there and hobbled towards the dormitory intending to retrieve the plastic pink package of sanitary towels.

"Where do you think you are going?"

It was Dr Shalt. I found myself too uncomfortable to meet her eye but then I thought underneath that uniform she was basically a girl, so she might understand.

"It turns out you were right." I tried to meet her eye. "I got my period."

"I'll take you to get something." Her lips stiffened. "And you can talk it over with the Doctor when you next see him."

"Why do I need to tell him?" The Doctor knew too much already. The stuff that was out of sight and down there, periods and the like were none of his concern.

"Because you'll need to store your things somewhere other than your dormitory where, as you know, you're not allowed during lesson time."

"But... but... actually, I've got something on my..." Saying the words inside my head was one thing––knickers, underwear, pants––but I was too embarrassed to say them aloud. "Where should I put them?" There was no way on earth I wanted anyone else to see my blood. I looked away. "I mean, should I throw them away?"

"Talk to the Doctor," she said. "He will need to order you more things."

Order you more things.

Now, I couldn't look at her for a different reason––she'd said something that never got said. She'd mentioned new things were ordered, meaning deliveries came to the island. And if boats brought things, then they must leave, too. My legs trembled, uncomfortably aware of the makeshift padding.

"The Doctor. Ok," I said. "He'll get what I need..." I risked a glance, but her expression had already shifted back to calm––a window blind snapping shut. Did she realize what she'd let slip?

"You'd better go now."

I hurried towards the dormitory, knees squeezed tight, savouring the new knowledge like a sweet. No wonder they had that old shed on the beach. If boats came to the island, they must leave too.

18

So Little Blood

Heli

IN THE MORNING, WHEN the bell rang and the lights flashed, there was something wrong––body smells––which was ordinary enough; although, it was more than that. An undertone disturbing the hard chemical scent of the Facility. I sniffed, reaching my feet out from under the covers where they flinched at the change in temperature. Today, the smell of the dormitory had achieved a new sourness, like milk left out of the fridge.

"Hey?" I pulled on my socks, slipping a sanitary towel into my pocket for later. Maybe it was me that smelled? I sniffed again. I had so far refused to discuss my period with the Doctor. The pink plastic packet resided at the back in the bedside drawer. I could manage things myself until they ran out. "Can anyone else smell something weird?"

But every other person was absorbed in the act of dressing, and nobody responded.

"Something's not right. Hey," I said, louder this time. "Sira." I moved towards her bed, trying to reach her arm. "What's going on?"

"Nothing," she shrugged me away to pull her hair back into its everyday ponytail. "Just get in the bloody line, will you? I'm hungry." She patted her tummy, her cheeks twitching, before trying to direct my shoulders towards the door. "Get a move on."

"Hang on. I've got to do the curtain first." First, I put my finger up behind her back before my hands reached––this time––for the thick grey cloth of the curtain.

The other kids joined the line, one by one from the boys' side. Except Mal. Where was he? Cai approached Mal's bed, the last one in the row. And for goodness' sake, the boy was still in it. The other kids made enough fuss whenever I was slow to get out of bed––especially Sira––why hadn't she noticed this?

"Hey, Mal," I called from the back of the line, rolling my eyes. "Get a move on, someone's hungry." I eyed Sira as the beginnings of a twitch settled over her features.

"Come on, lazy bones." Cai reached the near side of Mal's bed. "There's no time for a lie-in. Bell's gone ages ago. Someone will be here any second to..."

Cai's knees hit the floor, a dull thud reverberating through the still dormitory. A gasp escaped his lips, and I hurried over, my pulse accelerating. The silence around Mal's bed thickened.

"What's going on?" My voice was thin and high.

"Don't look." Breath rasped inside Cai's throat––in and out––and out again. "Don't fucking look. Oh. My. God."

But I wasn't listening.

"Mal, Mal." *Oh my God*. Mal's head was unmoving on the pillow, a terrible stillness. His eyes were wide and staring; scabs formed at bitten lips; dark cheeks cold to touch. I pulled the sheet back slowly, my body trembling with each breath. His hand slipped free, cold and lifeless, a thin line of blood crusted at the wrist, a wicked shard of glass caught the light, gleaming with intent. I stared at it, realisation dawning. He'd done it. Mal was gone.

So little blood; I would have expected more.

"Oh, Mal." I couldn't breathe.

"Is he hurt?" Joe left the line to approach the bed. His steps were soft and slow like he didn't dare make a sound.

"What's wrong with him?" Sira appeared, her hand pinched my sleeve, and I shrugged her off.

"I said don't look." Cai's voice was a blade piercing skin.

Breath squealed inside my throat, shattering the silence.

"Why Mal, why?" I dropped to my knees at his side, my hands shifting as though if they were quick enough, they could shut out the horror. A scream left my throat. I knew why.

"Get up, Heli." Sira pulled my arm, her cheeks spasming. "Don't make this about you."

But panic had seized me, clawing at my throat, burning my eyes. In a heartbeat, everything had changed.

"Wait," I said. "Someone should close his eyes." I gulped air, pushing Sira away and getting up to lean over the bed. "It needs to be his friend."

Mal's eyes, the darkest shade of brown, were so familiar. Usually, they were full of sarcasm, humour, and a spark, like he knew stuff about this world and was waiting for the rest of us to catch up. My fingers hovered over the thin skin of his eyelids, fluttering and uncertain. His eyes looked the same but different. I wondered what it must be like to unsee things. Sure, sometimes he could be sulky, in a mood and refusing to talk. It made you feel bad just to be near him at those times. But when he listened, he really listened. When he got you, he really got you. And now he was gone.

"His eyes," my voice broke, a ghost of itself. I would be the last person to see his beautiful eyes. "I can't bear it. Oh, Mal."

"Heli. Stop it. Don't touch him. Someone's coming." Sira tried to pull me away. "For god's sake. Get in the line."

"So what?" I brushed Mal's cheek with my lips. Cold, so cold. My fingers trembled once more before descending to close his eyes. "Goodbye, my friend," I said, tears spilling over my hot cheeks. "Goodbye, Mal."

I lay beside him on the bed. I didn't care what anyone thought. My cheek snuck onto his chest, just like the time down on the beach after he'd saved me from the sea. Except, this time, Mal was cold and stiff.

"I'm sorry, Heli," Sira's voice was in my ear, her hand on my arm as she knelt on the floor beside the bed. "I shouldn't have said that... I was in shock. I mean––what the hell? Bollocks, bollocks."

My gaze travelled back to the other kids together in a tight line, their mouths open. A tremble went through them, and they gripped each other. Things at the Cerletti Facility would never be the same. Not ever. My hand rose to hold my nose. It had been grim before. But it would be worse without Mal. When Sira slipped her hand into mine, I didn't even mind.

A key card broke the silence, and the door opened. Dr Shalt entered.

"What is going on?" she said. "Why aren't you––" She gasped, her gaze taking in Mal's body, inanimate beneath the sheet––a faint smear of blood––his face distorted by a grimace. Eyes forever shut. Sira and I huddled together next to him.

"Go to the dining hall." Dr Shalt's voice was cold even as she steadied herself against the wall, her fingers fumbling for her alarm. "You too, Heli. Sira. Get up. All of you. Go. Now."

Cai led us along the corridor, reaching his hand back. A line of us, snaking together, our feet stumbling one into the back of another towards the dining hall. We didn't mind, moving as one body, each of us holding hands with the person behind. I blinked; my eyes so clouded I couldn't see. A terrible buzzing filled my ears as our line gathered tighter. Sira's hand was twitching in mine. I pressed closer, and we trembled together.

Inside the dining room, our breakfast was already laid out. We took our usual places at the table on autopilot rather than a desire for any food.

"Children," the Doctor appeared before us as we picked over pieces of cold toast––fingers moving dry quarters from one side of the plate to the other––our eggs uncracked inside white cups. Mal's plate of food had already been brought to the table before our arrival and sat untouched: as cruel a reminder of his absence as his empty chair.

"A tragedy," the Doctor said, his voice devoid of emotion while tears pricked at my eyes. "But we must remain focussed. Together we will persevere for the sake of science and progress. Let this be a reminder of the importance of discipline and cooperation."

I stopped listening. Forced the Doctor's words out of my head. My gaze moved across both sides of the table, trying to avoid Mal's place, the place he would have sat if he hadn't been dead. I thought for a second, someone sat in his chair. But no one would dare, and it must have been the blurring in my eyes or the shock.

Cai was at the table's far end where he always sat next to Sira. Her eyes were glazed, her cheeks spasming like she couldn't get them under control, while Joe's shoulders shook, his hands in angry fists on the tabletop. It was weird because I'd never seen Joe show any feelings other than violence. I supposed he looked murderous now, but I kind of understood it.

Mya and Sophia were crying, pausing only to take great juddering breaths or wipe their faces on their sleeves. No one was listening to the Doctor and his cold comfort. When Cai met my eyes, my defence collapsed. I took a gulp of air and made an ugly sound in the back of my throat. Hot tears spilt over my cheeks.

"It's time for school," the Doctor said. "Clear up, first. Remember your roles. Order," he paused, "follow the processes. They have been put in place to help you."

"I'm here for you," Cai mouthed across the table as chairs scraped back, and we assumed our places to clear the uneaten meal.

There was a part of me that longed to throw myself into Cai's arms and bury my face in his shoulder, cry my tears into him. Let him absorb me, to share the burden of my grief. But it was too soon, and I shook my head; I wasn't ready to talk.

But the Doctor hadn't thought of the most basic problem that arose from the terrible change that had taken place that morning and Mal's job was not reassigned.

The Doctor paced an outer circle around us as though it were him and not us that was the caged animal—unused to direct supervision—his hands twitched as though searching for a pen.

"That's better." Air whistled through his nose. "With the school day, you will find peace in the order of things."

The strange moaning came from the back of my throat again and I searched for the distraction of my role. There was no one to bring me the plates, so I forced myself to move back to the table, assuming Mal's job again, and clearing them myself.

I left his plate for last, removing it from the table with the greatest of reluctance. And it was the thing that broke me, carrying what should have been his breakfast, the last meal prepared for him, to the bin. I sat on the floor and wept.

The Doctor handed me a cup of something warm and coaxed it down my throat. It must have had a sedative of some sort in it because it was really hard to follow his instructions after that. My legs and arms felt dislocated, hard to control like after pins and needles.

"Routine," the Doctor said––as though the word had lodged itself in his throat––when the bell rang for line up. "It will hold us all together."

The Doctor was wrong. The routines needed to be changed, not just to accommodate Mal's absence, but the Cerletti Facility building changed too as they took things away, stripping anything that might constitute harm from out of our way. The mirror came down from the bathroom wall and one of the others––a porter, sometimes two of them––worked through the long days that followed Mal's death to nail down everything that couldn't be taken away.

"It wouldn't have stopped him," Cai said when we passed the other staff at work in the corridor. "Removing the means doesn't change the will."

"They're pretty thick," I whispered back, "for doctors."

In the dormitory, although he had gone, my friend's bed remained. Empty. That night, we stood together in a circle around it. Most of us cried. I don't know who reached out first, but we were all holding hands. Even Joe, who'd normally spit you in the eye rather than touch you. I stared at his hand entwined with mine. There was a scar on the back of mine where he'd stabbed me once with a pencil.

"It's my fault." My throat spasmed. I hadn't planned on speaking.

"Don't be soft," Cai said.

"But I didn't sleep well. If only I'd checked on him."

"It wouldn't have made any difference," Sira said, her arm twitching until Mya had to release her hands. "Sorry, sorry, sorry," she said while I took the opportunity to drop Joe's hand. "Mal would have found another time, done it a different way. Waited til you were asleep."

"You sound like one of them." I shuffled towards the curtain. "For God's sake, he was just a kid."

"We're all kids," Sira said. "He shouldn't have done it."

"Take that back," Joe rounded on her, punching her shoulder, then the side of her ribs; he was clever enough to know where to aim, places where the doctors wouldn't see bruises.

"Stop it," Mya said. "You're hurting her."

"You might not like hearing it. But it doesn't stop it from being true." Sira pulled Joe down with her to the floor.

"Hey," I said, even though I would have quite liked to punch someone myself. I didn't think Mal would have liked it. "For fuck's sake, Joe. Get off her."

The bell rang then, and we trudged to our beds. I could hear Sira crying, because of Mal or Joe, I didn't know.

"He's an arsehole," I said after a while. "Not worth your tears."

"It's not about him," she sniffed.

"Mal was my friend," I said. It was petty, but it seemed like there was more upset over Mal after he'd died than before.

I flipped my pillow over, searching for the relief of the cool side, and found it. A note from Mal. Paper he must have ripped from his exercise book. The edge was a perfect line, like even at the end, in his last hours, he didn't want to get into trouble. The letter said:

It's tough to write this. I can see your face... Don't look up. I can't really. Right now, you're asleep. But I can imagine you--how you might look--as you read this. I'm sorry I can't stick around to help. And I've only got this one, crappy bit of paper, with no room for mistakes, to tell you that.

Remember the day we went swimming? That was the one good day here. Even though we nearly drowned. For what it's worth, I wanted to help you find out about your sister. But I've worked one thing out for you. In this place--this fucking awful place--you are the good thing.

I wish I knew if you could get well, but I don't. I do know you shouldn't follow the Doctor's path, stick to your own and never look back. Learn to like the mad girl within--fuck it--love her. Love her for the both of us. If you manage that, I reckon you might work out how to get out of here. It's how Mollie did it. Last thing she said to me was stop trying to get out, focus on how you're never going back in.

I didn't really know Mal had liked me that much. Loved me even. My heart hurt and I pressed the paper, thin and lined, over my cheek. As though I could imprint his words into my flesh. Somebody loved me, once they had; it felt like enough.

19

My Bad Side

Sira

AFTER THE DOCTOR'S SPEECH, Mal became a ghost, his presence erased. But he lingered in our whispers and the empty chair in the schoolroom that no one dared touch. Bit by bit, they removed his things too--his egg cup, his clothes--until all traces of him were gone, except the ones we secreted away.

Our memories.

I've never told anyone else before, but I helped him out early one morning when he'd messed himself. I heard him creeping about, trying to clean up. We didn't talk about it afterwards; we didn't need to. In that moment we were just kids pretending we worked on the space station, turning something humiliating into something bearable. I guess you had to be there.

In our break from schoolwork, Heli and I huddled together with Joe and Mya, whispering what we remembered. Although, I kept my memory of the imaginary space station overflowing with excrement to myself.

We talked about the things that Mal had done, the way he used to listen to your problems, the good times when he hadn't been shitting himself. We were squashed together in the corner of the dining hall, sitting on the floor, banana peelings and juice cartons between our crossed legs.

"None of you like me, not properly." Joe paused and looked around; I tried not to react and not one of us contradicted him. "But Mal, you know, I think he actually did. God knows why."

"Here it comes again." Heli sucked her drink hard until her straw made a gasping sound. "The famous self-pity."

Joe's jaw tightened, his hands clenching the juice carton. "Pack it in," he said, his voice low and ominous. Then before anyone could stop him, he kicked her side, hard enough to make her flinch.

"Hey," I put my hand out, a threat I suppose, in case he did it again. I was growing tired of his violent strops. "Stop it."

"I don't care what you say," Heli looked Joe right in the eye, "or what you do; you're an animal. Mal was my friend."

"Yeah, well, he was my friend too." Joe leaned in. "You know, he told me once, he was used to early starts in the morning because of his swim training. His body clock was stuck. But he wouldn't say anything else."

"He wasn't much of a talker." I shook my head. It was hard to imagine that Mal and Joe had been friends. Mal was the kind of kid who would carry a spider outside rather than squash it. Not that you could do that here.

"I think he was training for the Olympics or something like that," Heli said, her face sad and serious in the low light of late autumn; she rubbed her side, frowning. "Mal was amazing in the water. But he just stopped wanting to do it one day. Even before he came here, I think. He never really talked about it. Except once."

"You'd think it would have given him something to live for," Joe said. "You know, having such a big talent. I wish I had one."

"He wasn't comfortable in his body." The words slipped and slid around in my mouth, taking hold as they spilt into the confessional space.

"Yeah," Heli said, a faint smile flickering over her lips. "We talked about it the day he rescued me from the sea."

"I was pretty sure he had a crush on you," Mya pointed at Joe whose cheeks went dark.

"Fuck off. I'm not gay."

"That doesn't mean––oh my God," Heli took a deep breath, her cheeks were flushed a furious shade of red. "He had better taste than you."

"Don't do that," I said, raising my juice carton. "He was a good kid. To Mal."

"To Mal," Heli raised her carton and knocked it with Joe's.

He looked surprised when juice squirted at his face then he laughed. Heli turned to me and knocked her carton against mine.

A smile pulled at my cheeks; it was what was expected. I didn't feel much like it though. Life without Mal in the Facility was worse; his loss highlighted how doomed the rest of us were.

I'd spent a long time trying to do what the Doctor told me to. But now I worried it wouldn't be enough to get me out of here. There were the secret visits to the toilets with Joe, too. Even after the Doctor had caught us, we kept doing it. I tried, but I couldn't make myself stop. It was the only outlet I had, better even than drawing. Without that release, I thought I might explode. It was my bad side, but I hid it as best I could.

When the bell rang, we filed back to the schoolroom under the gaze of Dr Fiennes. There was someone else in the corridor, which was unusual.

The Cerletti Facility didn't go much in for surprises. A man, or rather his feet, was perched at the top of a ladder fixing something. His torso and legs were clad in the white and black uniform of the porters and janitors who worked here––the ones who were not doctors––a tool belt hung down around his middle. The chisel glinted under the fluorescent lights, perfect for carving my pictures on the walls. My fingers twitched with the urge to grab it. But one wrong move and I'd lose more than my chance of freedom.

"Mind the ladder."

"Alright." I missed a step in surprise.

"Nice day out there, eh?" He climbed down from his ladder and wiped his forehead. "You kids been out?"

The porter must not have got the Facility brief that *silence was a virtue.* Not, as the Doctor was fond of explaining, in the old-fashioned religious sense. Silence bred order, and order was a necessity for the healing routines of Cerletti.

"No," I said, joining the line outside the schoolroom door. I stood on the first of the black vinyl spots. The porter could work it out for himself when we started the chant. *Silence is healing.* This was no ordinary place.

In the schoolroom, our books were laid out, different ones from earlier. The other kids bent over their work. My book about algebraic equations had been replaced with a lesson on rivers and valleys and something called an oxbow. I smoothed the map out and found a fresh sheet of paper in my book. But I couldn't concentrate, and I watched as first Joe and then Mya were taken out. I wanted to tell them, warn them. There was someone in the corridor, a talkative someone. But I couldn't find the words.

"Problem?" Across the room, Dr Shalt stood over Heli. I blinked; I hadn't noticed she was with us in the room instead of Dr Fiennes.

"No," Heli said, her smile almost as convincing as Dr Shalt's. "I was thinking about the helicoidal flow. It's kind of like my name. You know Heli means sun, but I think helicoidal means a spiral and––"

"Fascinating," Dr Shalt said. "But work must be silent. You've had a warning already this morning, so now you will stay in through exercise time and complete the rest of your work in silence."

"No, please, I didn't mean to." Sometimes begging worked. "I'm really sorry."

"Do you want to do this the hard way?" Dr Shalt's voice dropped, sharp and cold. "You know how that ends, Heli."

Heli lowered her head to the desk, her body convulsing with sobs. "Help me," she whispered, and I watched her, unsure whether this was one of her episodes or whether grief had caught up with her again. She twisted from side to side, tears coming to a stop on her chin.

"Something is wrong," I said. "Dr Shalt, please?"

"That is enough." Dr Shalt pressed her device. "Sit down. You too, Heli, until someone comes."

"Stop it, Cai," Heli kicked her desk. "It's not worth it."

"Back to work," Dr Shalt said. "You too, Sira."

I kept my head down when the Doctor came for Heli with his needle. Resistance wasn't worth it. It only made things worse. I should know that by now. One time, when I first arrived, I got upset when I found out about Mal and the chair, and they put him in isolation. Because I shouted, they punished Mal. You learned quickly after something like that.

Across the room, Heli gasped as the syringe hit her skin, puncturing her flesh. I tried not to look, concentrating instead on the exercise book. Her pain filled the room, a counterpoint to the silence. I kept my head down, but something was brewing inside my chest. There were places here she hadn't even experienced yet, isolation or the chair. I wanted to comfort her, to tell her if she did what she was told, it would be easier, get better even. But I knew better than to speak out. Resistance only brought more suffering––but the feeling inside me refused to go away.

20

Hot chocolate

Heli

It had been a few weeks since Mal died, and one afternoon after school, the Doctor did something strange. He cancelled our chores and served us toast and hot chocolate. The sweet, milky smell was out of place against the cold, chemical air of the Facility. We ate in silence, glancing at each other, waiting for the catch.

Then the Doctor sent us outside. I walked with Sira, holding hands and whispering about things we once had but no longer understood--makeup, music, and boys. How things might have changed. New haircuts, different jeans, a fashion for piercings. And how would we know?

"Could we ever belong in that world again when we've spent so long in this one?" My voice drifted across the landscape, colours losing their shimmer as the day faded. The thought felt foreign, like childhood memories buried and blurred at the edges. I felt the tug of darkness, but I held onto the inconsequential conversation with Sira as hard as I could.

"Will we ever get to go back though?" she asked. "Home. And if we do, will we get those things back?"

"I don't know that I want them back." It was true, after the time spent at Cerletti, phones and fashion mattered less and less. What I wanted back was my freedom.

"You don't think you'd like to be kissed one day. Meet a boy?" Sira giggled, her face flushed.

"Who says I'm into boys?" My face flushed as thoughts of Cai simmered.

"Aren't you?"

"Alright, I am." I smiled, my head spinning in the soft light. "But I could kiss a boy here if I wanted."

"Really?" She smiled. "I used to think you and Mal would--you were so close--but then I realised he wasn't into girls."

"No," I said, "he wasn't... It wasn't like that. We were friends." I let my breath out and darkness closed in.

Mal.

It was hard to think about him, painful to hear his name. I gazed out over the water, where it stretched in an indistinct line away from the island. It was hazy with a dark mist today like the discoloured glass housing the Doctor's oldest body part--the convict's brain.

"You know, at first I really missed my phone," I said. "Couldn't imagine coping without it. Now I--"

"Don't think about it at all?" Sira squeezed my hand and for once I didn't mind. Just for a moment, the two of us together made me less lonely. "Me either. It's weird, isn't it?"

"Yes." Sometimes my Gran used to blame my behaviour on having a phone. The things that had been done. My wrongness. As if such a thing could be attributed to mobile signals.

It's interfering with her brain, she would say. *We managed without them in my day.*

"Heli?"

"Sorry." It was hard enough without Gran's voice inside my head. "You'd have to be here to understand."

"About that kiss," Sira giggled again, the noise sounding as though it was coming from somewhere deep inside her chest: heavy and sleepy. "You know something, I kind of like Joe––"

"Desperate much."

"Heli," a tremor ran through her, from head to shoulders and beyond. "Joe and I... sometimes we, you know––" Her voice faltered, and she looked at me, cheeks twitching, waiting. "It's the only thing that makes me feel normal."

"No. Don't tell me. I don't want to know."

"Stop judging."

"But Joe's an actual pig. He punched you that time after Mal..."

"He's just messed up like the rest of us."

"Oh, Sira." It wasn't an ordinary emotion for me to feel that someone else knew less than me.

"He really listens," she said.

"Oh, please."

"Alright, it's because he's gorgeous. And––bollocks, bollocks, great, big toad bollocks." Sira paused, her face caught in a spasm. "What else is there to do? We've got no phones, no life. You can't blame me for wanting something."

"I just can't believe you haven't been caught."

"Actually, I was caught that time––remember when I had to stay indoors with you?"

"That's why you were in the boys' toilet. My God, have you actually done it?" I gasped as Sira's cheeks contorted. "But what about getting pregnant?"

Her face relaxed. "Hands can't get you pregnant."

"Gross," I paused. "But what about... I mean--you could get pregnant from stuff flying about?"

"Stuff can't fly. And sometimes we use a sock or--"

"A sock? Stop, please. I do the laundry."

"If you had to, then," she nudged me. "Who would you pick?"

I would pick Cai. But I didn't want to talk about him with Sira, not after her talk about socks, and I pulled my hand away. It was complicated

"Where do you think he is now?" I asked, my hand felt heavy and light at the same time.

It was dusky as we headed back to the Facility, the air thickening around us, full of fragments, pollen, leaves and other matter. It was like falling snow, only dirty.

"Who?" Sira's hand reached again for mine.

"Mal. Where is he now?" Since he'd been gone, it was hard to concentrate on anything else.

"I like to think he's at peace."

I pulled my hand free. "I mean him--the actual him--his body. Where've they put it? Do you think they put it in the sea? Because he wouldn't have liked that."

"Oh." Through the darkening light, now I could only see the outline of Sira, her hand reaching again. "Please," she said. "We need to get back. I don't feel so good."

"But what if the Doctor took something first?" My voice dropped to a whisper. "You know how he is... He might have cut a part--for his collection."

I couldn't find the strength to finish my thought, which was just as well, because Sira threw up on the path.

"Sorry," she said.

"It's ok, we're nearly back. You can clean up in a minute."

At the Facility, we were told to line up inside on the corridor spots outside the schoolroom.

"Quickly," Dr Shalt said. "We have a visitor."

"Please, Dr Shalt," Sira said, her face pale. "I feel sick. Just now, on the path, I've already been––"

"I think you can manage a few minutes longer." Dr Shalt pushed her headband backwards, the wiry, grey hairs in her dark brown bob caught under the light overhead.

Like sheep we shuffled onto our spots, casting our eyes downwards while we waited.

"Silence," Dr Shalt said.

"Silence is healing," we repeated, and I clenched my fists, digging my fingernails into my palms to ground me.

"Full attention, please." Dr Shalt put her hand up to stop our chanting. She smiled as she indicated the Doctor was approaching with someone new. "Here's our special visitor."

I didn't know when the visitor had officially arrived on the island because she had no suitcase or other stuff with her. She had short legs and a slow stride. It was hard to judge her age; her skin was wrinkled, but her posture was stooped like that of an even older lady. If we'd known she was coming, Sira and I could have spent exercise time trying to find her boat.

"This is Heli," the Doctor said as he worked his way down the line, introducing us. "Stand up straight," he squinted through the bright artificial light of the hallway. Under his scrutiny, I tried to unfold my spine, but my limbs were heavy. It was ironic he should be concerned with my posture when the woman who accompanied him had a much greater need. "She's been with us for just over ten months now."

What a liar.

I didn't correct him. None of us did. We stood with our heads dropped low; it must have been the hot chocolate rendering us more mute than usual.

But it couldn't have been ten months. Could it?

The intense heat a few weeks ago. And now it was growing cool again. Ten months meant I'd missed my birthday. I shook my head. How long ago had Mal died? I shook and shook but I couldn't remember.

"They are very quiet?" the visiting doctor said.

"Of course, they do not cope well with change." The Doctor tapped the pen in his pocket. "They will get used to your presence. Now perhaps you'd like some refreshment. Or a rest?"

"I'd like to speak with them, if I may?" Her eyes crinkled, but it was not a question.

"Of course, please."

"Children," she said, her voice clipped and professional, "it is a privilege to assist with your journey to better health. Together we are contributing to a greater understanding of the adolescent mind. The principles of Cerletti are that we practise and use silence to ensure that everyone has an equal opportunity to know themselves better and advance towards their goal. We use silence as a sign of an ordered mind in the understanding that order leads to good outcomes. Now, raise your fists, please." She scanned us one by one, gesturing with her own hands. "That's it," she said, a half-smile flickering over her lips. "Listen to the options, and when I say show me, I'd like you to demonstrate your choice."

"We haven't introduced these checks yet," the Doctor spoke in a quiet, confidential tone.

"They will pick it up." The visitor turned to us; her own fist raised high. "One finger if you think we use silence to create a disciplined environment because we love authority, or two fingers if we use silence to show our ordered mind and to create good outcomes."

I wasn't sure whether to laugh or to scream. But my fist twisted to show the new doctor two fingers, in the careful, polite way she modelled.

"Very good," she turned to the Doctor. "We will need to practise until we have one hundred percent."

"Of course."

"I would like to refresh myself now." She began to walk back along the corridor. I squinted. The Doctor had tried but it was obvious who was in charge.

"Oxford University, eh?" he said, as he followed her. "You must have had an early start."

Dr Devitt had this theory about the magnetic force we were trying to prove. It was the best thing about being here in the Facility, time spent thinking about puzzles. I was lifting magnets one by one, connecting them in a chain and testing for resistance. Cai couldn't understand it, but I was turning into a science nerd.

The Doctor and the visitor appeared together in the room. I hadn't heard them come in.

"Have you got Emma's card?" The Doctor asked.

Emma?

I was so surprised I dropped the magnets I was working with.

"Pick those up." The Doctor's tone was terse.

"Yes, Doctor."

From the floor, I watched as Dr Devitt removed a small machine from a drawer in the corner and printed one of their special cards for opening the doors. The things I could do with one of those. I watched extra hard where the machine was returned to.

"Thank you," the Doctor said as he left. "Next time, please, think of these things in advance."

"Good of you to join me," Dr Devitt said when I stood as though I'd been sitting under the table all the time. "Shall we get this experiment finished before we have any more interruptions?"

I nodded, uncomfortable at the crack in Dr Devitt's usual manner. Perhaps he did not like the arrival of this new doctor––Emma––either. *Emma.* It was a strange name for a scientist.

On the return to the schoolroom, Dr Devitt's device beeped. He lowered his head and pressed a button to speak.

"Dr Vanardsdale, how can I help?"

There was a long pause while I pretended not to listen.

"Of course," he said: "Emma it is. Yes––there are eleven." His eyes travelled to me and back to the device.

"In a––if you could just give me a moment," he said. "I can talk more freely."

The lines on Dr Devitt's face went still.

"That was a short-term side effect. Although, it has been resolved. Time and persistence," his voice was odd. "Yes, just a moment. I will be back with you. No more arrivals expected for the time being––no."

Later, when I was walking with Cai during exercise time, I repeated to him the encounter with the Doctor and the card machine and also Dr Devitt's one-way conversation with the special visitor.

"Imagine if we could print one of those things for ourselves," I said, "and blow this joint." My heart fluttered, excited to be thinking about escape again. Now I'd seen the machine; possibilities shifted like butter-flies inside my mind.

"Blow this joint," Cai said. "As easy as that, eh?"

"Why not?" We passed through the gates onto the dry muddy track, heading towards the beach.

"Heli, getting out of the building isn't the hard part." Cai stuffed his hands deep inside his pockets. "It's getting off the island, isn't it? We can't just walk away."

"I know that," I said. Mal's note had said the same kind of thing. "But we can't just give up. I don't want to die here." *Like Mal.* Where was he now? I still needed to find out what the Doctor had done with his body. There had been no memorial; Mal had deserved more. I thought about the Doctor's collection of glass jars and shuddered. "I really want to get out."

"Me too." But Cai's voice was quiet, and I knew it would be down to me to plan it. My teeth ground together, the top onto the bottom ones. It had been the same with Mal. I was the strong one, the risk taker, the planner.

"Tell me what you know about Mollie," I said, remembering Mal's note. His advice to be like Mollie: to learn to love myself.

"You've heard it all before," he said.

"Tell me again."

"She was smart, funny, rude, loud. You'd have liked her."

"What are you trying to say?" I shifted inside my coat. It was warmer than expected outside. Warm with a coat, too cold without. The seasons were changing again. How long had I been on the island? Could it really have been ten months?

"Mollie hated it here," Cai said. "She talked about escape all the time. Then she was gone."

"Like Mal."

"Not like Mal. I don't know what she intended. But she made it out of the building."

"How do you know?"

"Mal told both of us. Remember? He found her coat on the beach, didn't he? Tucked in the rocks near the lighthouse. You know the bit down below––the gap near the path?"

"Let's go and look there. Maybe there will be some other clue."

"Heli, it was so long ago."

"There's no harm in looking." I pushed my hair out of my eyes. The sun was bright. "Do you think there's any chance she survived?"

"Only if she found a boat. The Doctor thinks she drowned."

"Did he say that?"

"It's obvious what he thinks."

"There are boats though aren't there?"

"Are there?" he asked. "I've never seen one."

"One, there's a boatshed. Maybe Mollie knew about it." My face flushed, recalling how I'd thought the boatshed was a perfect place to go with Cai. But I wouldn't let myself be distracted. "Two, Dr Shalt talked about ordering new things and them being delivered to the island."

"What things?"

"What does that matter?" My feet faltered. "Let's just see what we can find."

The sky was a brilliant blue, no clouds; the sun was too bright to look at. Back home I would have gone back for sunglasses and changed my coat for a jumper. But there were no sunglasses in the Facility, no shorts, nor any other concessions to the changing seasons. We each had one coat that was cold in the winter and hot at other times. I followed Cai's lead and unzipped.

Down on the beach, we picked through the pebbles and scraps of seaweed looking for something left long ago by Mollie, finding only shells, dried seaweed, plastic remnants and occasional sea glass.

"Funny, isn't it?" I sieved a handful of detritus. "How it ends up a treasure, but it starts as trash."

"Eh?"

"Sea glass."

"Oh."

"Sorry if I'm boring you..."

"You're not boring me, your highness. I'm just thinking."

I raised my eyebrows and we both giggled.

"What about?"

"The Doctor says this is my purpose."

"No." I pushed aside a mound of pebbles. "It can't be our purpose, can it? It's wrong what they do."

"Thing is," he nudged me, a gentle movement and then his hand kind of stayed where it was, "I don't believe it. Just. Sometimes I think it'd be easier, if I did."

"I get that," I said. "Giving in doesn't work for long though." And we sat like that for a moment, his hand on my arm as the sun shifted in the sky over our heads, I leaned towards him and rested my head on his shoulder.

It was about as clear a signal as I was prepared to make, and after a moment, his arm snaked its way around my waist and drew me tight against his chest. When I rested against him, his body entwined with mine, my pulse accelerated like before a race but there was a kind of peace like I'd never known before.

21

RED FUZZ

Heli

WE BROKE APART AND started sieving through pebbles again––cold and lifeless, like Mal's hand when we found him. I knew searching was pointless, but since his death, purpose had slipped away like the tide.

"Is it ever going to be ok again?" I looked at Cai, his hands buried in his pockets.

"Do you mean Mal?"

I was filled with loathing for the purple flush of heather that banked the sides of the path across the island's edge; the insipid white drift of clouds; the tight pinch of my shoes. I hated not knowing what to do.

"What are you doing?" Sira called from where she climbed the rocks. Her face caught in a shifting grimace. "Hurry up––the sun's on the harbour and I want to skim stones."

"Get lost."

"Why are you so angry?" Cai asked.

"This place is getting to me." I kicked a pebble.

"You know," Cai said, his voice higher than usual, tense, tight, "Before. Before it happened, you were telling me about the kids at your school. The shit bags. What did they use to say to you?"

"I don't want to talk about it." I turned away.

Sira's ponytail floated in the distance as she ascended the last section of rocks and pulled herself onto the small jetty.

"Made it," she waved her arms. "Come on, Heli. I've got a pocketful of pebbles. It'll take your mind off whatever's going on with you today."

"Talk to me," Cai said, putting his hand on my shoulder. "Please."

As if this day wasn't bad enough. Sira wanted to skim pebbles and Cai wanted to talk.

"It's not an excuse." My voice was so quiet. I wasn't sure Cai would even be able to hear it. "Being bullied is no excuse."

"For what?"

"What about this special visitor?" I asked. I'd already said more than I'd wanted about my past. "Like, who's in charge now––the Doctor or her?"

"Talk to me."

"You know, earlier––Sira told me she fancied you."

"Stop it. Please. Just. Talk to me."

"I am."

I was about to say something else when he touched my face. And his fingertip rubbed my cheek in a slow, soft circle, easing the words from my mouth.

"It wasn't so bad really," I hesitated. "Stop it. I don't want to think about it." My throat tightened, swallowing the words.

His finger tickled across my skin. And I made a silly, child-like sound.

"Trust me," he said.

But I didn't trust anyone. My own body betrayed me.

What a shame about that red fuzz, My Gran had said.

"Talk to me."

"They called me a freak." The past spilt over my lips while I tried to make it stop. "Even my family went on about my hair. It's not the word. I was such a disappointment to everyone——after perfect, Cinderella-haired Peony."

"I know how that feels."

"It's the way they used to say it. Like I was dirty. A filthy freak."

"It's a nasty word."

Freak.

Kids at school spat the word like the crack of a whip. But it didn't sound like enough. Not enough to trigger my condition and all the things I'd done. The teachers didn't think it was enough. Not enough to do anything about it. Not when other kids had pushed me, kicked me, and broke every rib. Not when they forced things into my mouth: leaves, mud, dirt, filth. Called me dirty. Shame swam through my guts. There were other things, worse things, things I wouldn't let myself remember. The Doctor doesn't think it was an excuse either——my sickness was my own making.

"I thought at first my hair had started it," I said. "But really, I was just an easy target. Because I was different, you know? A mad girl."

"Why would they pick on your hair?"

"As if you haven't heard of a ginger getting picked on. You've probably done it yourself. Back in the real world."

"I haven't," he said: "I would never. You're mean sometimes."

I looked down, ashamed, feeling like I did back then. Dirty and alone. Of course, it wasn't my hair that started it. It was me they didn't like. The mad girl.

"Heli," he said, "I really like your hair."

"What do you want?" I rolled my eyes. "A fucking medal?"

It's not ginger, my dad used to say like that was the issue, *it's red.*

"Cai," I shifted my feet, "it's not actually about my hair."

"It's like fire," Cai said, spots at the centre of his dark cheeks glowing hot and pink as shades of sunset. He didn't look so pretty right now--sweaty and awkward. "Look at you," he said, "so colourful. Red hair and green eyes."

"Green eyes?" Perhaps he didn't get the bit about me being mad. "Is that the best you can come up with?"

"They're the colour of spring, of sea glass--you know--the kind you love finding and," he said, "the colour of dragon skin."

"You're an idiot."

"I think you're beautiful." He leant forward.

For the briefest of moments our lips touched.

"You're not bothered about me being mad?" I held my breath.

"Don't worry," Cai said, taking a gentle hold of my chin. "Because we're all mad here." And then he leant forward again but it was no good because I was laughing too hard.

"That's a line from a t-shirt," I said.

"No, it's from Alice in Wonderland," he hesitated. "And I was trying to kiss you."

I was so uncomfortable; I could feel the sides of my face distorting. "Why would you want to kiss me? You just called me mad."

"It's a turn of phrase. A clumsy joke. You're funny and gorgeous even with your face all wrinkled up like that."

"I have wrinkles now?" But it was no good because I couldn't keep up the pretence. I was laughing, almost crying. "Hey," I said, my breath catching. "Kiss me then."

His hands tangled in my hair, his breath soft and warm and at some point, his tongue met mine, and we melted together. It sounded sappy, but there was no other way to describe the heat of it--the feeling of your body meeting someone else for the first time. For a moment, it was an escape, a fleeting break from the reality of this place.

"First time?" he said.

I shrugged, too embarrassed to confirm or deny anything. "You?"

"I've had a few girlfriends. Nothing like this."

"I'm not your girlfriend."

I pulled away, heading toward the jetty where Sira waited with her pebbles, refusing to look back. A part of me feared Cai's feelings came from pity or that he was desperate for any connection. But more than that, I feared that getting together with him would make me want to stay.

Before bed, I went all the way up to Dr Shalt. She was flicking through a book at her desk in the corner of the reading room.

"Can I see the Doctor?" I hadn't made any progress on an escape plan, and I hoped there might be another way off the island.

Dr Shalt lowered her book, its cover was jet black against her white coat. "Why?"

"I need to talk to him." I paused. "I'm worried about something."

There were two words the Doctors used to get your attention. Need and Worried. I *need* you to do something. I'm *worried* that you won't. When the doctors said them, they expected you to jump right to it. But when I used their words, they had no effect.

"You'll have to wait until tomorrow," Dr Shalt shook her head. "It's time for bed now."

She placed a bookmark in her book and stood to ring the bell, the smile never leaving her face.

But in the corridor, the Doctor was waiting outside the bathroom. His hands were entirely still. For once, his pen was absent; his top pocket empty and sagging against his chest.

"What is it?" he beckoned me to stop while he ushered the others into the bathrooms. Looking tired, he removed his glasses to pinch the bridge of his nose. "What are you worried about?"

"Nothing." My mind was too full to speak. Full to the brim with injections and medication and wondering where my dead friend was; with fire and nightmare; burning with the knowledge that no one wanted a dirty girl; a new doctor in the building who might change all the rules and the small, dark room with a chair no one talked about. Most of all, I was absorbed with wanting to kiss Cai and the terror it made me feel. I had wanted to ask the Doctor to help me with my thoughts––to slow them down––but now the opportunity had come, words failed me.

"You asked to speak with me." The Doctor gave an impatient look over his shoulder; his tone was off.

"Where's Mal?" Anger replaced confusion with a tick of his watch. The Doctor's face hardened, and I thought I saw a flicker of something beneath his usual calm––irritation or even fear.

"You know where he is." His breath hissed in and out through his nose. "He's dead."

"But where is he now? What's left of him, that is?"

"My God." Colour stained the centre of his cheeks. "Is it too much to ask..." His fingers reached for his glasses, yanking them from his nose. He cleaned them on his coat––quick, impatient gestures. "Of course it is," he said. "Heli, I don't want you to mention him again. He has been put to rest. His choice. Not mine. Now, it is time for you to go to bed."

"It's just——"

He leaned close. "You think you still see him?"

"No." I couldn't say anymore.

The Doctor said I saw things, hallucinations. A sign of my troubled mind. The funny thing was, I'd welcome seeing Mal again, even as a flicker in the dark. In a place where reality was thinner than paper, Mal would have grounded me.

22

THE VANARDSDALE EFFECT

Heli

IN THE LAUNDRY CUPBOARD, I heard them come in. Freezing, I crouched down, hiding myself behind the large plastic tubs of detergent that lived under the worktop. I lay flat against the floor, my heart pulsing, pulling dust and lilac-scented washing powder up my nose. I don't know why I hid; truth be told. I was trying to follow the rules.

"You haven't been this way before?" The Doctor's laughter triggered a skittish echo deep within my chest. "This is, of course, the laundry."

I didn't think I'd heard him even attempt a laugh before. There was nothing amusing about laundry. I wondered what had provoked his mood.

"I can see that, Matthew. And she's not here?"

The door to the storage cupboard opened and then shut.

"No, apparently, she is not. She must have been assigned to a different chore." The Doctor tutted, his humour vanishing as quickly as a mouse in the cat's shadow. "It doesn't matter, we can speak with her after dinner."

"Of course. But Matthew, if I may?" There was the soft sound of rustling and footsteps, and I expected to hear the door again as they left when the voice of Dr Emma Vanardsdale continued from the other side of the plastic tubs. "Of the children you have in your care, none of them appear to have recovered enough to leave, is that right? Because when we spoke before my arrival, I was clear I would like to take one back with me."

"I didn't say none of them have recovered."

"Well then, exactly how many of them are ready?"

"If you think it best you have a demonstrable outcome to exhibit..." His voice assumed a sickly, oily, cool note. "Perhaps there is one possibility."

"I see."

"And there will be others. Given enough time, of course. All of our methods have been scrutinised; they are the product of years of rigorous research. This Facility is revolutionary––we are taking strides for science––you said so yourself."

"It is not our methods I'm questioning."

"We are breaking new ground here," he said. "You'll find nothing unorthodox in my notes."

"How many of them are on track to recovery, would you say? Responding already to their treatment?"

"My research is based on the work of Cerletti and the principles you yourself helped to establish. Everything here has been approved from above. You know that."

"How many?"

There was a long pause in which the flow of blood from my heart was so loud, so furious, so insistent it seemed impossible neither of them could hear.

"All of them will recover––given enough time. Except perhaps for Heli. Her case, as you know, remains an," he paused to clear his throat, "an unorthodox one. The hallucinations are proving trickier to fix than we'd anticipated, which is why now is a good time to advance her plan. And, in time, our most famous patient will make for a brilliant case study."

"Do you see any need to re-evaluate at this point?" For a moment her tone shifted, and I dared hope she might stop him, but then her voice turned cold again. "Any other changes you intend to instigate?"

"No, Emma. I will continue with the plan as it is. I have been given time to observe the efficacy of my methods. That time is not up. We cannot hurry these things––nor should we."

"Some might argue we could expect to see more results by now."

"I didn't say there were no results."

"Matthew, please."

"In this Facility, we are dealing with the highest level of need. Out there––on the mainland––under the existing psychiatric health model, the expected life chances for these children are extremely poor which is why we are trying something new. If I am right, the outcomes of the Cerletti Facility will be a vast improvement. But you must give me my time."

"Of course. It is what was agreed. Although, if one of them were to––"

"There has been no incident. The necessary time to check our hypothesis is all I ask. Eleven children, who would otherwise be up to God knows what, are perfectly safe while we conduct our experiment."

"Very well," she said, and I wanted to scream at her to check again. We were not safe in the Doctor's hands. "You understand that it is my job to test you."

"Of course."

The Doctor had said *eleven children*. But there were thirteen of us. Weren't there? Fourteen, if you counted Mollie. So why didn't Dr Emma ask about the missing kids? How many of us would the Doctor disappear before he was done? We were at risk and vulnerable while the Doctor's experiment was given free rein.

"Of course, you must test me. It is as I would expect," the Doctor said, his voice and tone had been the same throughout their conversation. Cold and sickening. To him, we were work, research, an experiment; we were science. "I will keep them safe and report on my findings as agreed."

"Very well," she said, although her tone––if I could trust my instincts from behind the laundry tubs––had become wary. "I accept your judgement and will write up my report. Providing the children come to no harm, of course, the Cerletti Facility may continue its work."

"And the new direction for Heli," he paused to swallow, and my heart pulsed, "that we discussed?"

"Absolutely, yes. As she has been unresponsive to your other efforts."

"Good. Good."

"One last thing, Matthew."

New direction. I barely had time to process the blow when she continued.

"There is an element of paranoia to Heli's symptoms. Not to mention her anosognosia."

I stuffed my hand inside my mouth. They were talking about me. My heartbeat somersaulted like that time I had sniffed something on the playground. *Anosognosia.* Blood pumped in my ears. What did that mean?

"If we were to find that electricity triggered the anosognosia further, I would strongly suggest abandoning the experiment with immediate effect."

"Of course." the Doctor's tone shifted, this time he was subdued and trustworthy. "You are the expert. Our theory is the electric current will positively affect her current mental state. If you would like, we could monitor the first experiments together. Before you leave."

"I confess, I'd be interested in the results."

"As you'd like to observe the session in person," he said, "I see no reason why we can't proceed in the next day or two before your boat is due."

"That would be very agreeable." Dr Emma's voice was warmer now. Although her words, as they left the laundry, stuck like ice, cloying and cold against my skin.

I listened for the hiss of the closing door before I crawled out from behind the washing powder containers. My God. I pinched the skin of my forearm, afraid to trust my senses. Had I really heard what I'd heard? *Electricity* meant... the chair. There was too much to process, but I knew I was in danger. They had drawn a target on my forehead, and I needed to find Cai, he was the last one left who could help me.

"Cai?" He had finished his chores and was in the reading room with the other kids. "Thank God you're here."

"Reading only please, Heli." Dr Fiennes looked up from his device. "Find your book."

"Yeah?" It was a moment before Cai looked at me, his eyes skimming the last of his page. He placed a bookmark between the pages and smiled. "What's the matter?"

Words flashed through my mind, all the things I needed to say. Where to begin? I dropped my face into hands that had become boiling hot. It had been cold in the laundry room; my skin must have heated during my race to find him.

"I am in danger."

"What?"

My words sounded ridiculous, melodramatic, even to me. I tried again.

"Cai, they're going to put me in the chair."

"That's a reminder. I won't give you another one, Heli," Dr Fiennes's voice intruded. "Fetch your book."

I made a show of finding my book, even though the Victorian world of Pip and his problems no longer held any interest. To be truthful, I hadn't read a page since Mal died.

"The Doctor said the chair isn't part of your plan yet." Cai had appeared beside me. "Besides, no one's been in it since Mal. Or... maybe Joe, once or twice. But I think even the Doctor has realised it doesn't work."

"No, he just said, *not yet*, about the chair. And the Doctor absolutely thinks it works. And they don't know about Mal, do they? Or the new doctor doesn't anyway. No one is talking about him at all."

"She must know about Mal. He will be part of the records for this place. Slow down. You aren't making sense."

I flinched; it was one of my pet hates--a grievous knife to my heart. I loathed being told I wasn't making sense.

"Please." I tried to control the pitch of my voice: "I told you the Doctor lied about it. He made out the incontinence was some other boy. He won't talk about Mal. Maybe he meant it had been Joe or even you who'd been shitting yourself." Blood pounded again in my ears, this time with hot, white anger: "I can't believe you don't believe me."

"That's not what I said."

"You sound just like the Doctor."

"That's not fair."

"What's the point?" I rubbed my chest, it was heavy––everything felt heavy––and my cheeks were burning. "I've done everything you asked. Therapy. The tablets. I'm doing better. I've let the Doctor stick his nose inside my every thought. And you don't believe me."

"There's always going to be things that you see differently—

"You don't trust me." I backed away while he crept closer. Shuffling on my beanbag all the way to the far corner of the room. It was a betrayal he could doubt me after everything we'd been through––and our kiss outside.

"It's not right in this place. We are an experiment to them––strides for science. That's what this place is, the great Cerletti experiment. I'm telling you; they are going to put me in the chair. Just to see what happens."

"But––"

"They don't care what it does to me. What it did to Mal or anybody else."

"Heli," Dr Fiennes said. "That's enough. Someone will come and get you."

"Don't you get it?" I whispered to Cai. "Weren't you listening about the chair?"

"Calm down," Cai wriggled his beanbag towards me. "Go back to the beginning. Tell me everything. Again."

"The Doctor said I was unresponsive. And he lied, Cai." My voice was an urgent hiss, stinging my throat. "About Mal, the numbers here. All of it. He said the chair was a last resort. But now he wants to put me in it."

"Maybe if we go to him together——"

"Piss off."

And I could hear them as I got up, the other voices. In the playground back at school. Voices, not like the ones in my head, other voices. Memories of them taunting me, pushing me to the ground. A foot in my back. The crack in my ribs. Voices from back at school. *Freak. Schizo. Dirty little Ginger.*

Even Cai didn't believe me. My greatest fear. I was not trusted; just a girl crying wolf.

But if you stopped believing in yourself, then you were left with nothing. And I wouldn't be nothing. Mal didn't want me to be nothing. I thought about his note, the things he'd said to me; I had to keep trying.

"Dinner time." Dr Fiennes stretched his back out as he stood. "Put away your books and line up."

Dr Devitt came for me after dinner. Even though I'd been expecting it, it was a shock. I was too angry to prepare myself, to hide, or run away. I had thought there would be more time.

"Come with me, Heli," he said as the other kids were instructed to line up on the spots.

"No chance."

In that split second, I had decided. To resist. What other choice was there? Because even after the warning, I wasn't ready. There was no plan, no way to escape. I glanced at the out-of-reach window, tears pricking my eyes.

"No," I wrapped my arm around the chair as though it could protect me. I would stick my teeth into it if necessary, cling to it with all my might. They would have to pry me away, one tooth at a time. I glared at the dirty plates; we hadn't even tidied up. I wasn't ready.

"Let's not make this anymore unpleasant." Dr Devitt's hand reached for my arm.

"You admit it will be unpleasant." With my spare hand, I threw a glass.

"That's enough." Dr Devitt didn't flinch as the shards of glass crashed over the floor.

"Are you taking me to the chair?"

He said nothing. His hand met my shoulder, heavy and unwanted.

"Are you taking me to the chair?"

A sigh snorted out from his nostrils. "You're upsetting everybody else."

"You're going to take me to the chair." My voice was shrill. The other kids were frozen on the spots. Pieces of glass stretched across the floor between me and them——waiting. "I'm the one upsetting people?"

"You'll be sedated. There won't be any pain." His hand hardened and squeezed my shoulder.

"Tell them you couldn't find me." My voice cracked with fury. Every muscle was taut, ready to fight. "I'll scream so loud they'll hear me on the mainland."

"It won't hurt."

"You don't think it hurt Mal?"

Dr Devitt looked between the door and Dr Shalt who was watching us, her grey eyes cold. But there was no Dr Emma in the room, so he must have judged it safe to reply.

"Heli," his voice was low. "Mal's reaction was unusual."

"I'll scream." Once they put me in the chair, it wouldn't just be my body they'd take. They'd strip away everything——thoughts, memories, until there was nothing left but their experiment.

"You have three seconds to get up and come with me. Before I sedate you right here."

I threw my plate across the table; shoved my chair away until it squealed. Heat flooded my cheeks as my scream tore through the room. I gripped the chair like it could anchor me. But nothing could stop what was coming. It wasn't even worth the look on Cai's face--the shock, the realisation of how wrong he'd been about the chair, about everything.

-

23

GOOD GIRLS

Heli

DR DEVITT CLAMPED HIS hand tighter onto my shoulder and pushed me towards the door.

"Can you manage on your own?" Dr Shalt said from the other side of the dining hall.

And I thought it was probably her suggestion she would lend her weight to forcing me out of the room that compelled my feet to start moving on their own. Like I didn't even need Dr Devitt shoving me forward. The only thing worse than being taken to the chair would be being taken to the chair by Dr Shalt.

In the corridor, the Doctor was waiting with Dr Emma anyway.

"Good choice, Heli," he said, his hand reaching to pat me as we passed. "You've made the right decision."

Saliva formed in a bubble inside my throat. I was trapped somewhere between the desire to spit and trying not to choke. Tears streamed from my eyes and something hateful brewed in my chest, like a hiccup, only more explosive.

"Please," I tried to swallow my outrage like a good girl and beg. But I couldn't contain whatever was building, and liquid bubbled from my lips, dripping over my chin. "I don't need the chair. Please," I gasped for air. "You said not yet."

"We will take good care of you," the Doctor said like I hadn't just begged for a reprieve with no thought to my personal dignity. "There will be a lovely sedative when you get there. This is part of the plan. It will help your reformation and ease the burden you've been carrying."

"I don't," I snorted like a sick pig, "want to."

The Doctor took hold of my other arm and together the two of them marched me along the corridor. Dark thoughts gathered and I sobbed until my face was bruised. But they didn't let up.

"Here we are," The Doctor said. "Emma, if you will."

They lifted me onto the chair, and with a hiss of sound, it lowered. My ankles and wrists were contained in some kind of contraption designed for disobedience, and my mind emptied. Raw like the aftermath of a long scream. It reminded me of the day I'd nearly drowned out at sea, the helpless clutching of white water and desperate splashing.

"There you are. Now, this will relax you," Dr Emma murmured, her needle biting into my arm. A sharp inhalation followed, like she was savouring the sight of science, fascination overriding any empathy.

Shock ripped through me like a phantom; an invisible invasion reaching every nerve ending. It pulsed, shifted, and intensified. I clung to an image of Mal, his laughter on the beach. But as the ghostly chill seeped beneath my skin, memory faded into something less real. If they took my mind, what would be left? My limbs twitched, shadows of movement beyond my control. A buzz of sound and excruciating cold.

Then it receded, leaving me with a lingering ache and thoughts that scattered--uncatchable, like mist.

"How often do you sedate them, Matthew?" Dr Emma asked. "Other than for the chair."

"Not often," he said. "Perhaps when a patient is hysterical, for example."

"And on mass?"

"Almost never."

"When I arrived," Dr Emma paused. There was no mistaking the edge of authority in her tone. "They appeared subdued then."

"They are unsettled by change," the Doctor said, with his usual calm, but there was a flicker of something else--deference or maybe unease. "Action taken pre-emptively has proven more efficacious than after an outburst." He chuckled. "I trust you're not questioning my judgement?"

"Evaluation is part of the process of science. You of all people should know that."

"Of course," he said. "Your job is to test me."

I imagined him removing his glasses, regarding her with his face, unprotected, an impression of vulnerability.

"I must seem somewhat uncivilised," he said, "how quickly one falls out of the habits of society."

"And Heli--how do you expect her to respond to the electroconvulsive therapy?"

"As you know, her case is complicated, but I would expect things to turn a corner and for us to begin to see the fruits of our labour. To calm her at the very least."

"What outcome are you expecting for her? Eventually?"

"Best case scenario is total rehabilitation."

"I see."

"Except of course…"

"Yes," she said. "Except for that."

Except for what? My brain raced to fill the gaps. A failure. A fatality. Something they couldn't say aloud.

I wanted to scream at them to tell me. What did they mean, *except for that?* My eyes fluttered, impatient with being kept in the dark.

"One last thing. A curiosity more than anything." I heard the rapid movement of her lips in the darkness. "You see them as delinquent, don't you? To you, the children are delinquent, not just mentally unstable."

"The two present together. Look for example at the case of this patient. Setting fire to her grandmother's home."

Delinquency. As if I needed further proof the Doctor was an arsehole.

"Perceptive," he said. "But the routines are not there to be, as some might say, punitive. A disciplined mind is the first step towards recovery. That is the central tenet of everything we do at Cerletti."

"And the incontinence problem of your first patient. Has the side effect impacted anyone else?"

"All resolved," he said. "An early problem, quite over now. Joe has settled into the treatment well." He cleared his throat. "There is something I would like to mention," he said. "I must ask for some relief staff to alleviate the signs of cabin fever. Dr Devitt, for example, is younger, not as experienced as the others."

"And the support staff?"

"No. They already have a rota; two weeks on, two weeks off the island."

My eyes rolled backwards, sleep hovered, ready to steal me. I tried to hold my breath, to force myself to stay awake and hear this secret conversation, lies slipping from the Doctor's mouth like diarrhoea.

"There is a doctor I have in mind for the opportunity, a specialist in electroconvulsive therapy. Subject, of course, to your ongoing funding being approved."

"How likely would you say green lighting our funding is?"

There was a pause, before Dr Emma answered. "I have seen nothing yet that gives me undue concerns for your continuation." Her tone lost its hesitancy as she continued. "In fact, I am curious to see how far this process can go. As you know ECT--"

"Is your field of speciality," his voice dripped, slick like oil. "Would you like to stay for her second treatment?"

Second treatment. The terrible notion of enduring this again settled in my gut. If the first treatment could do this much damage, what would the second one take from me?

"It is not too soon to safely repeat the process?"

"We can do it--every third day."

"Perfect," she said. "If we can schedule it for Thursday morning, my boat can leave afterwards. I will check if the tides are still agreeable."

Once was bad enough. I didn't want any more treatments. If I stayed, I would end up dying here. Or worse, I would become incontinent. I needed to get out. I needed to talk to Cai again--make him see the truth before it was too late. And I had two days and three sleeps to manage it before they would strap me into the chair.

Again.

24

DARKER

Sira

THE DINING HALL WAS dim––the bulb in the strip light flickering, near enough burned out. I avoided Joe's chair, sat down, and started scooping sausage and mash into my mouth. Sometimes, eating helped calm my twitches. Of course, we knew it was tempting fate to use the bathroom before meals as the doctors' presence intensified during transitions. But––my shoulders started to relax––it had been worth the risk now that we seemed to have gotten away with it.

When Heli sat next to me, her body hit her chair like one of those heavy sacks of plant fertiliser.

"Alright?" I said, allowing myself to look at her.

While I'd been flirting with Joe, Heli had been in the chair. I felt sorry about it. We all did.

First, Mal had been in it, then Joe a few times, and now her. I wanted to ask if it hurt. But from the state of her, you could see the chair made you sick more than anything else. It had made Mal incontinent. I squirmed in my chair at the thought.

"Urgh," Heli said, pushing her food away.

"It's like Halloween, isn't it?" Joe pointed at the light above us where the bulb was on the brink of burning out. "Or like how Halloween is in the movies."

"That's hardly Halloween." I stared at my plate.

Did Heli want to talk about the chair? Mal had always clammed up; Joe never wanted to answer any questions either.

"It's just a joke." Joe lifted his eyebrows at me like he was convincing me he was trying with Heli. Trying to distract her.

"What do you mean Halloween?" Heli thumped her hand on the table. "There's no pumpkins or witches or––"

"I think we're the pumpkins." Joe smiled.

"For God's sake. Something bad is happening," she said. "If you stopped thinking about yourself, going on about Halloween and all, you'd see it too. Just shut up."

I looked between them, unsure of what to say; it was ironic when it was Joe who stood the best chance of being able to help her with how she was feeling right then. If she let him.

"What's wrong with you?" he asked.

"What's wrong with me?" Heli squeezed her hand into a fist and pressed her fork against the tabletop until it bent. "My stomach hurts like hell and my forehead has a weird, cold, itchy sensation. What's wrong with you?"

Joe looked at her and it seemed like he was about to say something but then he picked up his knife and cut his sausage into neat slices. He's not much of a talker.

"He means well," I said.

"You haven't said anything about them putting me in the chair either." Heli scratched at the side of her temple.

She had a wild look in her eyes, and to be truthful, it made me nervous like all the times I tried to tell my momma I didn't want to do the pageants anymore.

"Heli, I'm sorry." I scratched around for words of comfort. "I didn't know whether you'd want to, you know, talk. I thought maybe you would bring it up."

"I don't want to talk about it." She dropped the fork with all its tines bent out of line. "Except they said," she paused, "not they, he, he said the incontinent kid had fully recovered."

"What?" Joe was distracted by his food, skewering his sausage pieces with a look of reverie on his face. He was weird about food. I looked around the table. Everyone else was listening to Heli, wondering what she was going to come up with next.

"That's not all," she said. "The Doctor said you, Joe, were the incontinent kid."

"That's not true," he made eye contact with me for the briefest of moments, his cheeks colouring. "It was Mal who shit himself."

"Exactly," she said.

"Exactly what?" Joe speared his next mouthful onto his fork.

"It's just a sausage." Heli's snapped, her voice rising. "You bunch of greedy pigs. Mal is dead and the Doctor is telling lies."

"Calm down," I indicated Dr Shalt in the corner. But she was already on her way over. "You'll get us into trouble."

"If you'd just listen. You'd know I was already in trouble. The Doctor just fried my brain with electricity, and he's planning to do it to all of you. That's if he's not too busy lying about who's dead and who's incontinent."

25

TWO DAYS AND THREE SLEEPS

Heli

THE OTHER KIDS AROUND the dining table looked away, like whatever it was that was happening, they were afraid it was catching. I scratched my forehead, but the weird itch couldn't be soothed. Footsteps approached. An irritating click-click of a regulation-size heel.

"Heli?"

Dr Shalt's shadow loomed.

"That's a warning," she said. "Table manners and quiet conversation only." She pushed my plate toward me. "Eat up. Now. Be a good girl."

Sausages: there were two of them, thin and pink-skinned on one side, curled together in an unappealing shape. Mashed potatoes towered beside the scattering of tiny, round peas, all of it untouched. My guts lurched. I was certain, Dr Shalt and I would have different ideas about what a *good girl* was.

For a moment, I was tempted to throw the whole plateful at the wall. Better yet, I could throw it at Dr Shalt. It might be worth the punishment to see the greasy combination slide over her stupid, smiling lips. But I needed to tell Cai what the Doctor had said about a second treatment and the ticking timebomb waiting in the shadows. I needed someone to help.

"I'm sorry," I whispered, avoiding the looks from the other kids at the table.

Sira looked the angriest. Her hand hovered above her plate, fork slumped to the side. I remembered her hunched face last night when Dr Devitt took me. I tried to smile, but she shook her head. My throat struggled to swallow. Why would Sira be upset? The Doctor's pet wasn't the one who'd been put in the chair.

"Sorry--what?" Dr Shalt said.

"I'm sorry, Dr Shalt." I took a deep breath, trying to ease the tension from my muscles. "I'm sorry, everyone."

Dr Shalt nodded and returned to her table near the corner, sitting and crossing her legs. She glanced once around our table before turning to finish typing her correspondence. A muscle pulsed in her forehead as her fingers flew over the keyboard, her smile spreading, slick as syrup across her face.

"What are you going on about?" Cai leaned close. His face pale, and eyes wide. "What happened?"

"Oh, are you listening now?" I cast a glance at his empty plate. "The Doctor was talking to the visiting doctor, this Emma Vanardsdale, and he said the incontinent boy has now fully recovered."

"What?"

"Can you stop saying *what*? Don't you know any other words?"

He pushed his plate away, gazing at the emptiness for a moment like he was sad he had finished all his food.

"Are you sure?" his voice wavered. "Maybe you misheard."

My hands clenched and I resisted calling him a pig again. Time was too precious. I needed to make him see.

"I was right last time," I said. "Wasn't I?"

"Sorry," he paused. "I just don't get it. Why would the Doctor say that?"

"Because he is a liar."

Cai expended his breath, and it squeaked like a hot sausage over the fire.

"But," I stiffened, a cold shudder travelling across my spine. "I don't get why he'd want to lie about that?" My gag reflex worked overtime. The sight of greased sausage skin wasn't making it any better. Two patches of skin on my temples itched where they'd attached the electrical things. "I mean, seeing as Mal, as Mal is... Not here. How else can the Doctor explain that?

"Are you sure that's what he said?"

"Yes." My fingers reached for my fork. Not to eat, just for something to grip hold of. Something solid. "I think the Doctor is pretending Mal was never here."

"Heli," Cai dropped his voice to whisper, "you know sometimes what I see and what you say aren't always the same." His eyes flickered across the other kids at the table, they were watching me. Lips slick with sausage grease. Plates near enough empty. "Do you get me?"

"Not really." The fork was hard. Its ends bent.

"Are you taking your meds?"

"Sometimes. I mean, I'm trying to, but I don't like the things they do to me. The trembling and... and the other stuff."

"You have to take them," he said. "This place, there's some weird stuff going on, and how are you going to know what's what if you're not taking your tablets?"

"You don't believe me." My throat was dry. I could feel the cold sting of the electric current again, travelling through me. Strange because I would have thought that electricity would burn. "Even after what they did."

The thought that Cai, of all people, didn't believe me made everything worse. Slipping from my grasp, the fork clattered onto my plate, and I held my nose instead. Around the table, the faces of the other kids were hard and angry. They looked like they hated me. But why? What had I ever done to them? Mal's chair--sat empty, neatly pushed under the table--and no longer required. I couldn't make this stuff up.

But how was I supposed to know what was real and what was not when no one would talk to me? My face folded. I missed my friend, Mal. Most of all, because he would have believed me.

"Hey," Joe poked his fingers into my side. "Don't do that. We'll get into trouble for breaking stuff."

"What do you think you're doing?" I shoved his hand away.

"That's quite enough, Heli." Dr Shalt appeared at the table. "Come with me. Now."

"But I wasn't doing anything. Why don't you do anything about his violence?" I lunged towards Joe, but he dodged out of the way while Dr Shalt slid her hands under my armpits and dragged me back.

She must have pressed her alarm too because Dr Devitt was in the room with his needle ready.

"Please no," I said. "I wasn't doing anything."

Across the table, I caught Sira in the middle of rolling her eyes at Joe and I stuck my fingers up.

"I hate you," I said, my voice was limp, a sad old teddy with no stuffing.

Dr Devitt's hand tightened on my arm and there was a sharp sting.

When I came around, I was in my bed in the dormitory. The other kids were moving around, the whisper of talking and opening drawers.

"Hey," I said to Sira when she got close enough. "Is it morning?"

"No," her ponytail shook, backwards and forwards, more than was necessary, before she got it under control. "Bedtime."

"Great." Now I had three hours less to plan my big escape. Hours, when I wouldn't be able to sleep, my only company, the darkness.

"Do you want to talk about the chair?" Sira whispered, sliding into the bed next to mine.

"Not with you."

"It was hard over dinner," she said. "Dr Shalt is a bitch."

"You seem to like the doctors plenty when they're around."

"Oh, Heli," she said, her voice hollow and sad.

"Don't feel sorry for me." I wriggled to the far side, as far from her as possible. Even though I could hear Mya holding her breath from her bed, on that side. All of the other kids were waiting to hear what I might say. Of course they were.

I could have told Sira––I could have told all of them––how I was sedated when they did it. Immobile and without consent. But I didn't want to talk about it. What was there to say? I had no words of comfort for the others. They'd find out soon enough when their turn came.

I touched the skin on my forehead. I supposed if there was one thing I would say, if they asked again, that I'd expected it to burn. Electricity was like fire, right? But it turned out I was wrong. Electricity was cold. Unbearably cold, and I had only a few hours before I would have to feel it again. I closed my eyes. Even though it was dark, and they couldn't see me, I felt exposed under the microscope of their interest. Sira reached over and patted my arm.

"Get off." I was in that delicate state––on the edge of sobbing.

"I'm just trying to be nice."

"Don't bother." I turned over, feeling for the comfort of Mal's note inside my pillowcase. I would spend the night planning my way out.

At first, I thought I needed to make one of their cards––to find an opportunity to use the little machine in the science lab. And thanks to the arrival of Dr Emma Vanardsdale, I knew where it was kept. But how could I get there without a card?

The possibilities and impossibilities chased around as I scrubbed my fingers around my eye sockets, digging at the sands of sleep. Then it occurred to me, just like Mal had said in his note. Instead of trying to break out after exercise time, I would not come back in.

26

Pretending

Heli

I closed the shower stall door and continued to plot my escape. The sound of water blocked out the chatter of the other girls. During the exercise hour, I would need to find a place to hide. Eventually, the tides would be right, and Dr Emma's boat would come, then I could stow away. We could stow away together, because if I was leaving, Cai had to come, too.

I'd stopped blaming him for doubting me about the chair. This place messed with your head. Our relationship might not always make sense, but I knew things were better when we were together.

"Get a move on, Heli," I jumped when Sira banged the cubicle door. "Time's up."

"Fuck off."

It was hard to imagine, according to the Doctor, that I'd been in the Facility for nearly a year. I'd missed my sixteenth birthday, spending enough time here to make friends and lose them. If I could have looked, if they hadn't removed the bathroom mirror, I was sure my face would carry an echo of the time, the same way my arms bore the scars from the fire.

"I mean it, Heli." Sira banged the door again: "I'll get Dr Shalt if need be."

"Hang on. I'm washing my soap off."

The only mirrors left were in the lab––fragments designed for cutting things in half. Twisting, I traced the strange tribal-like markings on my hips, changes etched into my skin. Stretch marks, mum once said, would fade to silver.

"That's it," Sira said. "I'm getting Dr Shalt."

"Don't be such a bitch. I'm coming."

When I unlocked the cubicle door, Sira was there, her arms folded across her chest, her cheeks spasming. I'd known she would be. No one called for Dr Shalt––not even Sira.

"All yours," I said. "You can get nice and clean for your boyfriend."

After breakfast, while the others made their way to the school room, I was summoned to the Doctor's office. Dr Devitt accompanied me along the white-walled corridor, but neither of us spoke. Inside the room, the Doctor was arranging papers behind his desk. My heart pulsed, what if I'd got it wrong and he intended to put me in the chair right now?

"Take a seat," he joined me at the small table at the centre. "Thank you, Dr Devitt, that will be all."

"This isn't my day for a session." My breath was loud inside my throat. "Is it?"

"Would you like to talk about Mal?" The doctor adjusted his pen, a fat round barrel, the deepest shade of burgundy.

"Not really." I glanced at the corners of his room, but she was not there. The Doctor's walking shadow, the one that had come to judge us.

Where was Dr Emma? There were too many thoughts jostling inside my head. Escape, loneliness––stretchmarks. "I thought that you…"

I was about to tell him I knew he hadn't told Dr Emma everything, not about how he had kept Mal a secret. But something made me hesitate. I had an advantage. Knowledge was currency. Even if I couldn't figure out how to use it.

"Why, not really?" he tilted his head.

"The last things I said to Mal… I was distracted and I didn't notice."

"You're not to blame. He was a troubled young person and—"

"I know that." My fists clenched on my lap. My skin pale, like cream, with a smudge of freckles and a circular scar on the back of one––thanks to Joe.

"Survivor's guilt is common. In fact," the Doctor leant forwards, "Soldiers after the first World War experienced such profound––"

"I don't blame myself." How dare he presume.

"We aren't always aware of why we feel the things we do."

"I blame you."

He clicked his pen, placing it to rest on the clipboard on his lap.

"What would you like to talk about?"

"Why are you pretending to the new Doctor that Mal was never here?" I hadn't meant to say them; words that hung in the space between us.

"That's," patience stretched across his face. "That's not exactly how it is. It is better, for now of course, that we concentrate our efforts on those patients that we have right now in the Facility. That is what matters in the evaluation of the efficacy of our service. Anything else you'd like to discuss?"

"Nothing." It was always the same with the Doctor; his answers never matched the question.

"And yesterday's treatment," the Doctor said, "how has that made you feel?"

"I said, nothing."

"In that case," he lifted his pen and clipboard, folding one ankle across the other, "why don't you make your way back to the school room."

I tried to leave the room without revealing how surprised I was that the Doctor was trusting me to walk back across the corridor unsupervised. It was only a short distance, but he had never done this before. *Never.* Perhaps my comment had wriggled under his skin after all. *Good.* He deserved to suffer.

My heart fluttered. What if the Doctor had to pretend Mal had never been here at all? That there were no suicides in his Facility. What if he needed to pretend that to secure his precious funding? To greenlight his experiment to continue. The mystery of the Doctor's behaviour almost made sense, before it fragmented, and understanding cracked apart like a broken glass.

I lingered in the corridor, my gaze fixed on the front door, a pulse flickering like electricity from my heart to my neck. But without a swipe card, I had to bide my time. Tomorrow morning they'd put me in the chair again. My fingers curled into fists as I stared at the door, my resolve hardening with each passing minute.

The Doctor deserved to suffer; the thought crowded out the others. An urge to take his things, like I used to take Peony's, and burn them, crept under my skin. Fire was art, if you could control it. But it would only trap me in the Facility. I needed to leave with the others at exercise time and then not return. For now, I had to stay focused, so I returned to the school room. It was only a matter of time before I could leave for good.

27

Never Going Back

Heli

During lunch, I pushed away my half-eaten sandwich and leaned close to whisper in Cai's ear.

"I could have escaped earlier."

"As if," he lips twitched, amused.

"I'm serious. The Doctor let me walk back to the school room, alone."

"Why didn't you leave then?"

"Because the door was locked." My cheeks flushed while a muscle pulsed above my eye. "You can't just walk out. But if you listened, I could tell you my plan."

"Calm down," he grinned. "I think someone couldn't bear to leave me behind."

"You idiot." I could tell Cai thought I was crazy. "It's this place," I said. "It's making me worse."

He nudged my arm, and I blushed, remembering what it had felt like to kiss him. I couldn't recall how long ago it had been. My memory was unreliable before the chair, but what would it be like now? I thought about kissing him again.

"Cai?"

He turned his face towards me.

"Yeah?"

"I realised something." I leant closer until my lips brushed his ear, my breath skimming warm skin. I wanted to kiss him, but I wasn't about to tell him that. "All this time," I said, "I've been wondering about how to get out of here. And the funny thing is, we don't need to worry about that. We never did."

"What?"

"Instead of escaping the building. We just won't come back after exercise time."

"We won't come back," a grin spread across his face. "Genius. When shall we do it? We'll need to save food and water--"

"Today," I paused. "I'm getting out today. I'm waiting for Dr Emma's boat and I'm never coming back."

"Boat?"

"Yeah, she's leaving." And I squashed down what she'd hoped to see again before she left.

But when exercise time arrived, I was partnered with Sira. It wasn't just that Sira would be hard to shake off, I was sick of her too. Her quiet compliance, how she was the first to agree with the Doctor and the first to do his bidding. Although she'd asked about the chair, she was only being nosey; she didn't really care.

"We're meant to stay together," Sira reached for my sleeve as I hurried out from the metal gates onto the muddy track.

"Hurry up, then," I said, waiting. There was a distant roar from the ocean. "Get a move on." Irritation itched; how would I ditch her?

We sat on the edge of the lighthouse cliff, listening to the waves crash. The sound used to calm me, but today it couldn't cut through my nerves.

"The Doctor said we're getting trainers," Sira said.

"So what?" I didn't feel good. There was no choice. But now the moment had arrived, I was scared.

"Trainers; it's a good thing."

"Is it?" My tongue flicked over dry, salty lips, irritated by Sira's acceptance of everything. "Doesn't it make you angry? Like the Doctor wants to buy you."

"They could buy us, but they don't." Her touch on my hand was as light and damp as a dog's nose. "They subdue us."

"Why are you smiling?" I glanced around for Cai, but he'd vanished to the other side of the harbour.

"It's not so bad to give in. These shoes hurt my feet," her far shoulder twitched. "Trainers are easier for climbing rocks."

"I guess." I looked at the jetty where it stretched along the water. The splash and spray of waves hit against the old wooden struts. "Where is he?"

My hands stiffened. There's a feeling in my guts, that's new. A different way to avoid returning to the chair. It sang to me. I peered over the edge at the drop to rocks and blue water. The feeling pulled, tempting me to loosen my grip. If I angled myself the right way, I might avoid being scrambled. Although I shuddered because my lungs filling with salt water was a spectacularly shit way to die. I thought about Mal--and how he'd rescued me that day, saved my life, and the note he'd left behind. I owed it to him to find a way to take down the Doctor.

"We need to get back," Sira stood up, the faint ringing of the warning bell in the distance. "Are you ready?"

"Sure."

I got up while light grey-blue waves smashed together like a giant set of teeth. While we walked back, clambering over the last of the rocks and up onto the path, I wondered why I didn't do it. Perhaps I didn't want to ruin Sira's day, or maybe I didn't fancy a cold or painful end. But maybe there was also hope that things would change. *They subdued us.* Even Sira had worked that out. The Doctor couldn't get away with it.

"I could have run away earlier," I told her, as our feet covered the path back towards the Facility. The sun was sinking beneath the cloud line.

"You wouldn't have got very far," her cheek twitched. "There's no point in trying."

"I know," I stuffed my hands inside my pockets. I didn't have time for nose-holding. I needed to act now before we returned to the Facility and the door closed.

"Sira," I said. "I need to go to the toilet."

"We're nearly back."

"Can't wait. Sorry."

"Be quick then."

"Go without me."

"We're not allowed to go on our own," her voice was a whine. "Come on, can't you wait? The Facility's just there."

"No."

Sira reached for my arm, but I was too fast for her.

"Go without me." I slipped out of her reach, wrong-footing her.

"Stop messing around."

I started running back along the path towards the beach. What did it matter if Sira was on to me? She might as well be the one to report it to the Doctor. He'd know I was missing soon enough.

I sprinted towards the rocks, my heart pounding. At the boatshed's edge, Cai waited his face tense.

"How d'you get away?" Relief flooded my chest. I couldn't face the chair again, I'd rather die. But with Cai, there was hope––hope we could escape together.

"Said I needed the bog, didn't I?"

"That's what I said too." I grinned. "You should have seen Sira's face."

"Do you think they'll find us?"

"I guess the boatshed is a pretty obvious place to look." My heart pulsed, but where else could we go? Hiding places on the island were not plentiful.

"But they don't know that we know about it." Cai took my arm.

"Even so." Anxiety gnawed at my guts. "Shit," I glanced at the rocks. It was too late to change our minds, and what other choice was there? I didn't want to go in the chair again.

Inside the boatshed, there were some ropes, nets, fishing tackle, and not a lot else. But it was out of sight of the Facility. Somewhere to wait until Dr Emma's boat arrived tomorrow, and we could stow away. Outside the wind shifted, carrying a faint sound––footsteps? Voices? I shook it off. We were safe. For now.

Cai wedged an old fishing net under the door handle. "It won't keep them out for long," he said.

"At least we'll have some warning if they come."

"Are you cold?"

When I nodded, he put his arm around me, and his breath was fast. I waited for him to recover. He whispered in my ear, a tickle of pleasure.

"This is nice," he said. "How long has it been since we tasted freedom, eh?"

The warmth of his breath soothed me, but the reality of what lay ahead pressed at the edge of my mind. Tomorrow wasn't a promise––it was a threat. What would happen if we didn't get away? I clung to Cai, holding onto the moment of peace.

"What's this?" I whispered. "You came here for another sex talk?"

"I do want to talk to you," he said.

"What about?"

"I saw you earlier," he said, "on the ledge. Pushing yourself forward. What were you thinking––after Mal?"

"I was desperate, wasn't I? I don't want them to keep sedating me. Sticking me in the chair."

"Heli," his hand reached for mine. "I've got you."

"I don't trust the Doctor," I said, my heart beating too fast at his touch. "He said *except for.*"

"Except for what?" his hand stroked along my arm.

"I don't know." As I tucked my hair behind my ears, a memory scratched beneath the surface. "It sounded bad. Like everyone was going to get to go home, *except for* me."

"Heli," he lifted my chin: "I won't let them send you away, you're stuck with me." His fingers were soft against my skin. "But you've got to promise to hang on."

"I will."

"Both of us," he said, "can leave this place together."

"They are going to put me in the chair again." I looked at my hands, drifting past my nose. I shuddered.

"No," he said. "They won't."

"You don't know that. They'll catch us and then––"

"I won't let them."

"Will you kiss me?" I whispered.

"Sure."

When we kissed, his mouth touching mine, excitement flickered, dancing over my skin, light as the wind and laden with a new feeling. His fingers traced under the long side of my hair, grazing the skin at the back of my neck, and I wanted it to be more, for his touch to last longer. I took my clothes off and lay down beside him, needing to feel the heat of him. My skin against his, bringing us to life. It was my first time, and I kind of thought it was his too.

We dozed for a while afterwards, my cheek against his chest, his arms across my back. Cai's coat covered our naked bodies until the sound of waves came closer, and darkness pressed into the gap below the door.

"Cai?" I whispered while seagulls squealed where they nested in the space above the boatshed.

"What?" His voice was muffled with sleep.

"Are you scared?"

"There's nothing to be afraid of." His arms held me tighter.

"What if the Doctor comes."

"Everything will be alright," his breath was soft in my hair. "As long as we're together."

Fists hammered the door to the boatshed, the old net giving way under the force.

"Cai," I screamed as the door burst open, his arms ripped from mine.

We had nothing to defend ourselves, only scraps of rope and a broken net. Just the two of us, naked and vulnerable. Our clothes folded in the corner.

The Doctor entered, along with Dr Fiennes and Dr Devitt.

"Get up, Heli. And put this on." The Doctor handed me his coat.

I looked at Cai. "What shall we do?"

"Game's up," he said, his voice deeper than usual. "Put the coat on."

"It's not a game," I said. "Do something. They're going to put me in the chair again. You said you wouldn't let them--"

"Heli," Cai reached for my hand, his fingertips grazing mine.

I tried to hold onto him while Dr Fiennes put his hands--cold and hard--under my armpits and dragged me upwards.

"Don't forget," Cai said, his voice raw.

"What do you mean?" But he didn't reply. "Cai?"

I started to sob. I didn't even care I was naked while the Doctor wrapped his coat around me. All I wanted was to be left alone with Cai.

"Speak to me." I cried, smacking the Doctor's arm. "Where's Cai?" I trembled beneath the scratchy fabric of his coat. "Why've you taken him first? Don't leave me alone. Cai?" All I could think about was him, his touch, his voice--they were all I had. Now there was only a terrible silence.

28

The Chair

Heli

I TRIED AGAIN AS they dragged me out of the boatshed toward the rocks. The Doctor gripped my ankles, while Dr Fiennes and Dr Devitt heaved beneath my shoulders, their breathing ragged.

"Where's Cai?" I demanded, my voice cracking.

"Wait, Heli," the Doctor replied, struggling to steady his breath. "Until we get back. We'll discuss things there."

"But where's Cai gone? Who took him?" Panic surged through me, making the doctors stagger under my added weight. "Cai?" I screamed, my voice tearing through the air. "Please, where are you?"

Dr Fiennes shifted his grip, his voice dropping low as if I wouldn't hear if he whispered. "Shall we just——"

"Can't do any more harm, can it?" Dr Devitt muttered. "Doctor?"

The Doctor's grip tightened around my ankles, turning his hands into cold manacles. It was a shock after the intimate warmth of Cai's touch.

"Heli, do you think you can walk?" His tone suggested a reluctant compromise, but his hands told another story.

"I'm not doing anything for you, not after you took him away." I kicked out, calling again, "Cai? Where are you?"

"If you can walk back by yourself to the Facility," the Doctor sighed, as though he was making the ultimate concession, "you can see him there."

"Do you promise?"

"Yes."

"Really––do you promise?" I pulled at Dr Devitt's hands. I didn't trust the Doctor, but I hoped he might keep his word.

"Yes, Heli," Dr Devitt replied, his gaze fixed straight ahead. "I promise."

Back at the Facility door, the Doctor swiped his card and tapped in the code.

"Where is Cai?" I asked, their hands heavy on my shoulders as they pushed me inside. "And where are you taking me?"

They marched me through the long, sterile corridor––away from the dormitory, away from the other kids––towards the building's far end where the science zone lay.

"What are we doing here?" My heartbeat pounded in my ears, over and over. "Please, you promised I could see him."

But none of them answered. Just before the main door through to the science zone, they shoved me into a small, stark room––a bed, a high window, and a toilet in the corner. It was made for isolation. I'd never noticed the door before, though there were so many in this area.

"Where's Cai?" Tears burned as the doctors hovered at the threshold. "You promised."

But the Doctor was an expert liar, and as it turned out, Dr Fiennes and Dr Devitt weren't truth-tellers either.

"He's not here," my voice broke. I should've known better. "Wait, please don't leave, Dr Devitt." My hands banged against the door as he closed it.

"You promised I could see him. Cai? Where are you?"

Their footsteps echoed down the corridor, fading into silence. Alone in the room, my rage boiled over, and I hurled myself at the walls. The cold, chemical air clawed at my skin. When that didn't help, I curled up on the bed, the plastic-scented pillow pressing into my face. I couldn't sleep. Hours crawled by, maybe it was morning when they finally took me to the chair.

It was another kind of punishment. Without Cai, I faced it alone. Gloom seeped into the room, along with the cold hum of electricity. Shadows shifted with the movement of hostile feet. I tried to move, but my arms and legs stayed pinned. My mouth opened; a scream lodged in my throat. I had tried everything to escape, and this was something I couldn't fight.

"You have to understand, Heli, it's for the best." The Doctor's voice seemed distant.

But I didn't understand. Not when he slid the needle into my arm. The urge to scream twisted, the sound dissolving before it could break free. I thought of Mal, his dark, serious eyes. I tried to reach for him in my mind as if remembering him could bring him back. Mal and Cai blurred together in my thoughts: friendship, teasing, the same warm gaze.

"Please don't," I whispered, tears snaking into my hair.

"This treatment is a last resort."

"What about Cai?" I asked. "Is he here?"

"It's just me, you, and Dr Emma," the Doctor replied from his chair, "in the room."

Dr Emma Vanardsdale leant forward, flipping a switch on the machine. A buzz filled the air. I reached out for Cai's hand––Mal's hand––anyone's. I hated being alone. For a second, I thought I saw Dr Vanardsdale's hand twitch, like a brief flicker of compassion, but it vanished just as quickly.

The first cold jolt tore through me, freezing every nerve. I squeezed my eyes shut, gripping the image of Cai stepping into the room. His hand in mine felt real but the cold buzz of the machine shattered the illusion. I couldn't tell what was real anymore, and that terrified me most of all.

Afterward, they returned me to the small room. I lay on the bed, fingers tugging at my hair until I started braiding it in tiny knots, like the ones Peony and I had done at the beach one summer. I paced the floor, tried to jump up to the window, but I always ended up back on the bed, too drained to even cry. Time drifted. Meals came, but no comfort.

"Dr Devitt, please," I said when he brought chicken noodle soup. "How long have I been here? Is it sunny?" I added on a whim. "I thought I heard rain last night."

"It's dry," he said.

"Can I come out, please?" My voice cracked. "I––I hate being alone."

"Eat your lunch," he replied, backing out of the door. "We'll see."

The next day––maybe later, it was hard to tell––Dr Fiennes took me towards the domed centre of the building. I hoped I was going back to the schoolroom, to Cai and the other kids, but my breath caught in my chest as he led me through the forbidden door––towards the doctor's indoor basketball court.

"Oh," I said. "I thought––"

"No," Dr Fiennes cut in. "You won't be allowed back with the others for some time. And even then..." He gestured to a new treadmill in the corner. "Walk, run, get some exercise. Then I'll take you for a shower."

"And even then, what?"

"Treadmill first. Follow the rules."

The hot water of the shower stung, the soap harsh and unscented. Loneliness gnawed at me. I traced my name in shampoo on the tiles, knowing it would fade. Like everything else.

"Is that it?" I asked Dr Fiennes as he led me back down the corridor. "Back to that room?"

"Not quite," he said. "The Doctor wants to see you."

"Oh," I said, my heart flickering. But it couldn't get any worse.

"Where's Cai?" I asked as the Doctor instructed me to sit. "You said I could see him."

"It's as I suspected," he said. "We will proceed with isolation and the chair until we see some progress."

"What?" My voice quivered; he spoke as though I wasn't in the room. "Why aren't you talking to me?"

"Agreed. There's no alternative," Dr Emma answered, and the Doctor nodded.

"No, please, not again."

But they didn't listen. Between them, they marched me back to the science zone, and into the room with the chair.

"Do you understand now?" the Doctor asked when the sedative wore off later.

I met his gaze, although my tongue felt swollen, frozen by the electrical current.

"Heli," he said, releasing the straps on my wrists. "Where is Cai now?"

"Gone."

"But do you understand now, about Cai? About whom he is?"

"Yes." My fingers traced the knots in my hair. I did understand, at least enough to keep quiet. Any other answer and they'd put me back in the chair.

"Yes, what?"

I forced myself to look up. "Yes, Doctor." It wasn't hard to sound beaten. The electricity had shrunk everything inside me. "I understand."

"Good," the Doctor said, smiling. "We're making progress."

"Will I see him again?" I whispered.

"Who?" His tone was clinical.

"Cai."

"I would hope not," the Doctor said. "Cai wasn't real. Not seeing him is a sign you're improving."

"But..." A tear slipped over my cheek. "But I didn't get to say good-bye."

"He wasn't real," Dr Emma echoed. "There was no one to say goodbye to."

Cai wasn't real?

The words were a lie. Just like the Doctor's lies about Mal. Cai was real. He had to be.

29

ISOLATION

Sira

I PUSHED TANDOORI CHICKEN and rice around with my fork, the red-brown goop mixing into a sludge that turned my stomach. As far as I knew, I was the only one who knew where they'd taken Heli.

Isolation.

You see, I'd been there once myself, the night the Doctor caught me and Joe in the bathroom. It's a room so small you can't stretch your arms out, with a bed pressed against one wall and a toilet in the corner. A cell, if you will.

The novelty of solitude doesn't last, not when you've spent every night in a dorm, listening to whispers and breathing in the dark. There's a loneliness to the silence that makes you jump at every little creak. Worse than that, though, is the fear the Doctor might come back in the middle of the night, his footsteps too quiet on the laminate floor, his voice too smooth when he starts asking questions you can't answer. The threat sits on your chest, pressing down until you think you'll suffocate.

After the night Heli tried to escape, things changed for everyone. First, Dr Emma hung around, coming into therapy sessions and making everyone talk about reformation and "common goals", whatever that means. Second, the Doctor tightened his rules, like he thought he could squeeze the trouble out of us. And then, they put Heli in that small room and locked the door. They called it isolation, but it was punishment, pure and simple.

No matter what anyone said, I knew it was my fault she ended up there.

We were eating dinner a few weeks after Heli was found. Joe sat across from me, his fork clinking against his plate as he picked at the rice. Wiley couldn't sit still, bouncing in his seat and talking about nothing in particular. I kept thinking about Heli, picturing her alone in that cell, wondering if she was staring at the ceiling like I used to, counting the cracks in the paint.

"When are they going to bring her back?" I pulled the end of my ponytail, although no one answered. "Well?"

"Who says they will ever?" Joe finally said, tearing into his chicken with his teeth. A greasy trail of sauce smeared across his chin, and he wiped it with the back of his hand like he didn't even care.

"She was funny," Wiley bounced a little harder.

"She was crazy," Joe said, his tone so cold it made me shiver. "That's what she was."

"As if you're not," I said.

I liked Joe, sometimes I really liked him. But back when my momma was dragging me from one beauty pageant to the next, she used to say a winner had to be beautiful inside and out. And there were plenty of times when Joe's insides were pure ugly.

"Don't feel bad," Mya whispered, leaning in so Joe wouldn't hear. "It's not your fault."

"Turd balls," I muttered under my breath, my legs starting to jitter under the table. "Turd, turd, turd."

"Sira," Dr Devitt's voice cut through, sharp like a slap. "Sit down, please, or it'll be a warning."

Joe reached over, putting his hand over mine. "Calm down. It's okay. No one blames you." He shot Mya a glare, but she was too busy staring at where his hand touched mine to notice.

"I don't feel bad," I insisted, aiming a glare right back at Mya. "The Doctor knew she hadn't come back, didn't he? I wasn't telling him anything he didn't already know."

But deep down, I wondered if there was something more, I could have done to keep Heli from that room. I hadn't told the Doctor about the boatshed we found, about how it was probably where she went. If it had been me, I'd have gone there too. I thought maybe I was helping her by keeping my mouth shut. But the Doctor found her anyway, dragged her back, and locked her away.

30

Her Signature

Heli

WHEN DR EMMA STEPPED outside the room, I called to where the Doctor lingered in the doorway, his silhouette sharp and black in the crack of light.

"Doctor?"

"Yes."

"I want to talk about Mal."

"I have told you, Heli, Mal belongs to the past. Focus on getting better. That's why we're here, to help you." He stepped closer, his tongue flicking out, wetting his bottom lip. I couldn't look away from that small movement; it felt like a warning.

"But Cai––"

"Your subconscious provided what you wanted, borrowing from your surroundings." His gaze slid to the door left ajar by Dr Emma. His voice dropped, curt. "When you're ready––please put your things on."

I swallowed, my head heavy with the chill left by the shocks. My thoughts tumbled, tangling in the Doctor's lies. Brown eyes——Cai's, warm and teasing, or Mal's, dark and serious? I wasn't ready to let either of them go.

Sitting up, I winced at the sharp ache in my joints. My body felt brittle like it might snap if I moved too fast. They left me alone to pull on my jumper and shoes, as though the privacy was some kind of courtesy after everything they'd done. As if a few minutes to dress could erase the feel of the cold metal against my skull, the zap of electricity that twisted my thoughts until I wasn't sure where my fears ended, and their lies began.

I finished lacing my shoes when both the doctors appeared at the door, shadows stretching into the room like a threat.

"Let us have a talk, Heli."

The air in the Doctor's office was thick and sour, heavy with secrets. Dr Emma sat in a new chair beside the Doctor, her back arched, watching me with those pale, watery eyes.

"How are you feeling?" The Doctor's tone was smooth, practiced.

"Fine." My voice was steady but tight like a thread pulled taut. I needed them to think I believed their stories——about Cai, about Mal——if I ever wanted to see the other kids again. If I wanted a chance to stop the Doctor's lies and find the truth. I had to play along, even though the words tasted like ash in my mouth.

"Any side effects we haven't discussed?" Dr Emma's pen hovered, mirroring the Doctor's movements. Her eyes darted to me when I hesitated. "Any tummy troubles or——"

"No. I am fine." I forced myself to keep my gaze steady, even as the memories of Cai twisted inside my head, mixing with images of Mal. Mal shitting himself after they'd put him in the chair.

They both had brown eyes. Deep and dark, like the ocean at dusk. I remembered the letter Mal left for me. I pressed my hands underneath my thighs, sitting on them until the urge to hold my nose faded. Cai wasn't just a figment of my mind; he couldn't be. Not when I could still remember the warmth of his breath and the way he'd smiled in the dark of the boatshed. He'd said my eyes were green like dragon's skin. It was sweet and kind of dorky; there's no way I could have made it up.

"You understand, don't you? Cai was a fabrication of your overstimulated mind," the Doctor said, his tone cool.

"Yes," I lied, shutting him off before the words could cut deeper. "Yes, I do understand that, Doctor."

I tried to hold onto the pieces of the truth that still felt real. But shame burned through me, hot and raw. They said they'd found me naked and alone that night in the boatshed. The Doctor could twist the truth, but I wasn't going to let go of Cai.

"And his absence, how does that make you feel?" The Doctor's voice pressed at the edges of my mind, trying to slip in between my thoughts.

Lost. Angry. Afraid. I wanted to scream I remembered everything just fine. Cai and the schoolroom and the faces of the other kids, the games we played in the dormitory. But I swallowed those words, forcing my eyes open again.

"I feel fine," I said.

"Now that we've established a stable path of medication, you're finding the changes," he said, as though it was a fact I couldn't dispute.

"You knew?"

"Did I know you weren't taking your medication? Of course. Your anosognosia remained unaltered. When we administered your medicine through injections, there were small signs of improvement."

I stared at him, my mind scrambling to make sense of the words. Everything felt different, but my hatred for him hadn't changed. "Anosognosia?" I repeated. "What does that mean?"

"Anosognosia is an inability to accept your condition, coupled––in your case––with a strong, delusional tendency. Now that you're on stable medication and following your course of electric shock treatment, you will feel much better."

He was lying again; I could see it in the way his lips twitched and the way his eyes gleamed with pride. But I didn't feel better. I felt like pieces of me were slipping away, scattering like sand. If only I could speak to Cai. If I closed my eyes, I could almost feel him beside me, the warmth of his hand on mine in the darkness.

"I am not your enemy," the Doctor said, as though he could read my thoughts. Dr Emma smiled, a private joke passing between them. "You can trust me."

"But you don't like questions," I snapped, grasping at the one thing that felt solid. "You never answer any of them."

"Fire away," he said like it was some kind of game.

"What happened to Peony?"

"She's with your family. The last I knew––when they agreed to your care here."

"If I could just see her," I pleaded, turning to Dr Emma. "My sister must remember. She knows the fire wasn't my fault."

Dr Emma's smile was thin, almost pitying. "There are no visitors on the island, Heli. I think you know that."

"Yes, I do know that," I said, frustration boiling inside me. "But one day, when I get out of here, I'll explain it to my family. I need to."

The Doctor slid a paper and across the desk. "Your mother's signature," he said, tapping the familiar loops and swirls.

My stomach twisted as I stared at it. She'd signed me away.

"It wasn't her decision, really," the Doctor offered, as though he was being kind.

"What do you mean?"

"The court ruled you needed serious medical intervention after the fire. She didn't have a choice."

But that was the thing. The fire wasn't my fault. I needed to tell someone. I needed someone to listen. But they wouldn't believe me. No one ever had.

"Please, I need to talk to them."

"There's no contact with home," the Doctor tapped the form. "It's all in this contract."

Then he showed me the newspaper clippings. Headlines screamed at me:

Wild Girl Sent Away for Treatment

Firestarter

Danger to Herself and Others.

Each word burned inside my head.

That's when I understood, I wasn't a person anymore. I was the Doctor's experiment, as much a piece of the Cerletti Facility as the wires they strapped to my temple. And they wouldn't let me go--not until he'd finished with me.

31

PLAYING THE MAD GIRL

Heli

FOUR WAS A LOOSE number for a building such as this one; walls and edges spread across the island landscape like mould. It had been a place of captivity from the outset and yet there had been some relief, at least at first when Mal had been around. But isolation brought new meaning to the word prison.

"Prison," I whispered the word aloud.

It quivered and I said it louder. Once. Then over and over, rolling onto my back to laugh. In that moment, I became the maniac they'd always seen me as.

I stretched out, loneliness flooding me like caffeine. I clawed at my blanket, trying to tear it with my hands and my teeth. Wrapping it around myself, slithering across the floor snake-like. My face twitched--an imitation of Sira's--but after a moment, I put the blanket back, folding in a perfect pile. The mad act was over.

I couldn't pinpoint when Cai had left. In the boatshed or when I was in the chair. But he was gone.

I said it aloud, "Cai is gone. Removed. He has left me." And then I hesitated, comforted for a moment he was no longer confined inside this place. "But why did they have to take him away?"

I tried for a while to imagine him out in the real world, living his own life. Somewhere, I could find him again. One day in the future. But it was no comfort, all I wanted was for Cai to be here with me now.

I closed my eyes. Inside my head was a very dark place to be, and I longed, longed for the light of Cai. Without him, I was just me. And it wasn't enough.

The memory of the letter from Mal came to me then. And I wanted to see it again, proof that the Doctor lied, and that Mal was real. He had lived here in the Facility. I needed to get back to the dormitory and check to see that the note was there, to hold it in my hand as evidence. The Doctor was a liar.

"Heli." The door opened, and a figure entered the room. It was Dr Devitt, carrying a tray. "How are you?"

I looked at him but wouldn't speak. Once I had thought Dr Devitt was better than the others, but he had lied too.

"Lunch time." His voice held the fraudulent cheer of a teacher.

I waited for him to leave. On the tray, there was a bowl of white soup and two slices of bread—no butter. I wondered how Dr Devitt dared to wait in the space between the bed and the door so long after yesterday. Cai would have liked to hear about yesterday. Then Dr Devitt said something, and I looked up, surprised again to find him still there.

"How about some fresh air, Heli?" His voice was tight. I stared at him, wondering if he could feel my contempt.

It was true, *Silence,* according to the Doctor, *was effective.*

"Some fresh air." Dr Devitt said it again, "Would you like that?"

My freedom, from this room at least, rested in the hands of weak, guilty men.

"Sure," I began eating the soup, maybe I should ask him questions. He might talk if his remorse was strong enough.

"Well," Dr Devitt rolled backwards and forwards on the balls of his feet; his hands burrowing away inside his pockets. "Much better than yesterday. I was a bit nervous about bringing you soup again." He smiled as though he'd made a joke.

"If you're sure you don't fancy another shower," I picked up the bowl and made a pretence of throwing my food at him. "It's lovely and hot." We both laughed. A stupid, forced sound. There was no choice other than to play nice if I wanted to get out.

"I will speak to the Doctor," he said. "Tell him how well you're doing today."

"That's great," my face twitched.

"You don't mean that."

"What?"

"When you tell a lie, Heli, your face twitches. It's your give. Your tell. If you ever want to make it as a poker player, you'll need to mask it." Dr Devitt laughed, another forced sound.

"Like Sira?" I asked, her name a whisper on my lips. My heart pulsed, afraid that he would tell me I'd made her up too. And all the other kids.

"Not exactly," Dr Devitt paused, "although I concede the twitch is beyond your control."

"Oh." Relief was so strong it nearly suffocated me. I thought for a moment how even Sira's company would be preferable to my own––not to mention the pressing need to see Mal's note again. "I would like to go back to the dorm with the others if you think I'm ready."

"Don't worry," Dr Devitt removed his hand from his pocket, his fingers tensed, "the good bit is still true. You're following the rules. Despite yesterday, you are doing well."

"Wait," I said. "Dr Fiennes said something about things in the rest of the Facility. I thought that maybe... He actually said *and even then.*"

"I'm not sure I understand."

"It was the way he said it--like things had changed. What did he mean?"

Dr Devitt's sigh was audible. "Heli, I suppose he might have meant the rules have toughened up a little."

"They were already tough."

"What did you expect after your escape attempt?"

When he was gone, I finished the soup and made my plan. *What had I expected?* The Doctor punished everyone for my escape attempt. And now I had to laugh at jokes I didn't find funny and be compliant--a good girl--for stupid men. The doctors were just people, and they wanted things too. Dr Devitt felt guilty, and the Doctor wanted proof his routines worked. In their own ways they both needed me. If the Doctor's routines worked, they did at a terrible cost. Mal and Mollie had gone. Cai too. And I planned on being next.

I wished the Doctor hadn't told me about my family; it had been easier not to know. The fire wasn't my fault but none of that mattered as much as getting out of here. And I held that knowledge, along with all the other things I had learned.

I was going to follow Dr Devitt's advice even though he hadn't meant it in that way. I would learn how to control my twitch--what he'd called my *tell*. I would stop fighting--so that one day they would let me go. I would learn to love myself and find a way back to Cai. First step, get out of isolation and check the letter was still there––proof that Mal and our friendship had been real.

32

NUMBERS

Heli

THERE WAS ONE PART of isolation I'd kind of appreciated––sleeping in my own room, to close my eyes and drift off without the sounds of the other kids. Joe's snoring and Sira's farting. Or maybe it had been Wiley's farting and Sophia's snoring. In the dark, it was hard to tell.

"You can return to the dormitory," the Doctor said. "And your lessons."

"How long has it been?" I looked at him. If he wanted gratitude, he had another thing coming.

"Since your attempt to leave?" The Doctor pocketed his pen. "It's been six weeks."

Long enough to recover from surgery, to build a house or learn to knit. I shook my head. It had felt like longer. But who knew whether he was telling the truth?

Once the Doctor decreed me fit to be returned, the first thing I did in the dormitory was read and reread the note from Mal. The words were imprinted into my brain. At night, I lay with it in my hand, listening to the noise of the other kids sleeping. Until worried that the note would spoil, I slid it under my pillow.

It's tough to write this. I can see your face... Don't look up. I can't really. Right now, you're asleep. But I can imagine you--how you might look--as you read this. I'm sorry I can't stick around to help. And I've only got this one, crappy bit of paper, with no room for mistakes, to tell you that.

Remember the day we went swimming? That was the one good day here. Even though we nearly drowned. For what it's worth, I wanted to help you find out about your sister. But I've worked one thing out for you. In this place--this fucking awful place--you are the good thing.

I wish I knew if you could get well, but I don't. I do know you shouldn't follow the Doctor's path, stick to your own and never look back. Learn to like the mad girl within--fuck it--love her. Love her for the both of us. If you manage that, I reckon you might work out how to get out of here. It's how Mollie did it. Last thing she said to me was stop trying to get out, focus on how you're never going back in.

I lay in the dark considering how Mal's advice to never go back hadn't worked.

In the morning, I went to pull the curtain, but Sira beat me to it.

"It's my job now," she said, stepping closer like she was expecting an argument.

"Fine," I replied, falling into the silent line as the final bell rang. "Hey, Wiley. You forgot your--"

"Shhh," he hissed as the door swung open and Dr Fiennes strode in.

"I was only trying to--"

"Ten minutes docked from exercise time, Heli, for talking during line-up," Dr Fiennes said.

"But I--"

"A second infraction and you'll lose all your time outside." He glared at me until I mimicked the others, lifting my finger to my lips. "Very good."

Dr Fiennes inspected us one by one, checking the insides of our mouths and pockets before sending us to the dining hall where Dr Devitt waited to check us again. I wanted to roll my eyes, to exchange a look with the others, but they'd adjusted to the stricter routine; silence pulled their backs straighter.

Later, Dr Emma walked me from lunch to the Doctor's office, and I glanced at the line of kids returning to their spots outside the schoolroom.

"Come along, Heli."

"Yes, Dr Emma." I'd just have to get through this session, put one foot in front of the other, hold myself together, and be the quiet, compliant girl they wanted.

"I'd like us to agree on a common goal." The Doctor's pen hovered over his clipboard. Shadows flickered across the display cases behind him. "For your recovery."

"I'm not sure I understand."

Dr Emma cleared her throat, leaning forward with her hands clasped.

"This is your chance to suggest something we can all work towards."

"I thought you were leaving," I said.

"Don't be rude, Heli." The Doctor's pen jabbed against his clipboard. "Infraction of our code of conduct will result in the loss of your exercise time. Answer the question."

"But I thought we were already working towards something." I folded my hands in my lap, trying to look compliant. And I wanted to go outside.

"Sira, for example, has set a goal of having a stabilised mood," Dr Emma said. "She answers questions about her mental state, aiming for a six on her chart."

"A six?" I had no idea how a number could represent stability. And why six, when everyone knew seven was the lucky one? "Okay," I took a deep breath. This should be simple. "I'd like to work towards my release."

The Doctor shifted in his seat.

"That's right," I pressed. "I want to leave."

"You could answer the same questions as Sira and work towards a six," Dr Emma said.

"I'd prefer to aim for my release." I couldn't grasp what they wanted from me or where they were leading me.

"Here are the questions, Heli. Take a moment, read the first one, then give me your number. We'll track your progress each week."

"But you said it was a common goal?"

"It is a common goal." Dr Emma unfolded her hands, pushing up her sleeves to reveal thin, bony arms marked with age spots. "Are we in agreement?"

I turned my gaze away. Dr Emma brought changes, new methods in these sessions. The common goal wasn't mine to decide, even if she wanted me to think it was. I might be mad, but I wasn't stupid.

The Doctor checked his watch while Dr Emma cleared her throat, her face taut with a frown.

"Heli, are we in agreement?"

"Of course, Doctor," I paused. There was nothing else I could say. "I agree."

Later, I was paired with Sira for exercise. It was the first time I'd been allowed outside since the night I escaped with Cai. My throat tightened at the thought of it.

"Come on, Heli," Sira took my arm, smiling at the Doctor. "Keep moving," she whispered. "Before they change their minds."

We walked in silence all the way to the harbour. I wanted to ask her what had changed while I'd been kept isolated, though I thought I'd pieced some of it together. We sat on the old wooden jetty, feet dangling over the waves. I turned to her a few times; she did the same, but neither of us spoke. I had things to say but couldn't find the words. Maybe she did too––about the weeks I'd spent alone, about Cai leaving––but she kept quiet. I thought about asking her why she'd chosen six instead of seven. But she never listened to me.

The sun warmed my back, but it couldn't soothe the ache. Losing Cai hit harder than Mal's death, or maybe it just enforced his absence. Either way, I felt smaller, lonelier, a shadow of myself.

"I'm leaving," Sira said suddenly, her shoulder twitching as she tried to steady herself.

"But you can't," I said, my heart racing. After everything that had happened: Mollie, Mal, Cai. "It's too dangerous, you––"

"Not like that," she said. "I'm leaving with Dr Emma when she goes back."

"Are you better then?"

"They say I'm stable."

"Oh, right. You're a six." I said, waving my hand. "I thought maybe seven would be... Never mind. That's nice. You'll see your family."

"No," she shook her head. "At least not at first. I'm staying with Dr Emma at Oxford University––going to some conferences."

"They're parading you around?" It was like Mal had predicted. No future, just a showpiece, even if they said you were better.

"It's not like that," Sira's eyes narrowed. "It's just a few weeks, and I might even get a phone."

"They're showing you off like a prize pig."

"Why are you always so mean?"

"Speaking the truth isn't the same as being mean. I'm trying to warn you."

"Well don't. Be happy for me. I'm leaving this place."

She scrambled up and headed back along the rocks to the path.

"Wait," I called. "Where are you going?"

"Like you care," she paused. "I'm going back. The early bell's ringing. We lost ten minutes, remember?"

Just before the gate to the Facility grounds, I caught her hand.

"Hey Sira," I said. "I am happy for you."

"Liar." But her lips softened.

"Just... be careful, okay? Whatever they say, sometimes six isn't the right number. You could be a seven. Think about that. Don't trust them completely."

She leaned in, her breath warm on my ear. "I don't. But pretending has got me this far."

Her words echoed as I forced down dinner--lukewarm parsnip soup and crusty bread. Pretending might be my way out, too. Forget numbers and common goals--delusion? That, I could do.

33

Pretending

Sira

Under the harsh, schoolroom lights, we followed the headset instructions. Page after page of exercise books filled with graphs with diminishing lines, and hard pencil points. My temples throbbed as I tried to keep up. Heli was back with us, her pencil scribbling faster than anyone else's as though the harder she pressed the more time she could make up.

If there had been a clock, I would have checked it––again. But they'd removed it. I had nothing but my instincts to measure the passing minutes of my last full day at Cerletti.

"Shall I collect the books?" Heli raised her hand, looking at Dr Shalt.

"Yes, thank you."

I sat back, arranging my things on the desk. Heli picked up my book as she passed. It didn't surprise me; she was trying to impress the doctors. It had taken a year, but she'd learned the only lesson we needed, do as you're told.

In the dining hall, her good deeds continued. She poured us all water from the jug.

"What's up your butt?" Joe said as she passed.

"I've changed." Her eyes flickered, betraying uncertainty. "I'm a good girl now."

"As if," Joe shoved Sophia, hard enough to make her yelp.

"Hey," Heli said, her voice low and sharp. "Stop that."

"Whatever." Joe rolled his eyes, dismissing her.

I wanted to glare at him, but I couldn't risk a scene and jeopardize my departure with Dr Emma. At Cerletti, you did as you were told, and you did it quietly.

Heli's hand shook as she finished with the water jug, her frustration almost spilling over.

"Joe, that's ten minutes deducted from exercise time," Dr Shalt appeared at the table, noting the offence on her tablet. "Now, say sorry to Sophia. Any more trouble and you'll stay inside with me for the whole hour, understood?"

"Yes, Dr Shalt," Joe mumbled, his gaze fixed on his plate, hands tucked beneath the table. "I'm sorry, Sophia."

Heli stared at the scene, wide-eyed, as though she couldn't believe what she was seeing. It was lucky she'd poured all the water because the jug drooped at her side, threatening.

Back in the schoolroom after lunch, there was more maths and then history. My hand ached, switching between pen and pencil, the skin on the side of my middle finger indented and reddened. I counted the pages of equations and history notes I had written, five neat pages in my book. There was nothing in my lessons that could cause issues with leaving the island.

"Heli," the Doctor said, stepping into the room. "Come with me, please." Dr Emma followed like a shadow.

How did I feel about leaving under Dr Emma's custodianship? I didn't care. Whatever it took to get off the island.

In the evening, Heli returned as we filed into the dining room. She looked forlorn, lost, like she'd just finished watching her things burn to ash in a blaze of fire. Guilt sank through my gut like a lead weight. Would it help her if I stayed? We weren't friends exactly––she'd tell you that too––we were more than that.

"Now who's feeling sorry for themselves?" Joe nudged Heli, harder than I would have liked. "I missed some exercise time too, and I'm not bothered."

"Hey." I lifted my hand, hoping to quell things before they got out of hand. They just needed to keep the peace for one more night. Nothing could go wrong now; I couldn't bear it if it did.

"What's your problem?" Heli rounded on him, her voice trembling with suppressed rage as if she'd like to punch him, if only she could summon the energy.

I glanced at Dr Shalt, but her back was to us.

"Stop it––both of you," I said. "It's my last night. You could at least make an effort."

"Sorry," Heli sank into her seat, her back slumped like it was being dragged by an unwanted anchor. "I forgot. Tomorrow, really, that's..." She broke off, her fork hovering over her bowl of noodle curry. "That's so soon. When does your boat leave?"

"With the tide." A shiver ran through me as I imagined stepping onto the boat––the weight of freedom. "Around midday."

"Sira," Heli whispered, her voice unsteady. "Do you have any regrets?"

I shook my head. But I did. I regretted leaving the other kids behind.

"I meant about pretending," she said, her tone bitter. "But I guess you've got what you wanted."

"Hey." A hot blush crept up from my neck, and I glanced over at Joe.

"I've got no regrets." It was true, I had got what I wanted.

"Oh, God," she said. "You're not still?"

"Yes," I replied, the weight of my emotions settling in, a mix of nostalgia and longing. "I'm really going to miss him."

"Ew." She made a big show of pretending to be sick.

If I'd thought she'd listen, I'd tell her again: keep your head down and play the part. But Heli's never been good at pretending.

34

The Great Fix

Heli

THE ROUTINES AT CERLETTI continued: long hours in the classroom, meals in the dining hall, exercise, chores, and evenings spent in the reading room. Days ended with sleep behind the heavy grey curtains of the dormitory. Except Sira was gone now.

As promised, Dr Emma had taken her back to the research centre at Oxford University––her prize pig. I tried to picture them together on stage, the stooped form of Dr Emma lecturing while Sira sat quietly, a ribbon in her ponytail, fidgeting slightly. But Sira wasn't better, was she? She had learnt to shrink behind a mask.

Still, Sira's departure stirred unexpected hope. It wasn't that I wanted to share the stage with Dr Emma, nor did I think the Doctor would release me for some other purpose. Rather, Dr Emma was no longer overshadowed by the Doctor. Perhaps, if I could find a way to send her a letter at the university, I could tell her there used to be more of us––fourteen, if you counted Mollie. If I found a way to contact her, would she believe me? Away from the Doctor's explanations and deceit, there had to be a chance to be heard. Yet, Joe and the others' refusal to see my changes gnawed. Could I truly get better if no one believed it was possible? But I had to try something to end my sessions in the chair. Mal had wanted me to try.

Remembering Mal's trick, I tore a page from one of my exercise books, slipping it into my pocket during a quiet moment in class. I also tucked a pencil away, although its absence would be more noticeable. Later in the reading room, I started to craft a letter.

Dear Dr Emma,

I'm sure you remember me from Cerletti--it's Heli, and I need your help.

I might have smiled at the absurdity of the situation if I weren't trapped in its grim reality, alone in the Facility. There was no gang to back me up, not even a dog to brainstorm with. With Sira gone, I felt more isolated than ever.

I need you to know the Doctor lied; there were more of us kids once.

Silence enveloped, my voice echoing through the room. Why would Dr Emma believe me? I had no proof. The Doctor had convinced her I was the liar. But Dr Emma wasn't just another flunky; she had the power to think for herself. Mal and Mollie's names would have to suffice--it might be enough to make her question the Facility, enough to change the recommendations in her report and challenge the Doctor's routines.

"What are you doing? Making all this noise?"

The Doctor's voice was calm, unruffled. My hand froze around the pencil, a makeshift weapon in my grip. I leaned my elbow over the scrap of paper and looked at him defiantly.

"Put that down."

I held the pencil rigidly between us, refusing.

"Where's Mollie?" I asked.

"I don't know." the Doctor hesitated, then added, "She left, and that was that."

Liar.

"There was a body," he continued, and I flinched, finding myself in a confessional. The pencil slipped from my grip. "She drowned."

"She's dead?" I didn't want to hear about Mollie's fate; her act of defiance had given me hope.

"It works," the Doctor said. "What we do here works. Look at Sira. And I'm not prepared to have kids like––"

He took a deep breath, his jaw relaxing.

"You should be getting ready for bed."

That was it; he believed he was right, and nothing, especially not a kid like me, would derail his grand vision for the Cerletti Facility.

"You're making a good recovery, Heli. In time, you have a chance at a normal life. That's why we do what we do––to give you that gift."

"But I didn't want Cai to go." My words trembled. "You never asked what I wanted."

The Doctor's gaze was detached, unyielding. "My goal is to make you better. That should be your goal, too."

"I just want to leave." I whispered, the weight of the Facility pressing down, heavy and unrelenting.

"We need to share the same goal; to make you better."

"But that's not your goal either." I was sick of his lies.

"How many times do we have to go over this?" He reached across and pocketed my pencil. "That's a ten-minute deduction from your exercise time tomorrow."

"It's not your goal," I repeated, my voice rising, while fury coloured his cheeks. "Your goal is to prove your theories right––that routine and electricity work. The Cerletti Facility is about you, not us."

Hatred flickered across his features as he shook his head.

"Dr Emma has granted us an extension of our capacity. Soon, we'll be able to treat two, maybe even three of you at once with electroconvulsive therapy. Isn't that welcome news?"

Then he turned and walked away.

I barely had time to slip the forbidden paper into my pocket when Dr Devitt appeared behind my chair.

"Time for bed."

I joined the others in the bathroom to wash and clean up. In the dormitory, I hid the scrap of paper in my drawer just as Joe approached my bed.

"Heli?" he said.

"What do you want?"

"Calm down," he shrugged, looking shifty. "I just want to talk."

"No, thanks."

"Why can't you give me a chance?"

I held up my hand, the silver scar he had given me glinting in the dim light.

"How many do you want?"

"But," his face contorted. "I thought because of Sira."

"What's this got to do with her? She could be annoying sometimes, but she never attacked people. You? You love hurting people."

"I'm trying––"

"I know about you and Sira, the things you did." I shuddered, looking him up and down, from his hair to his disgusting socks.

"Truth?" he asked.

"If you must." I sat on the edge of my bed, longing for the lights to go out and for the peace of sleep.

"I miss her," he took a long breath. "I didn't think I would, but I do."

"What do you want? A medal?"

"It's not my fault, you know." He rubbed his eyes as the warning bell rang. We had one minute until the lights would go out. "I didn't ask to be like this."

"Whose fault is it, then?"

"I'm 16," he paused. "And you think I'm doomed to be like this? No one will ever like me."

"She did." I looked at him; he was pathetic, trying to make me feel sorry for him after everything he'd done. "And you didn't deserve her."

"I know," he said, shuffling towards his bed.

Now that Sira had left, it fell to me again to draw the curtain. I glanced at the boys in their beds, from Joe to Wiley, all the way to Mal's empty one. What would he have made of Sira's departure and Joe's attempt at friendship? What would he think about the Doctor continuing his experiments? I hesitated with my hand on the curtain, knowing what Mal would have done. He would have laughed at Joe and about Sira. But he hadn't found a solution for the Doctor; I was on my own with that.

From his bed, Joe turned and pointed. "At least I'm not a hypocrite."

"Say that again."

"You heard me," he replied. "But I will say it again: you're a hypocrite."

I slipped through the curtain as the light went out, keeping close to the wall to avoid the sensors.

"Say that again?" I leaned over his bed. "You're the one who treated Sira like dirt even though she stood up for you, defending your psycho behaviour. And all those other things she did with you."

"Yeah, and you know what?" The whites of Joe's eyes glowed in the darkness like a cat's. "I own it, Heli. I made out with her at first because I was bored. Now that she's gone, I feel like shit. And I don't know if I'll ever get the chance to tell her she meant more to me than that."

"On behalf of girls everywhere--what a great guy you are." I glanced back at the curtain, weighing my chances of making it back without detection. "Sira had a lucky escape."

"You don't get it, do you? I'm owning what I've done. I know better now. I miss her so badly it aches in--I don't know--my heart."

"You can't feel your heart, dumbwit."

"This isn't science, Heli," he breathed. "It's love. That's right; I think I love her." He paused like he was waiting for me to congratulate him on the one decent emotion he'd held in his ignorant head. "I never told her anything nice. So yeah, I'm a creep. An idiot. But you?" He shook his head. "You treated her badly, too, and you don't even know it."

"No, I didn't," I said, although deep down, I knew he was right. "Why don't you crawl back under your duvet and make out with your socks? That's right," I said, edging toward my bed. "She told me about that."

35

Missing Boys

Heli

THE DOCTOR'S OFFICE, COLD even in summer, now leeched warmth from the air, its chill seeping into my guts like a warning.

"It's been eight weeks since your escape attempt," the Doctor clicked his pen, ready to write. "Thinking back to that day, Heli, how does that make you feel?"

"Feel?" I said. How did he think it made me feel? I was trapped––and lonely. My hopes of escaping were lower than ever. And that was the heart of the problem with Cerletti, wasn't it? There were too many obstacles. "I feel fine."

"You're doing well," his pen stalled. "Since your numerous outbursts a few weeks ago, you have settled back into the routines of the Facility. You are making progress."

I smiled even though I hated him so bad. Terrified he'd know––some-how––what I was thinking, I averted my gaze and tried to keep a hold on my good girl persona. It had been a week since my last lost exercise hour and even though it was cold, being outside was the only thing that kept me going. But pretending to be good was harder than being the mad girl--squashing myself so small--keeping my face straight and my hands still. I held onto hope with my fingernails until I could work out how to stop the Doctor from putting any more of us in the chair. I needed to post my letter.

"Do you still think about escaping?"

"No," I said. My face didn't even twitch. What a liar I had become. What Dr Devitt had called my *tell* was under control.

"No plans at all to disrupt our processes? We have your full cooperation with our shared goal?"

I nodded. "You have my full cooperation."

"Then," he said, "given how well you are doing, how quickly you've adjusted to our ways, this time, we can include you in the plan and schedule another session in the chair."

"What?" The breath left my body with a squeak. The Doctor wielded the word *chair* like a punishment. "But you just said I was doing better."

"It's thanks to the chair that you've come this far," he smiled, although there was no warmth. "Progress comes at a price, but I believe we are on the right path to achieving our common goal."

My heart pulsed. My goal was to stop the Doctor and get out of here.

"Do we have your cooperation?"

My eyelids fluttered and I thought about Mya and Sophia, and Wiley, and even Joe. About how while the Doctor put me in the chair, the others were safe--for now.

"Yes," my guts squirmed at the memory of the cold touch of electricity. "Doctor," the question burst out, "will I ever get out of here?"

"Follow our programme," he said, "stop breaking rules. But," he paused, "I don't imagine us ending our days together on this island."

Us. The arsehole still hadn't answered my question.

"Thank you," I said, remembering that someone else was coming to help and the Doctor had been given the go-ahead to increase his use of the chair. Time was running out. Who would be next?

I looked at my trembling fingers. The veneer of compliance––of being good––cracking as easily as eggshell. Why had I thanked him? It occurred to me then, there was more than one way out of here.

If the Doctor saw the two of us bound together by his thirst for science, then his death would be an exit too. The thought shimmered like land mass appearing on the horizon––new and full of hope. But I wasn't wicked enough to let the idea grow and so I took the thought and put it in an out of reach place, hiding it deep inside of me.

"You know there was anthrax on this island once," the Doctor pocketed his pen. "They thought they'd never get rid of it. And here we are. Do you see what I'm saying?"

"Not really."

"If we follow our hypothesis, we can clean up even the worst of messes. Science gives us the answers you see."

"Are you saying that I'm, we're, like anthrax for you to clear up?"

"I think you understand the analogy a little. Now, our time is up. Would you like a sweet?" He pushed the bag towards me.

"No," I stood. Mad girls didn't eat sweets, and I was tired of being good.

Back to my lesson and I finished my essay on *Romeo and Juliet*. Before the conversation with the Doctor, the sixteenth century had been as far from my understanding of life as could possibly be––a time of patriarchy and peculiar fashions. Now I saw our stories were the same: selfish adults using kids to make meaning.

In the afternoon I had science with Dr Devitt. In the bowel of the building, the science lab was a place where many things happened. The experiments with the Doctor were always bad whereas science lessons with Dr Devitt tended to be ok.

"You know, I'm going to be leaving for a little while, Heli." Dr Devitt passed me a clean test tube. "Use this one, please."

"Oh," my heart throbbed. Once Dr Devitt's replacement got here, the Doctor had said he could increase his use of the chair. Was there any way to stop it? I glanced at the fire extinguisher. "Why do you need to leave?"

"Well, it will be good to have a little break. See some friends, go to a museum. Then after a while, I shall be back."

"But what about science lessons?" I had pretended to be good, tried my best but it was impossible. The Doctor always got his way.

"Well, the replacement doctor will take over my duties. And the Doctor thinks, given how well you've responded to the electro-convulsive therapy, that the new doctor can oversee the treatment of someone else in the chair."

"Who?" My heart pulsed. I should have been pleased at the idea of finishing my time in the chair, but I wasn't, I felt sick at the thought of someone else suffering. *More than one person.* The Doctor was unstoppable.

"It's not for me to say. I just wanted you to," Dr Devitt pushed his glasses up his nose, "to hear about my leave from duty from me, first."

"Oh."

That was when I saw it, in the moment between looking away from Dr Devitt and pouring the bubbling mixture over the table instead of into the test tube. The glass shattered in my hand as I gasped out loud.

Between the convict's brain and the floating appendix, there was a new clear glass jar. Inside an eyeball floated––a disconcerting shade of orangey-pink with a web of dark, veiny threads like spiders' legs. And in the centre, a black-brown iris stared, unblinking.

Mal.

Shock held the inside of my throat. The Doctor had added Mal to his collection.

"It is natural," Dr Devitt cleared his throat. I tried to, but I couldn't look away from the jar. "That after all this time you might feel abandoned by my departure. You find change difficult, that's understandable. It is the reason I wanted to tell you myself. But," he paused. "No, please don't get upset about the mess. I will clean it up when you've gone. Why don't you go and wash your face? It's lunch time now anyway."

"Dr Devitt?" My voice was strangled. "Is that new?" I pointed at the jar.

"Is that—ah…" Colour had the good grace to drain from Dr Devitt's face. "Goodness me." He removed his glasses from his face and wiped them on his shirt while the bell rang.

"How fucking dare he."

"It can be discomfiting when you have an emotional attachment, of course. But this is how we acquire knowledge. Scientists have been dissecting human bodies since time immemorial. Once upon a time, we called it natural philosophy," he pushed his glasses against his face, "we won't say any more about the foul language. But come on now. Lunchtime."

Unable to speak further, I followed him away from the lab.

Inside the dining hall, the image of Mal's dark eye floating inside a glass jar on the Doctor's shelf haunted me and I couldn't speak to any of the other kids, the world divided in two. Those who liked to dissect people and those who didn't.

There was something else that was bothering me. My sister Peony's eyes when they'd pulled her out from the fire. The firemen carried her from the building on a stretcher. I'd run over but her face was so black, she couldn't see anything. *I'm sorry.* I remembered saying it over and over. *You're a wicked girl.* My Gran had said, which wasn't true until I'd opened my mouth and told my lie.

It was Peony that started the fire.

By the time my parents arrived, I'd made up my own story until I believed it was the truth.

"What's got into you?" Joe said. "Can I have that?" His fork descended. "Suit yourself." He turned to prod Wiley. "Don't you think Heli looks like she's seen a ghost?"

"Leave me alone," I flicked his hand away from my plate. It was me that had started the fire that had hurt my sister. Driven mad by my own stories; I was as wicked as my Gran had always said.

There was no hope for me, but the other kids? Even Mal--what was left--needing saving. I'd known it all along; the Doctor didn't see us as people, we were science to him, *natural philosophy:* body parts ready for harvesting. I looked at the other kids around the table.

Who would be next?

The shock of what the Doctor had done spurred me on to finish my letter for Dr Emma. I needed to find a way to get us out. If I managed it, I could confess what I'd done to my family. They hadn't believed me anyway, but I wanted to see my sister and say that I was sorry. The plan I was sure was flawed; but I had to do something--hold onto something--so that I didn't dissolve.

During the afternoon lesson, I managed to avoid the watchful gaze of Dr Fiennes. Changing tact, I ripped my previous efforts from the top of the stolen page. If not for me, then I needed to do this for the other kids, there needed to be justice for Mal: atonement from the Doctor. I needed to stop him before anyone else was put in the chair——or dissected——in his thirst for scientific knowledge. I planned my letter and rather than risk stealing a pencil again, I wrote the words while we worked in the school room.

After our lessons were finished, I was sent to the laundry to do my chores. The floor tiles were cool where I laid on them watching the slow spin of water in the washing machine. The gurgling of the drier. My eyes opened and closed as I tried not to see the Doctor's collection: a new jar and the floating eyeball of my friend.

Mal.

I tried to think about him instead. The way he laughed at my jokes and saved my life in the sea——his quiet friendship——and I wished he was still here. He'd understand what was going on. He'd said I was the *good thing*. I was sure he'd want me to stop the Doctor any way I could.

I finished folding and separating clothes into piles when the woman walked in; her shoes, white and laced, squeaked over the floor.

"Hi."

"Oh," she paused. "I'm sorry, I didn't realise you were still here." She looked at her watch before turning, her hand already on the door. "I think you're meant to be getting ready for exercise."

My heart jolted, adrift inside my chest, my mind racing with possibilities. The other staff weren't supposed to talk to us; they did their jobs out of sight. This was my chance. Although I hadn't expected to encounter it so soon.

"Wait," I said, my voice sharp with desperation. "Just one minute. Please."

36

Choices

Heli

THE WOMAN LOOKED AT me, her eyes not unkind. When her lips parted, I shifted forward. I thought she was going to speak but my movement must have startled her because she scuttled backwards––mouselike.

"What's your name?" I kept my voice quiet.

"I'm sorry," she said, and she looked sorry too; her gaze darted back and forth to the door. "I can't talk to you."

"Wait. Please."

She hesitated, one hand frozen midway to the door; her face an agony of indecision. I knew she wasn't meant to talk to me, but I needed to make her break the rules.

"Please." I said. This wasn't for me. The Doctor had left me no choice. I had to stop him from expanding his use of the chair.

"I'm not allowed to talk to you."

"Can you listen then?" I made my hands hold still, even though they longed to force her. "If that's allowed. Please--I need to--if that's ok, could you just listen?"

"You know the rules." But she wrapped her arms across her chest, her eyes restless.

The rules were the other staff are not allowed to interact with us. But I wondered what they had told this woman that made her look so afraid. Her foot squeaked across the laundry floor tiles as she began to edge closer to the door and I held my breath, needing to act quickly before she slipped away.

"Would you mind posting something for me?" I asked. The other staff--the cleaners and porters--spent two weeks on the island then two weeks off; the Doctor had said.

"No."

"No, you don't mind?" I tried to smile--not the sly, sickly grimace of Dr Shalt--but the open smile of someone decent. "Or no--you won't help me?"

"You're not supposed to be in here. It's exercise time." The woman shuffled further away, and she didn't return my smile. "And dinner when you return, I've laid it out already." She turned away, reaching for the door handle. "I'm not taking a letter."

"Please. Please." This was my only chance, and I was neither ashamed to beg, nor lie. "It's for my mum. Just to let her know that I'm ok. You can read it, if you like." I pulled it from my pocket. The small piece of paper. What was left of the page ripped so carefully from my schoolbook, its edge sharp against my palm.

The woman turned, her back again to the door, and the note hovered between the two of us, while she stared, saying nothing.

"It's just a bit of paper. What harm could it do?" I leant forward––just to my tiptoes––holding the note within her grasp. The way children were taught to hold out sugar cubes or apple slices to horses. "Please?"

She had to have some thoughts about children being separated from their parents. All people must. Unlike the doctors, the cleaners had no motivation to be cold, ruthless, or scientific. Not everyone liked to collect body parts. I couldn't have got that wrong.

I edged closer until the letter touched the skin of her arms.

"Have you got kids?" I asked.

"I have to call the Doctor." But her eyes never left my face.

"Nieces? Brothers? Sisters?" I paused. "Anyone who you'd want to hear from if they were in a place like this? Just to know that they were ok."

She looked at me; her eyes round and helpless––a bunny rabbit's or a duckling's. "You're not supposed to be here."

"It's just a letter. Read it, and then you can say no. But I need to tell my mum I'm ok. Please," I whispered. "Please. She works at the University. I don't know the exact address."

On one side of the page, I'd written Emma Vanardsdale, care of Oxford University, Science Department and on the other:

Hi mum,

I wanted you to know that I'm getting better! And I forgive you for sending me here. The doctors are helping me.

Please would you let Mal Stephenson and Mollie Mulholland's parents know they're fine too? Everyone who comes here gets fixed––one way or another.

Love Heli

Although she put the letter in her pocket, I had no way of knowing whether the woman in the laundry would take pity and send such an innocuous-sounding message or whether she'd recognise the name of the only person who I hoped might help. I guessed it depended on whether, deep down, she believed it was ok to cut kids off from their families. And if she sent it, whether the letter would reach Dr Emma at the University--without a proper address or even an envelope and then--if at last it fell into her age-spotted hands whether Dr Emma would take the hint and check those names or not.

Before, it had seemed like a good plan: solid, promising, clever. It was all that I had. But as soon as I handed the paper over, the weight of all those--ifs--squeezed tight, and I worried it wouldn't be enough to stop the Doctor.

At exercise time, we were separated into five pairs, although I took little notice of who my partner was while we changed into our trainers and left the Facility building. Anxiety tormented me, dogging my every step, gnawing its way inside my head and pulling out the strands of my hair. Would the woman post the letter?

"Really?" Joe said. "This is our one chance to talk all day and you're just going to pull your hair out and ignore me. Typical. You know, I did wish I hadn't done that to your hand. I've said sorry, more than once, it's not my fault I get so angry... Don't look like that. I've seen you shoving people." He stepped forward, his face close enough to touch. "Alright, I'll say it a-bloody-gain, I am sorry."

I opened my mouth and tried--I really did--but no sound would come out. If I could have spoken, talking would have been a welcome distraction. Even talking to Joe. Instead, I traced over the events in the laundry with the woman. Dread made its way down, settling in my guts. If the Doctor found out what I'd done; would there be punishment?

As we jogged back, the sound of the bell in our ears, Joe pulled my sleeve.

"Come on, Heli," he said, "stop being such a bitch."

I looked at him, worried for a moment that somehow, he knew what I'd done.

"What?" The word burst out of my mouth, like a burp.

"I need to talk to you," he said. "It's about Sira."

"You told me before," once they'd started moving, my lips wouldn't stop. "Actually, I miss her too." A weight shifted. Maybe it was the memory of how desperate I'd been in the laundry for someone to talk to and how now of all people, I felt sorry for Joe. "I miss all of them. It's even more shit without them."

"It's too quiet;" he paused. "I know it's selfish, but I wish she'd come back."

"I get that." My eyes closed and I thought about Cai and how I wished he'd come back too, even though it was better for him not to be trapped in the Facility.

"Like," Joe said, his voice quiet, "if Sira were here now––I could tell her that she mattered––because she always worried, you know, that people saw her tics before they saw her. But I see her. And she matters to me." He bent forward, his hands on his knees while he caught his breath. "That's not what I wanted to talk about though; I'm worried."

"Worried?" My feet stopped on the path. "What about?"

"About what's happening to her. Out there with Dr Emma."

"You mean while she's the prize pig."

"She's a caged pig. She might have left but Sira doesn't get to go home. So, what happens to her?"

"I don't know." My hand tugged at my hair. Sira was another reason to put a stop to the Doctor. Even though she'd left, she was still under his jurisdiction. "I used to get so annoyed with her." My fingers twisted through my hair. "I could never understand why she sucked up to the Doctor."

"Just because you're sorry doesn't mean you have to think someone's perfect. Sira could be annoying." Joe licked his lips. "You must have unfinished business of your own. If you had the chance, what'd you wish you could say to someone?"

Joe's words kicked me in the guts. I shouldn't have stopped to talk to him because I didn't want to think about it.

"Anyone at all?" he said.

"If I had the chance?" Concentrating on each step, I kept my gaze on the looming spectre of the Cerletti building because I didn't want to talk about it. "Nothing."

There were too many things that needed to be said. Mal and Cai and Peony. I had unfinished business alright.

"Talk to me." Joe nudged my shoulder as we headed along the path, back towards the Facility. "What's the worst that could happen?"

"Do you think we're bad people?" I asked.

"You mean because we're here."

"Yeah."

"No," he shook his head: "Sira wasn't a bad person. Mal definitely wasn't. You're not. Maybe I am sometimes."

"I did a bad thing," I retreated from his arm. If I had the chance, the one person I wanted to talk to most, was my sister. "I told this lie."

"Everyone tells lies," Joe said. "Do you need to apologise to someone?"

"It's not like that," I hesitated. "It was me--I suppose--I lied to myself. And soon after, it didn't feel like I was lying, it felt just the same as telling the truth."

"Eh?" Joe leaned closer and I could see the strain my confession was placing on his tiny brain.

"Forget about it. We need to get back."

I picked up my pace towards the Cerletti building, where it waited in the distance. Joe wasn't the right person for this conversation. I wasn't sure, I understood it myself. I had been lying though, hadn't I? All this time––to myself.

"You know, I think what you said is brave," he touched my shoulder: "Lying is a tough thing to admit."

I shrugged, although his hand was kind of comforting.

"Tell me what you did."

"It started at my Gran's." It's hard to explain why I started to talk, except the feeling of Joe's hand on my back reminded me I wasn't alone. And that when you told someone to get lost and they stayed to listen, it meant something. "We went to her house every summer, Peony and I, to give my parents some time alone."

"Nice."

"No, it was horrible. My Gran literally thought children should be seen but not heard."

"She would have got on well with the Doctor."

"If we were too noisy, she would hit us with her slipper. Stuff like that. When we were little, Peony and I used to pretend we were trapped by the wicked witch from *Hansel and Gretel*. We'd bring sweets from home and make out we were eating the witch's house. You know, like in the storybook."

"Stories aren't really my thing."

"Doesn't matter. The last time we went, Peony was too busy sneaking out with her boyfriend to hang out with me. Too old for our games and so, I took all her stuff, and I set fire to it. Except, Gran's bin wasn't metal like the one I used at home and the fire got out of control."

"Shit," he said.

"I thought she was dead when they brought her out from the house. Her face was black, and her clothes melted."

"Your Gran?"

"No." A tear slid along my cheek, hot and unwanted. "It was Peony; she had come back. She tried to put the fire out. And then... I thought she was dead. So, I blamed the fire on her."

"Did they believe you?"

"No. But that's not the point. I believed me. Even now, things are kind of muddled. I just thought if they believed Peony had done it, they would forgive her. Whereas they would never forgive me. And... I suppose I was right about that bit because they sent me here." I paused. "You must think I'm a monster."

"I've done worse. Why'd you think my parents sent me here?"

"You stuck pencils in them too?"

"I said worse."

"But I'm not the same as you. I don't enjoy hurting people."

"I don't enjoy it," a pained look flickered over Joe's face. "I can't control it. I wanted this place to make me different but––"

"The chair didn't reform you?"

"That's not funny."

"Dr Devitt said it would be someone else's turn soon. But who?"

"The Doctor said something to Wiley that makes sense now." We passed through the iron gates, onto the narrow path towards the Facility door.

"Shit." Not so long ago, I was desperate for someone else to be put in the chair. Now, the thought of Wiley being strapped in made me feel worse.

"Not up to us though, is it?"

"I sent a letter," I whispered as we approached the Cerletti building, "to Dr Emma. Maybe she can stop the Doctor."

"Always hope," Joe grinned and put out his fist. After a moment, I lifted my fist, and we knocked them together.

"Do you think we'll see them again one day?" If somehow the Doctor was stopped, would we all be reunited.

"Sira?"

"And Cai."

He looked at me, a flash of pity in the turn down of his lips. "Who's Cai?"

"Do you think we'll see them again?" I bit my lip, unable to hear him properly. It was impossible to contemplate there was any truth in the Doctor's words. I only wanted Joe to say yes.

"Yes," he nodded, fists still clenched. "I think about it every day. I will see her again. I'm sure of it."

"Are you going to give her a big kiss?"

"Fuck off."

"Hey Joe?" I tapped his arm. "When you see her, will you tell her I miss her too?"

In the school room the next day, Dr Fiennes was at his duty at the desk, when Dr Shalt––an unexpected visitor––came into the room; her hair looked greyer than it had been when I'd arrived. From stress or the lack of a hairdresser on the island, I didn't know. They talked in hushed voices; her pink lips moved back and forth––a ghost of her former smile––while Dr Fiennes frowned.

What were they talking about? I tried to lip read but could only make out something about being *entitled to a break*. Even with Dr Shalt's fakery, it was obvious she was pissed. She stepped backwards, revealing the heavy red fire extinguisher hanging between them on the wall. Fire. I embraced its memory, blood whooshing in my ears.

When her heels clicked, clacked across the tiles, announcing her departure from the room, I looked up to find Dr Fiennes regarding his device with furious concentration. The sound of Wiley's pencil scratching across his page cut through the silence. My heartbeat accelerated. If it had to do with the letter the Doctor would have acted by now though, wouldn't he?

"Eyes down on your own work." Dr Fiennes glared around the room. "You too, Heli, or you'll miss your lunch."

I pretended to turn my attention towards my work. The voice-over had set me a task, but I couldn't remember what it was. I stared at my notes in the exercise book. It was supposed to be a history lesson; I remembered that much: a lost war and a maniac in a bunker.

They said Hitler had a breast. Didn't they? I pressed my pen down on the page, an imitation of writing. But how could you have one half of a pair? Could one survive without the other? Memory scratched. A whispered conversation under a blanket with Mal, once upon a long time ago. He'd told me something about a hand under the military uniform concealing something. Hitler's third nipple. Or had it been another General––a different war? Napoleon's hand maybe? That was it; I tried to picture his uniform. French? But I couldn't remember for sure. And there was no one left to ask. No one to separate truth from rumour. It bothered me. Joe was right. It was too quiet at the Facility.

The voice in my ear said time was running out. The source should have been read and digested. Ready for answering questions. I glanced at the words. It was a long piece of text and probably not about missing body parts. The others in the room stirred. Dr Fiennes's sigh from his desk was audible. Wiley's desk was next to mine. I glanced across at his workbook. He was answering maths equations--his dark hair casting shadows over pencil marks. Dancing to its own beat. The bell rang and I put down my pencil. *Body parts.* The words triggered the memory of Mal's eyeball through the glass; it shivered into view, and I squeezed my eyes closed. It didn't matter whether the Doctor moved it, knowing it was out there, was too dreadful.

"Just a minute, all of you," Dr Fiennes cleared his throat. "Stay in your seats."

Hunger swirled through my guts. Wiley's elbows hit his desk; his head cradled in his hands. Silence stretched over the room like spider web.

Dr Fiennes looked at me and my heart pulsed.

Why was he looking at me?

"Wiley, you are to go to the lab. Straight away. The Doctor is waiting outside to take you there. The rest of you, I will escort you to the dining hall. Pack your things away quickly. Then line up on the spots at the door."

The Doctor is waiting outside.

My pulse flickered in my neck; it was obvious the Doctor planned to put Wiley in the chair. But why hadn't he come in to collect him? Maybe he hoped this way would cause less of a fuss. Mal never went willingly, and neither had I.

I glanced at Wiley; he appeared unconcerned. Someone needed to warn him. There was a voice in my ear, and I jumped before remembering it was coming from the headset.

We packed our things away and Dr Fiennes counted the pencils twice while we waited--silent on the black, vinyl spots. But as soon as we left the schoolroom, our line snaking towards the dining hall, I asked to go to the toilet. If I could follow Wiley, maybe there was a way to cause a distraction if nothing else.

"There's no one to take you to the toilet, Heli," Dr Fiennes said. "You'll have to wait."

"But I can't," I said and then in a flash of inspiration. "Dr Fiennes, I've got my period."

"Do you think that's the first time I've heard that excuse?"

"Excuse? But Dr Fiennes, I'm not making it up. The bathroom is just there. Please, I'm desperate. Look, I——"

"Just this once," he tapped his device, "but I will call Dr Shalt to come and fetch you."

Inside the toilet door, I counted to ten, then made a break for it. All the way down the long, white-walled corridor towards the science zone. But what would I do when I got there? I didn't have a card.

I needed a plan. To do something——big or small. Maybe I could trip a switch and shut the power down. It was all I could come up with. There was no time for indecision, nor anyone to ask for help. My pulse tapped from the inside of my neck; whatever I'd tried before, the Doctor had proved unstoppable.

To my surprise, the lab door was propped open. My heart accelerated; something was off. There was the distant sound of voices. I had never been in the science lab alone. I stepped forward, crossing the threshold between out there in the corridor and inside. A tingle of wild energy swept through me and the urge to run through the lab breaking things, opening doors, smashing machines. I squashed the feeling down, inching across the floor. This wasn't the time for destruction. I couldn't let Wiley end up like Mal. I wouldn't. Not again.

On the side where they stored the test tubes, there was a drawer that held a box of matches. Matches were easier than electricity and finding a way to shut off the power. If fire had been my gateway into the Cerletti Facility, it could be my way out. Wiley's way out too.

The flick of a match could change everything. But there was a shiny, red fire extinguisher waiting on the wall. Fire wasn't freedom it was a trap.

There was quiet in the lab now; all the doors were closed. I approached the shelf with the Doctor's collection of body parts. There was something else I wanted to do––to reclaim a thing that should never have been taken. I could get rid of them all. His precious collection. But I started searching through them––for the important one––the small glass jar with Mal's dark brown eye.

I shifted the heaviest one with the convict's brain, it swayed back and forth in its murky fluid. I reached for the next one, the glass slipping in my shaking hands. Mal's unseeing eye stared back, a grotesque reminder of what had been stolen. Nausea clawed at my insides.

The door creaked, and the Doctor's shadow fell across the floor. He loomed, his voice cutting.

"What do you think you're doing?"

37

My Art

Sira

Walking to the harbour with Dr Emma was strange in ways I couldn't pin down. The bag at my side, held the bare essentials——a change of clothes, a hairbrush, and a toothbrush. That was it. My momma would have been scandalised to think the Doctor didn't consider her various beauty brushes a medical necessity. To her, appearance was everything. I wasn't returning home, but thoughts of my parents lingered.

At the end of the path, where a beach sloped one way and the harbour the other, a lighthouse jutted out, its beam flickering over restless waves. Less a guide, more a gatekeeper warning me of the danger ahead. Dr Emma cleared her throat.

"Can you manage by yourself?" she said.

"Of course." I was surprised by the question. What did she think we'd done every exercise session for over a year? "Oh," I stopped, my foot hovering--half on the muddy path, half reaching for the rocks: "Do you need help?"

The question was ironic. I drew in a breath, the wind whipping across my coat.

"It's quite alright," she pointed. "The captain is coming."

The wooden jetty creaked beneath my feet while I watched the man help Dr Emma over the rocks, her bag strung across his shoulders. In the white-topped waves, a small boat bobbed, tethered and waiting. Joe would've been thrilled at the sight of it; all the other kids would have cheered or jumped up and down.

The image of Joe made my chest hurt: the sweep of messy hair; his intense, gruff exterior and soft insides. It was hard to reconcile, I'd never see him or the others again. Joe's arms around me, the way he whispered my name before I left--it haunted me.

Heli's voice echoed too, nagging me to be a seven on Dr Emma's scale. To challenge their rules and expectations. I'd wanted to. Sometimes back at the Facility, I pictured letting everything go and drawing six big, fat penises for them to count. I could have drawn seven or eight if I had dared, but I'd followed the rules for so long, leaving Cerletti messed with my head.

At their approach my heart pulsed, even though I didn't know what I was alarmed at--Dr Emma changing her mind and sending me back--or never seeing the other kids again.

By the time we reached the mainland, the city's glow swallowed the last trace of the island. The Facility was gone, not even a smudge on the horizon, and yet, I couldn't stop thinking about it. Instead of freedom, it felt raw, swelling like a bruise.

"Change is unsettling," Dr Emma said. "A period of adjustment is natural."

But loneliness hung like fog. At Cerletti, I had Joe, Heli, and the others. Here, there was no one. Even the air was heavy, and Dr Emma's presence was like having the Doctor's eyes on me all over again.

I tried to draw, sketching in the notebook Dr Emma let me pick out. She didn't know about my art, how I'd draw ridiculous parades of dicks or worse. No one ever saw them. They were mine, a rebellion against a life that was limited, monitored, destined to be a number six. My art was the only thing that made me feel good.

"Sira?" Dr Emma's voice jolted me, and I snapped the book shut, yanking at the end of my ponytail. The old urge to pull at my hair crept in––a bad habit I couldn't shake.

"Can I sit?" She stood in the doorway, her silhouette backlit by the light from the hall. She looked uncertain, which immediately put me on edge. Doctors didn't do uncertain. They didn't knock either, but she'd managed to break both rules. Something was wrong.

"Sure," I said, my chest tight. Joe's name on the tip of my tongue. A string of the other kids' names. "What's happened?"

Dr Emma placed a hand on my knee, her touch careful, and it only confirmed my worst fear.

"Has someone died?" My voice trembled.

"We don't know yet," Dr Emma's voice was dead calm, rehearsed. "There's been an incident."

"Someone's hurt? Is it Joe?" My throat was tight. I clawed at my top, pulling it away from my skin. If I'd still been there, would it have made a difference? "Heli? Mya? Wiley––"

"Sira." She took my hand. "It's about the Doctor," her voice was steady, too steady. I gripped the bedpost, my pulse roaring in my ears.

38

THE FIRE EXTINGUISHER

Heli

"WHAT DO YOU THINK you are doing?" The Doctor repeated. It wasn't possible he had heard me earlier––the thoughts inside my head––my secret self and the call of fire.

"Where's Wiley?"

Anxiety squirmed through my guts. Was it too late? I glanced at the door the Doctor had emerged from, the one that led to the room with the chair. It was closed.

"Where is he?"

"Heli," he lifted his finger: "You're not allowed in here unaccompanied. You know that."

"The door was open."

"That's because Dr Devitt was removing some of his things––ready for his departure. At all times, you must follow our rules––stop looking for opportunities to break them."

"I haven't done anything wrong." I gripped the jar, trying to still the shudder in my hands.

The Doctor stepped closer, dragging the dark, black outline of his shadow over the bench.

"What are you doing?" He paused. "For goodness's sake. Those are not for you to tamper with."

"It's just one of the jars." I held it up. Mal's eye––as I remembered it: dark brown and urging me on.

"That is part of my collection. Put it back, please." The Doctor stroked his hand back and forth over the pen in his top pocket. "I have other things requiring my attention right now. You're not my only patient."

Wiley.

I looked again at the closed door; had there been time to strap him in? Administer the injection and turn the dials. I didn't think so. This was my last chance to do something. The glass jar was hard and solid in my hands, but it wouldn't be enough to stop the Doctor.

"Stop that. Do as you're told. At once."

The sun streaked through the high windows, casting shadows on the table; it should be a good day on the beach later, the tide low and the rocks warm. But I wouldn't be there. My throat tightened and the glass jar shook against my hands. Anger radiated from the Doctor like heat. I knew I wouldn't make it to the beach later.

"Sit down," he said, "and I will call someone to escort you back to lunch."

"This doesn't belong here. It doesn't belong to you."

"What are you talking about?"

"Mal." I straightened up; and the sun shifted until I was shadowless: "You shouldn't have taken his eyeball."

"I have no idea who you are talking about."

"Liar," I said. "How dare you pretend you don't know who I'm talking about. Mal Stephenson. Look," I shook the jar at him. The eyeball popped from side to side.

"We have been through this, many times; you are delusional. In Layman's terms, you make people up. You invented friends for yourself. Cai and," he waved one of his hands, raising his voice, "Mal did not exist. He wasn't real."

Rage hit me square in the face. How dare he lie about such a thing.

"Doctor?" Wiley's silhouette was faint in the doorway to the room with the chair, ghost-like. "You shouldn't say that. Mal was real."

"Go back in there," the Doctor pressed his device. "I will be just a minute."

"I don't want to." Wiley hesitated on the threshold. "I'm scared."

"Do as you're told." The Doctor glared at me as though Wiley's fear was my fault. "Exercise time is cancelled for the foreseeable future. Perhaps for you too, Wiley, unless you do as you're told."

"Mal was real." Wiley turned and vanished inside the gloomy room once more. My heart pulsed, relieved that Wiley had confirmed it for me.

"You're a fucking monster," I stepped towards the Doctor, my gaze searching the room for something solid while a thought uncurled. The violent one. I needed to do something bigger. Wiley wasn't safe for long; the Doctor must be stopped.

"Speak to me with respect," the Doctor jabbed his device. "Where is everyone?" he muttered, shaking it. "There will be consequences for your behaviour. Isolation proved effective last time."

"You're a menace." I had to find something stronger, heavier, something that wouldn't shatter––like glass––into a thousand pieces when I swung it at him. My gaze alighted on the fire extinguisher. It would be heavy enough. "You're an arsehole."

I threw the jar with Mal's eye, and it shattered at his feet. Embalming liquid sprayed the bottom of the Doctor's trousers while Mal's eye bounced towards the bench. I thought Mal might have approved of this––his last act.

"How dare you," the Doctor swept the glass together with his foot. "You will atone for that. And all of the other rules you've broken."

I counted the steps I needed to take to reach the fire extinguisher. Five, if I was fast, because only one of us was coming out of this encounter intact, weren't they?

I took the first step.

"Yes," he said. "I know all about that. Talking to the cleaner, damaging Facility property. You've been busy writing letters." His lip curled. "We have been too lenient with our methods here. I see that now. But you will atone."

"Yeah?" I edged again towards the fire extinguisher. I didn't care about his threats. The only thing that mattered was stopping him from going into that room with Wiley.

"You've made so much progress," he said, leaning in. "Why turn your back on it now? Don't waste your potential."

My hands shook while he messed with my head.

"No one would accept your word over mine." He pursed his lips to hiss. "You are delusional and not to be trusted. Always making people up. Mal is a figment of your illness."

"Liar." I inched forward another step.

He was making me doubt myself. But this time, he wouldn't get away with it. He needed to be stopped.

"A sedative now and be quick about it, Dr Shalt."

Dr Shalt had appeared in the room. She looked from me to the Doctor, her smile uncertain.

"I'm sorry to take so long. We were actually looking for Heli. She asked to go to the toilet and disappeared."

"Just get the sedative."

"Children died here." I took the last step, reaching to pull at the cold surface of the fire extinguisher. All this time I'd wanted to escape the Facility; I should have realised the Doctor was the Facility. "Children died. One day people will find out what you've done."

"There was no expectation that everyone would make it." Cruel lines encircled the Doctor's eyes, making them bulge. "You will go back into isolation except for your visits to the chair. You and Wiley both." His voice cracked, a rare slip in composure. "Step away now, Heli."

I swung the fire extinguisher, the clang against his skull echoing through the room. A burst of feeling flooded my guts when he grunted, his knees dropping to the floor.

"You won't get away with this," he said, groping for his device, his breath coming in jagged rasps.

So, I swung again, harder this time. The sickening thud silencing him, his head snapping to the ground.

"How does that make you feel, Doctor?" I repeated his stupid question from our therapy sessions, my voice steady. "Knowing it's over? Knowing you've failed."

There was no blood. I dropped the fire extinguisher, my heart hammering inside my chest. Looking at the Doctor's head--at close range--where he lay on the floor, he was older than I'd thought and weird without his glasses. His eyes were wide and startled.

I picked the glasses up, but when I tried to slide them back over his nose, they no longer fit. One side of his forehead and his cheek were swelling, turning angry shades of blue and purple.

"Doctor?" Dr Shalt was there beside me, the syringe trembling in her hands. "Heli! Don't touch him."

"We won't be needing that now?" I pointed to the injection.

"What have you done?" Her fake smile faded; her face unmasked. "You've ruined everything."

"He was a monster," I said.

I held my hand under the Doctor's nose, a gag rising in my throat. And there it was, a slight warmth. A dampness crept over the back of my hand. I hadn't hit him as hard as I'd thought. The old bastard was still alive.

"That's enough. Keep still." Dr Shalt said, her needle piercing my arm as the world tilted. The Doctor was going to survive, but so would I. "Now lie back," she said: "Quick, before you hit your head."

39

AFTERWARDS

Heli

I WAS IN ANOTHER place now. I suppose you'd call it a Facility, too, but it's not like the last one. This one was on the mainland with long stretches of green grass outside with trees that blossomed pink and white in the spring. And visitors. My parents and my sister came once every week or two. Some of Peony's hair had grown back, although the skin on the far side of her cheek was puckered with red. When she saw me looking, she shifted her hair with her working hand.

"I'm sorry," I said. *Sorry for the fire. Sorry for everything.*

"Are you?"

"Yes."

"I never thought I'd hear you say that." When Peony smiled, the room felt warmer, soft, like sunlight, not fire-warm.

"I guess I've changed."

"Tell her about the verdict, Dad." Peony combed her hair into place with her fingers before continuing. "The Doctor got what was coming to him."

"Oh yeah?" I remembered the Doctor's quiet composure the days I had been required to go to court. Should I have been the one on trial? I guess you'll have to decide that for yourself.

"We arranged an early visit especially to tell you," Peony hesitated. "You know when you were sent away, I was so angry, I blamed you for everything. But after what we've learned. You didn't deserve any of it. None of you did."

Her words settled, soothing me, releasing some of the guilt I'd been carrying.

"Go on then," I said, my heart pulsing in my throat. A memory of dark brown eyes; a chair that delivered ice cold shocks; grey seawater stretching endlessly and the weight of a fire extinguisher. "Tell me."

"The jury found the Doctor guilty of abusing his position. Of using his influence in the scientific community to wield undue power." Peony's eyes gleamed in the way they did when a person believed justice had been served. That she was on my side over this, despite everything, filled me with promise. I still remembered the way the courtroom had fallen silent when the Doctor took the stand, his voice steady as though he believed his lies could save him. "They also found him guilty of concealing the suicides of two of his patients. Guilty. Heli, you've got to feel good about that."

"Have I?"

"Yes," she shook her head. It was another look I recognised——the long suffering of a mad girl's sister. "The Doctor will be prevented from further practice. At least you've got to be pleased about that?"

"I am," I said. Justice felt hollow, it didn't account for the scars beneath my skin, nor the things that we'd lost. But it was something and maybe in time, it would be enough.

"There's something else," she said.

"Yeah?"

"We met someone who said they knew you. Wanted us to pass on her love."

"Who was that?"

"Tall girl with a ponytail. Sira?"

"Was she..." my heart pulsed. "On her own?"

"No, she was with that other doctor who testified. Dr Emma."

"Did she say anything else?"

"There was a boy, too," Peony smiled. "Very cute; I think he was her boyfriend."

"Oh really?"

"Joe, he said his name was."

40

Outcomes

Sira

There's a word that's used in therapy sessions a lot.

Outcomes.

They talked about the best ones or the poor ones, desirable ones and not-so-desirable ones. It made it seem like there were lots of options for the mentally unstable, when truth be told, our choices were limited.

"Thank you for coming," the therapist said. "It's been really helpful to have you here. To get your perspective on your time at Cerletti."

My neck twitched from side to side, and I concentrated on my breathing like I'd been taught.

"It must have been very triggering for you to relive it," the therapist pushed the tissue box across the table towards me.

"She doesn't need tissues; she's hardcore," Heli laughed in the chair beside mine. "Haven't you been listening?"

"Your transport isn't for another hour," the therapist said, ignoring Heli's jibe.

It reminded me of one of Joe's funny British expressions: *like water off a duck's back*. I started laughing too as I caught Heli's eye and we fell together, our shoulders touching.

"Would you both like to take a walk through the gardens?" the therapist smiled. "Have a catch-up, just the two of you?"

"I'd like that very much," I said.

"Cool," Heli said, getting up.

Outside, the leaves were falling. Soft colours of brown and orange in what the British called autumn, but I still thought of it as fall.

"You're still here then?" Heli said, her feet sinking into the overgrown grass.

"Do you mean here, as in Facility here? Or——"

"Aren't you American?" she scrunched her face.

"Oh. Then yes, I'm still here. My folks didn't get what they wanted out of Cerletti and Dr Emma's actually been quite helpful with things. She says I'm as fixed as I can be. And everyone will just have to live with the rest."

"She said that."

I laughed. "Sort of. In doctor-speak."

"Do you miss it?"

My heart pulsed. "Cerletti?"

"No, the States. Where were you from before?"

"Kansas."

"As in the Wizard of Oz?"

I nodded. "Yes."

"I didn't think that place was real."

"It is very real," I said. "It's nice here." I gestured to the garden. "I like the trees." Heli scrunched her face again and dug her hands into her pocket. "Are you happy?"

"When I'm not in there," she pointed to the window up high on the side of the building, which I took to mean when she wasn't in therapy. "Yes, I think so. Someone said something recently––about living with the rest––and I think that's pretty clever."

"Oh yeah?" I grinned, looking at the sun as it descended, spreading its rainbow of colour over the grass. There was a healthy smell outside in the garden, too, of grass and leaf mulch. It reminded me of the smell of the farms back home, and I thought maybe one day, I would like to go back. "Do you ever think about the Doctor?"

"All the time," Heli said wincing. "I still see him at the trial. You know, he just sat there, stone-faced. But his eyes... they were still scheming. But maybe deep down, he knew it was over."

"It doesn't feel real he went to prison." I looked away. It was hard to process it. I felt guilty when I remembered the Doctor like I should have done more. "It was good that you..." I paused. How could I say it aloud? "I'm glad that you stopped him. Thank you."

"D'you think he took his collection with him?" Heli turned, her hand reaching for my arm. "That's one of the things that still troubles me. Like, I feel he took a part of me, too, and put it in a jar. I just don't know which part." She dropped my arm and ran her hands over herself as though searching for confirmation that she still all there.

"I know what you mean." I stepped forward and took her hand. "But that's all in our heads. I think his collection, what's left of it, is the least of his concerns right now. It's prison where he's gone––not a hotel, Heli. He can't reach us anymore. Not any part of us."

"I wouldn't have made it without you."

"Me either," I said. "And now, we've got to keep going for them."

She nodded and squeezed my hand. "You still see the others?"

"Yes, Joe is in the same place as me. Dr Emma helped with that. Wiley too and Mya. They're ok."

"Good," she smiled. "I never did see what you saw in Joe, but I'm happy for you."

I smiled back. Considering everything, our outcomes had turned out ok. What I'd learned from the failure of the Doctor's methods was that even though our choices were limited, it was better when they left us with some hope.

"Thank you," I said. "For what you did."

We walked back to the Facility, the day's light fading as we went. It was reminiscent of all the walks we took on the island at Cerletti, except there was no bell ringing or spots to line up on.

"Tell Joe I said hi, would you?" she said when we hugged goodbye.

"I sure will." I squeezed her tight, uncertain whether we'd meet again. "You take good care of yourself, do you hear?"

"You too," she turned to enter the building, her hair a dazzling shade of red in the setting sun.

41

The Mad Girl's Ending

Heli

But I want a different ending to my story. One that doesn't linger in the shadow of the Cerletti Facility. And I think it goes something like this.

Cai and I walk in the green grass garden, hand in hand, passing underneath the blossom tree. The flowers are candy-floss colours and soft when we lie in them. From time-to-time, Cai leans in close and whispers things in my ear, although the things he says are not to be repeated––they are private things, held in our minds like secrets and kept out of reach. They are not to be repeated to doctors or counsellors. They are just for us.

Sometimes, we talk about our memories of the Cerletti Facility, the walks we took there on its pebble beach, and we remember our friend Mal and the other kids who shared the Doctor's routines and the island paths with us.

"What was it all for, Heli?" Cai says, his breath warm on my cheek, my ear, my throat. "Our year at Cerletti, what did it achieve?"

"Strides for science?" I say, laughing.

Sometimes, he asks about the day I smacked the Doctor around the head with a fire extinguisher. But I tell him the same as I tell everyone.

"I just wanted to stop him. To prevent him from using the chair on Wiley or any more of us."

And then Cai smiles, his dark eyes shining, and my heart beats fast like it always does when he's around. Because I am happiest when I am left alone with him and the things I make up inside my head.

MEET ROMANY HEARTFORD

One of five daughters, Romany grew up near the infamous dreaming spires of Oxford, England, in a small but loud household. Now married with three of her own noisy children, she finds solace walking and swimming along the beautiful beaches where she lives in Cornwall. She is a teacher of English Literature and creative writing and longs to see her name in print.

Mad Girl's Love Song is her debut novel.

www.ingramcontent.com/pod-product-compliance
Lightning Source LLC
Chambersburg PA
CBHW061344310726
48974CB00001B/192